TAKEN BY TIME

In the Möbius Loop

M. C.
Strayer

M. C. Strayer

I ask for your most valuable resource, time, in exchange for a story. Only you can decide if this tale is good or bad. My hope, however, is you look beyond good and bad, to ask if it serves you well or not. If you are searching for a happy story, look elsewhere. Indeed, I must warn you now this story will not be one of those. Forgive me for revealing the ending, but the traveler never returns home, the good guys do not win, and evil still continues strong after the last page. If this too closely mirrors the world around us for the reader, then you have this storyteller's apology. What the tale lacks in happy endings I can only hope it makes up for in happy moments, as well as courage through the painful ones. My hope is that this too will closely mirror the world around us.

Your Humble Storyteller

M. C. Strayer

Contents

Fire and Ice
　　Some say the world will end in fire,
　　Some say in ice.
　　From what I've tasted of desire
　　I hold with those who favor fire.
　　But if it had to perish twice,
　　I think I know enough of hate
　　To say that for destruction ice
　　Is also great
　　And would suffice.

-Robert Frost

CHAPTER ONE - THE PATH TAKEN

Excerpt from **The Road Not Taken**
Two roads diverged in a yellow wood,
And sorry I could not travel both
And be one traveler, long I stood
And looked down one as far as I could
To where it bent in the undergrowth
-Robert Frost

The boy stood at the fork in the path and weighed his fears. Going to the left would take him home where he knew questions about his tardiness would lead to the conclusion he remained a foolish boy. If he answered honestly about how he lost temper and his wits, he worried he would look as idiotic in his parent's eyes as in his own. The path to the right looked as if it could lead to a great view of the city and an excuse for this lost time. However, the boy cautioned himself, it might also lead to a big waste of time. In a country known for dangerous people and even more dangerous creatures, wandering deep into a forest felt like a foolish idea. Still, though nothing about the path implied any danger, the fear of the unknown persisted. Those two eternal fears of what the world would think of him and of what the world would do to him tore at the boy. As it is with most people, if he would have been able to step back, he would have admitted those fears to be quite small; but then when any of us look at the world we often feel quite small as well.

It was a Thursday that had appeared similar to any other day, and perhaps that was what allowed it to be so different than any other day. The sun didn't shine any brighter; in fact, it mostly hid between the clouds that brought a wetness to the day and kept the South American warmth in. There had been no signs of crows, no black cats and no strange dreams. There had been nothing so far that warned young Marcus this day would be the day everything in his life changed forever. The morning noises that had wakened him were no different than the previous day's or the days before that.

The sounds of his grandmother's cooking and his mother's cleaning, though both were being done for his benefit, annoyed Marcus. He heard his brother and sister running around being a nuisance as they did nearly every morning. He thought to yell at them to be quiet, but Marcus realized no matter how silent the house might be he would be unable to sleep anymore. When he finally got bored of lying in bed, Marcus rolled out of bed to face the day.

Marcus absentmindedly made his bed, putting in the exact amount of time he calculated would prevent his father from looking at the bed with disdain or his mother from complaining but not a second more. Marcus put on the short pants he had worn the day before to clean out the garage and found his cleanest dirty shirt. He wondered why his mother hadn't done any of his laundry until the numerous clothing piles in every location but the hamper answered his complaint.

The house was typical of southern Brazil. The concrete's prematurely aged appearance came from both the constant dampness as well as the frugality with which it had been poured.

Rugs covered tiled floors, not matching one another but each matching in some way with the overall ambiance of the house. The blend of South American warm hospitality and American cold utility gave the house a distinct character. Tastefully selected and placed, overpriced furniture stood draped with handmade blankets from a list of people whose names Marcus's mother could recite without pause. Electronics brought back from the USA rested on shelves next to a small painting of Virgin Mary and a carving of ocean goddess, Lemanjá. The house itself hid behind a smattering of fruit trees a short distance from the street and the sounds of trucks mingled with sounds of birds both tending to their own morning routines.

For breakfast Marcus's grandmother had prepared the normal regional fare, and Marcus enjoyed the fruits especially. His grandmother had put out the usual combinations of mangoes, papayas, bananas, and guava, as well as tapioca pancakes which Marcus always looked forward to when visiting. While the food in South America may not have been as varied as the diversity he enjoyed in California, Brazilian food made up for it in quality. Marcus ate last and so decided to try to make it appear he had put some effort into cleaning up the table. He hoped the attempt would inspire his grandmother into making some other delicious desserts he knew he would only get while visiting. Marcus's grandmother harbored none of the aversions to sugar that his parents did, and Marcus loved to devour a large bowl of some sugary fruit creation before bed. In truth Marcus did little other than pile dirty plates in the sink and brush crumbs from the table to the floor. Still, he left clear evidence of clean up, and Marcus hoped that it would go far.

Noting that his dad was already gone and his Mom was working on chores, Marcus couldn't help but feel that every day in Brazil had started exactly the same. He didn't know what tasks his mom was working on but he thought to himself that she would almost certainly be doing them again when he got out of bed tomorrow.

Marcus, on the other hand, often spent his time in Brazil doing as much nothing as he could. The adolescent convinced himself his life in California was too busy and vacation was his much-needed chance to relax. From what Marcus had seen Brazilians always did better than Americans at relaxing. In the time since Marcus had arrived in South America he had not done much except go to the market and to the park a few times. After eating he didn't have anything to do for at least a few hours and didn't know when he would have a chance to relax so much again.

Marcus's little sister called to him to help her with something, but Marcus immersed himself in wondering why his phone showed no missed messages from his friends back home who still wouldn't be awake for a few more hours. Marcus couldn't help but feel every time he left the States everyone forgot him until he returned. Marcus could see from pictures that they always had fun without him, and he vacillated between frustration with them for not needing him and with his family for bringing him on the trip. Either way he resolved to have enough fun in Brazil to make those in the states feel jealous at his pictures. Marcus also remembered he needed to take a picture that would catch the attention of his crush, Mary. He lazily plotted how he would accomplish this as he remained sprawled across the cloth couch, dividing his attention between his phone and the eternally muted television.

Marcus's grandmother came by and tousled his hair after kissing his head. She adored her three grandchildren, but Marcus suspected he was a favorite and the son she never had. "Obrigado pelas frutas, vozinha," Marcus said attempting to thank her for breakfast in his Portuguese without looking up from his distractions. His voice didn't carry any of the intonation of gratitude but rather the rote flatness of a formality.

"Tudo por você, docinho." His grandmother's reply, in contrast, sounded as full of love as four words could be. She disappeared again to help his sister with whatever task Marcus had successfully avoided.

"Marcus, will you go down to the street market and bring back seasoning? There isn't enough for barbeque tonight," his mother stated in the form of a question, though Marcus knew it wasn't a question at all.

"Mom, I have to meet up with Dad," Marcus protested, already knowing his protests were in vain. "We are going to pick up firewood, and he needs my help." The first part was true; the second part probably less so. Marcus harbored no desire to go to the market or anywhere else at that moment. In contrast he nurtured plenty of desire to continue in the idleness older boys who are about to become young men often enjoy. If he would have been honest with himself, Marcus would have admitted he enjoyed going to the market, especially by himself, but on principle he resisted his mother taking advantage of his free time.

"What time are you meeting Dad?" she asked in a way which clearly showed she already knew the answer.

"I think maybe around eleven," he answered although they both knew his father never did anything 'around' any time but adhered to a near neurotic desire for all things to be on time.

"And what time is it now?" his mother asked again knowing the answer.

"Almost nine..." Marcus replied in a mumble knowing exactly where the conversation was going as he rolled off the couch to get his belongings for the impending market trip.

"Mmmhmmm... So, you don't think you can go to the market, get spices and some fruit and make it back in less than two hours?"

Marcus noted that his tasks now included getting some fruit and wondered if he attempted to debate longer with his mother, he might end up being tasked with bringing home a whole pig. Instead of further arguing, he decided to take the money his mother had left on the table, wondering when exactly she had placed it there and how long she had been planning this trip of his.

As he went to leave she grabbed him for a hug, and he noted she appeared to be hiding a bit of sadness in her eyes. Marcus had not reached the point in his life where he felt comfortable asking his mom about her feelings and so didn't remark at all on it but rather tried to act too grown up for any displays of emotion and affection. Marcus remembered his dad had been acting strangely the past few days as well, though Marcus was annoyingly aware that his parents' troubles were not with each other.

"I guess I have to do everything..." Marcus whined as soon as he was far enough away that his mother wouldn't respond, but still close enough that she could hear.

Outside the house the sounds of both the nearby forest and the adjacent potholed street were magnified, as were the noises of children playing and a couple having a discussion which sounded especially heated for still being morning. Not educated enough to understand why the streets and sidewalks in Brazil didn't usually match the pristine smoothness of those in California, Marcus regarded them with disdain. He also wasn't old enough to appreciate the character those flaws in city planning and maintenance lent to the town. Perhaps no one can see scars and irregularity in a landscape as beauty and character until they can see those things in themselves.

Marcus had been to the local street market numerous times on previous visits. He had also been to plenty other street markets enough times that he knew there was nothing particularly special about this market. It didn't take him long to find the fruit stand, or for the vendor to mix the spices Marcus knew his mother wanted. He thought it might have been faster to buy pre-mixed and pre-ground seasonings but decided against it. He reckoned any time he saved would be lost debating the lack of quality in pre-made seasonings with his mother, or worse yet, his grandmother.

Marcus paid for the spices and didn't forget to congratulate himself for his magnanimity at letting the merchant keep the twenty centavos change.

Despite Marcus's protests earlier to the contrary, Marcus did think he had plenty of time. Getting a bowl of açaí and watching the crowd for the beautiful women for which Brazil is famous seemed like a good use of the morning. Marcus haggled over the price of a small bowl and protested over the lack of condensed milk the man put on it mostly to prove to himself that no one could take advantage of him. When he sat down to eat his treat, Marcus noted that it never tasted as good as the açaí made for him at home. He alternated between annoyance at the flimsy spoon and the wobbly table, but the variety of people at the market did not disappoint him. After marveling at both the beauty and the strangeness South America's combinations of ethnicities produced, Marcus stood up to find the fruit vendor. His not-quite-empty cup and spoon remained on the table as a testament to his teenage selfishness.

The people in the town were not as monetarily wealthy as the community Marcus lived in in the United States. Often at the market he would wonder how much more material wealth he had than the man selling fruits out of an ancient van wearing clothes which had probably been purchased before Marcus's birth. With his pocket full of money Marcus considered himself far superior to the working poor and wondered why the man always appeared so much happier than Marcus ever felt. "Probably because poor people are stupid and stupid people are poor," Marcus thought to himself with disdain, though it didn't quite convince or assure him. As he finished up buying a few pieces of fruit he knew would satisfy his mother, he headed out of the market taking in the sights and sounds of commerce at one of its oldest and most human levels.

All the vendor booths at this market were nearly the same. White plastic folding tables across as many parking spot size spaces as the vendor secured though payment or ritual. In the world of tens of millions of streets and millions of street markets with vendors taking money for countless chickens, fish, meat, vegetables, fruits, trinkets and sweets there are always sufficient charlatans taking money for nothing more than a sleight of hand or vague predictions of the future. Some believe their feats to be true magic, some just believe there are enough fools for the clever to make an easy living. This market had somehow lacked the con artists on Marcus' previous visits, but Marcus noticed a new addition remedied the deficiency. Traditionally the market terminated in a familiar set of folding tables with coconut water being sold in cheap flimsy bottles from a food truck. On this day a short distance past the truck sat a man at a small but sturdy wooden table.

The purported magician dressed rather plainly. Despite the heat he wore typical denim pants as well as a plain grey sweatshirt which he wore with the hood pulled up. Instead of the normal cotton of almost every sweatshirt Marcus had ever seen, this one was made from a heavier course material. The hooded sweatshirt concealed much of the man's appearance as did a dark beard grown long, though lacking in thickness or fullness. His left hand rested tucked into the pocket of the sweatshirt while his right hand appeared to be drawing shapes on his table with a piece of charcoal. As people walked by, Marcus heard him call out names and mundane facts. He spoke flatly as though in a conversation with someone in the middle of the walkway. The voice sounded to Marcus like it belonged to someone who had been saying or doing the same thing all day and had lost all interest or enthusiasm. While his behavior implied he was a lunatic, his words sounded clear and precise.

"Roney works at a bank," he noted as a light-skinned middle-aged man walked by.

"Nidda enjoys cooking with extra salt," he remarked as a woman with a bag of produce passed by.

Marcus noticed none of the market's patrons payed the man any notice. Marcus wondered if their aversion was due to the lunacy of inaccurate statements or the discomfort of accurate ones. Apart from the oddity of his diatribe, just looking at his clothing made Marcus feel uncomfortably warm in the tropical heat.

"Nana, trying to learn a new language," the man droned on as the tall dark-haired girl sauntered by.

Marcus resolved to not look at the man as he walked by and decided to remain focused on something far away in the distance. As he did he put his grocery bag free hand in his pocket and noted a ring there he had found the day before.

"Marcus has a ring in his pocket," the voice tonelessly accused.

Absentmindedly Marcus's the words almost left his mouth, "Yes, I do have a ring in my pocket." He could have easily kept walking not taking note, but as the man spoke Marcus felt that the sound of the market went perceptibly quieter forcing him to pay attention to what the man said. Like all skeptics Marcus tried to think of an explanation and quickly decided to attribute the perception to well-practiced powers of observation. Marcus admitted to himself the explanation though improbable, was still possible, which was enough for the skeptic to continue walking.

"A grey ring that appears to be made of rubber," the man in grey spoke with a more pointed tone, still lacking any spirit. Marcus immediately felt a surge of surprise. He rebuked himself for not only letting the simple street performer attract his attention, but now he was rather stumped as to how anyone would know the specifics of the ring in his pocket. He fingered the ring in his pocket as his feet turned him slowly in the direction of the voice. The practical side of the boy wanted to walk away, but he feared if he did so this man would know he had gotten the best of Marcus.

"I will tell you of your past and future, Marcus," the man spoke clearly to Marcus still without any inflection or emotion in his voice.

Marcus could not explain why he walked over to the table as he stood directly across from the fortune teller. From there Marcus could inspect his provoker better; or rather more clearly see he couldn't examine him very well at all. Despite the beard Marcus saw many tattoos and scars on the man's face. More tattoos, pockmarks of many small scars and a larger one just above the wrist marked his exposed right hand. Marcus at first tried to dismiss them as the cheap markings of a gang member or low life, but they were more similar to runes or primitive designs he remembered seeing in museums or history books. Still, Marcus decided they were fakes intended to add to the magical persona, which the man failed to exude very well outside of his overall strangeness. Cheap reflective sunglasses covered the man's eyes, which Marcus took solace in hiding from. The man appeared to be middle-aged in his late forties or so, but his skin showed the damage of one who lived a life exposed to the elements. The face did not show a sadness as much as a lack of happiness. His only possessions were a beaten weathered canteen and a large walking stick.

"So, you have magic powers, huh?" Marcus asked putting as much sarcasm and disdain in his voice as he could muster despite being more than a little thrown off by the man's earlier divinations. Marcus now hoped he would somehow be able to embarrass this street performer and prove his superiority in his own mind.

Ignoring the question, the man simply plodded on in his same empty voice, "Marcus was born in a place among the trees, but far from these trees."

"That could literally mean anywhere in the entire world," Marcus said to himself assuredly. Under his breath he added, "All these stupid predictions are the same nonsense."

The man either didn't hear or didn't care for the boy's remarks and continued, "Marcus used to look out the window and see the large trees as a small child," the man nodded down to the table where his hand had been busy while he spoke. On the table Marcus saw the man had sketched the view from the balcony at Marcus's first home. The trees, the rocks and the tiny stream behind them were drawn exactly as Marcus remembered. Understandably, seeing a sketch of one of his earliest memories done by a stranger gave him a shock. He searched for explanations but found only confusion and fear instead. The drawing was crude, done with a small piece of charcoal on a wooden table but remarkably close to what Marcus remembered. All the more impressive, he thought, since the man drew the scene oriented to where Marcus stood.

"How did you do that?" Marcus whispered more to himself than to the man. He wanted to reach down and rub the picture out to take back his stolen memory, but the man's sleeve quickly dispersed the drawing with a few quick movements.

"Marcus grew up along the sand playing in the sea, but far from this sand and sea," the voice went on again ignoring Marcus's question. Both statements the man made were accurate, though vague. He had been born in the forested North of California and lived most of his still few years on the beaches of Southern California where he hoped to be again soon. "Marcus almost believes in magic. He wonders about the forces unseen but doesn't believe they have anything to do with the world today. Marcus believes all those things are lost now, just like a little toy car." The man stopped talking as he placed a toy car where the drawing of the forest had been.

Marcus's shock at seeing this toy car was much greater than anyone not familiar with it could have understood. The car was a black 1982 Pontiac Firebird with a piece of plastic in the front that was supposed to simulate a red light. Many years ago, Marcus's dad saw one at a garage sale. When he went to purchase it, Marcus told him that he didn't really want it. His father smiled at him with nearly a laugh when he told his son the miniature car wasn't for Marcus. Marcus had been perplexed since his brother and sister weren't old enough to play with it. The car brought a smile to his father's face repeatedly, and a very young Marcus decided this meant it must be a wonderful toy which he had failed to recognize the importance of. He would beg his father to let him play with it, and always his father would acquiesce, saying only, "Don't lose it," which is, of course, what Marcus did a few years later. The memory always stuck with him, partly because he felt he had let his dad down, and partly because for years he remained certain he hadn't lost it. He remembered being at his Baba's house around the time the man died and lining up all the toy cars in his collection along with his Samoa Joe and Captain Poe action figures. He had meant it to be a funeral procession for the grandfather who had always shown him so much affection. When he went to collect the cars, the black one with the inexplicably important red plastic light in the front was gone. His father dismissed it as carelessness on his son's part and did not attempt to hide his disappointment which made the memory stick out so clearly in Marcus's mind.

And now here--almost ten years later and a continent away-- the car and its red plastic light stared at him from a wooden table. Marcus told himself it could not possibly be the same one, but he couldn't ignore how it matched his memory, all the way down to the dent in the door.

Marcus's shock at seeing the car put him in a stupor.

"One shouldn't leave valuable things lying around. But remember not everything that is missing is lost."

The words caught Marcus off guard, leaving him unable to rationalize anything about the conversation. Marcus's thoughts progressed from fear to simple disbelief. He started to feel a bit light headed and weak but fought against the sensations.

"Marcus is about to go on a very long journey which will take him far from everyone he knows and loves. Marcus must leave that life behind and accept pain and sacrifice to be successful."

Thoughts about the history of the toy car so consumed Marcus's thoughts that he almost missed what the man said. Marcus felt the man proved his point by getting under the skin of a boy who considered himself a man at fourteen. Desperately Marcus wanted to believe the entire exchange to be some trick and continued to search frantically for an explanation. None of this seemed to matter to the man whose measured monotone, unfeeling voice continued on. "Marcus's journey is very important, and though he will be opposed from both sides, and despite painful loss, Marcus must prevail."

"I don't know what you're talking about... Stop... just stop..." Marcus mumbled. Everything around him felt a million miles away, and he and this awful stranger and his table were in some surreal dream world. He searched frantically for more words to say. He wanted to curse at the man for stealing his memories and for making a fool of him. He also didn't like anything the man had said about some journey, especially if it meant pain and sacrifice. Most of all he hated the way the man made him feel; scared and confused. Marcus would have felt better if the man showed enjoyment at Marcus's suffering, instead his tormentor went through his dialogue with the emotional emptiness of a worn-out recording.

"You must not fear, Marcus." Marcus heard the man say the words he had heard from his father all his life but now mocked him and his fear. With his anger boiling over and the ringing of rage in his ears Marcus felt the desire to reach out and strike the man. He stared down at the man in his anger, but only his own reflection from glasses resting on an emotionless face met his gaze. Immediately the urge to be as far from the man in a grey sweatshirt overwhelmed the boy.

Marcus turned to go, almost stumbling. He left the market not quite at a run, but far from the cool casual walk he would have been proud of. In fact, Marcus payed no attention to what direction he traveled. He only wanted to put time and distance between himself and the disturbing experience. He could still see the man's face, still feel that violated sensation as the man pulled at his memories, and still hear the voice telling him he must not fear. At his frantic pace Marcus soon ended up on the edge of town nowhere near his home.

When Marcus finally calmed enough to realize the futility of his aimless walk, he found himself in a part of the city he did not recognize. The street he walked along on appeared to continue on for a long way in a direction Marcus knew would not take him where he needed to go. A quick shiver of panic came hand in hand with a feeling of shame for having let someone get inside his head and have such an effect on him.

As his fear subsided Marcus's practical side emerged. Like most lost modern people Marcus decided to consult the map on his phone for his location and a short way home. When he first opened his phone, the time glaring at him from the screen shocked him: 10:27AM. Marcus knew he should have returned more than half an hour ago. If he had still been at the fair, there would be enough time to return home by eleven, but when he saw his location on his phone's map the timeline for his return by eleven didn't look as promising. The small costal city formed a bit of a 'U' shape, according to the map Marcus had walked to the north east edge of the town. Although his family's home was also near the edge of the town, it was on the north west side. He would either have to walk back into town toward the market and around the undeveloped forest area, or he would have to walk through a short expanse of it which might mean very slow and difficult traveling.

Marcus didn't want to commit to either plan yet and so decided to walk toward the edge of where the town development ended to take a look. If the shortcut looked too overgrown, he would traverse around the forest through the town. "I'll just tell Dad I lost my temper and went crazy because a street magician without even a crystal ball scared me so much that I ran off to another part of the city. At least Dad will be happy to hear it involved that stupid black car." Marcus couldn't think of any better way of stating the events to make himself look less foolish in his father's eyes. He felt pretty stupid in his own eyes and kept replaying the events in his head trying to make sense of them.

As he began to convince himself of the lack of any real magic at the town market and the multitude of ways the man could have tricked him into seeing whatever the man wanted him to see on the table, Marcus came to the edge of the forest. He smiled to himself as he observed the beginning of a pretty clear path running through it. He convinced himself that after a brisk walk on a clear path, his day would be much more normal and hopefully filled with his grandmother's delicious barbeque. It made sense to Marcus that there should be a path here, as he felt sure he couldn't have been the first person to want to cut from one part of town to another without walking through the crowded streets.

The cell phone showed plenty of signal as he started on the path, and Marcus felt a tingle of joy as he watched a portly man come out of the trail. Marcus convinced himself that the trail could not be too difficult if a man carrying an extra half of a person worth of weight could make it. As he started into the forest he continued to replay his conversation with the strange man at the market. Marcus kept going over all that had occurred at the market trying to figure out how he would explain it to people in a way that didn't make him sound foolish or crazy. The more he thought about the time, the more he realized some explanation would be required when he arrived home. If he did not make it back in time to pick up firewood with his dad, he would have much more explaining to do.

Under the canopy of the large trees Marcus started to think he would use the walk through the forest as the excuse why he had lost an hour of his day. The plainness of the path, unfortunately, didn't offer any excuse as to why someone would lose an hour of his day on it. As he continued he came to a fork in the path. The main way was clear, and he could tell the other path wandered off to his right toward what the locals would call a mountain since the area around the town was so flat. Now Marcus had a decision to make; to return home a little late with no excuse or go to the top of this hill and find something worthwhile around it that would sound adventurous enough to warrant missing an hour or more of his day. Of course, if he made it home by eleven that would be all the better; he would have a great story and no grumpy reaction from his mom or dad.

And so, a boy came to a fork in a path and deliberated for a short time, weighing his fears. Many important decisions have been made by careful examination of the costs and benefits or of the possible gains and losses. This was not to be one of them. Marcus stared at the path and instead of making a decision consciously, his feet seemed to decide on their own accord. Without knowing exactly why, Marcus walked toward both a hill masquerading as a mountain and the strangest day of his life.

After Marcus made his decision to take the path toward the large hill in the little forest on the edge of town, he started to get the feeling common with travelers that he was going exactly where he needed to be. He checked a map on his phone and confirmed this little detour wouldn't take him too far and would in fact get him back about five or ten minutes after eleven o'clock. That would be close enough to eleven that his father would ask why he was late, but not enough to get him into so much trouble that he couldn't talk his way out of it. Marcus could then tell a story about an odd, but obviously not magical, charlatan at the market, as well as a great trail and hill just outside of town. A trail which he would claim had an amazing view, whether it did or not. He would take a picture; it would be a nice addition to the great ones he would show his family, friends, and maybe even Mary later.

As he got closer to the hill, he saw the path went directly up toward a pile of stacked rocks. He approached the pile of rocks hastily climbing higher for an improved scenic view of the area. Marcus continued to follow the trail when he noticed an entrance to a small hollow in the hill which would only pass as a cave to those who didn't spend much time in nature.

Marcus couldn't resist the desire to look in the cave and still climb to the top of the hill. Somewhat regular travel had worn a path to the cave, and Marcus reasoned it would take mere minutes to see the cave and the top of the hill. A legitimate excuse for lateness would be worth a few minutes of jogging later. Besides, Marcus's dad had developed a strange fascination with caves after his own father's death and this one might interest him. As Marcus got closer he saw the end of the cave from outside and felt certain going inside would be a quick and easy adventure. The mundane graffiti on the nearby pile of rocks assured him civilization was not far away. Marcus entered the cave with a quick glance at his phone that confirmed the cell phone signal remained strong and plenty of time remained if his walk turned into a trot.

Marcus shuffled along the cave's smooth floor making sure not to lose his footing. The cave wasn't very deep, and in just seconds Marcus walked to a few paces from the end. Stopping to look around Marcus saw the cave was only bare stone, with only bits of trash marking where others may have sought shelter from rain or society. Near the mouth of the cave the ground had been worn by habitual sleeping. "How badly do you have to screw up your life to sleep in a cave?" Marcus asked the absent tenant.

As Marcus walked forward he felt a deep sense of foreboding but brushed it aside. He thought he saw a shimmer like a heat mirage a few steps ahead but convinced himself it was his imagination. After taking another step he caught a glimpse of the phenomenon, which disappeared just as quickly. If Marcus would have been of a more superstitious mind, he would have run at that point. However, he couldn't imagine telling his father he was late because he had gotten distracted by a street peddler then been too scared to 'explore' a cave. Especially a cave which would prove to be no bigger than a garage. Admitting to being scared by an oddity his father would no doubt have a rational scientific explanation for would be even worse. His mother may be more open minded to any supernatural interpretation of events but less accepting of his fear of them.

Every hair on his body stood up as Marcus took the last few steps walking past where his mind had played tricks on him. At first Marcus rebuked himself for his fantastic imaginings, but it had been a very strange and surreal day and one more inexplicable event hardly struck him as out of place. A few more steps and he could tell his father about climbing a hill and exploring a cave in the forest. His story would avoid any talk about wandering lost in rage brought on by the tricks of a third-rate market magician.

Marcus symbolically touched the back of the cave and turned around. The light coming in through the mouth made him feel assured. He was taken aback by the way everything in the cave appeared to him slightly different when he turned around. The cave itself remained unchanged, but the walls, the rocks and the floor all appeared dryer and the rocks sharper than when he had walked in. It appeared to Marcus as though the natural wetness of the damp cave had instantly been soaked up. The trash that littered the floor had been replaced by small animal droppings. Marcus assured his racing mind looking at the cave from a different angle explained the difference. After the heat mirage coupled with his hair standing on end, and the odd transformation Marcus wanted nothing more to do with the cave. It would be unfair to say he ran out, but he certainly did not emerge at a casual pace.

As Marcus emerged from the cave and looked around, the whole area had undergone a subtle but noticeable change. The stones, for the most part, were the same although Marcus didn't see any of the vandalism he had noted before. The plant life, however, appeared notably different and more overgrown. Marcus began to doubt himself as he searched for the path which had led him to and then up the hill. He couldn't precisely identify what in the plants and trees appearance changed from his walk in, but they were all somehow more vibrant and lush. The forest also sounded much quieter, and he couldn't hear anything other than chirping birds.

Forgetting his plan to climb the hill Marcus continued beyond where he remembered the path starting. He looked back for the cave entrance and noted it was out of sight though he remembered distinctly seeing it from the path when he had approached. He walked back toward the cave entrance convincing himself he would find the path again, but already fearing he would not. When he did not, he decided to consult the map and GPS on his phone. He felt ashamed at having to do so again when he had been so certain he would not be so careless as to lose the well-trodden footpath. As he looked at his phone the words NO SIGNAL glared back at him. All at once the feeling came flooding in that whether it was with his phone or his sanity, something was very, very wrong.

Marcus scurried up to the top of the hill now believing in his head that when he got there he would see the town, the path, and all the sights to reassure him of his location. However, his heart warned him he would actually find himself far from anything he knew. Marcus nursed the belief that the phone would work better at higher ground though a feeling in the pit of his stomach told him otherwise. Fear has a way of stretching frozen moments and the climb to the top of the hill, which took him less than five minutes, seemed to last forever. At a flat spot on the hillside Marcus realized he had gained as much elevation as he needed. Marcus looked around emotionally overwhelmed by the beauty of the forest, but devastated at seeing no town, no road, and no cell phone tower. In fact, Marcus saw no sign of any human habitation. He looked down at his phone; 14 APRIL 2033, Marcus suspected was not accurate anymore, though the NO SIGNAL clearly was. It would be impossible to explain how lost he felt in a location that in some ways looked minutes from home. The fear of losing his mind combined with the beauty of the area he surveyed was too much for a fourteen-year-old boy, no matter how badly he wanted to be a man. Marcus collapsed onto a nearby rock and cried.

CHAPTER TWO - LOST

Not until we are lost do we begin to understand ourselves.
  - Henry David Thoreau

Marcus was not sure how long he cried before he grew tired of his tears. He decided rather than sobbing, he would eat the fruits in the bag he had been carrying since he left the market. The sweetness of the banana and the act of doing something productive improved his spirits immediately.

"I guess I better start rationing my food until I find some more," Marcus said to the bag of fruit. His voice betrayed his disbelief in his situation.

The landscape looked so similar to the one he had left that he believed fruit trees were bound to be somewhere nearby, although he couldn't see them from the hilltop. For a few moments Marcus stared blankly into the endless expanse of forest. The smell of the forest struck his senses as he sat in silence. Marcus did not remember ever smelling the forest before the cave, but now he smelled the subtle yet robust fragrance which sought to assure him nature was in control but meant him no harm. The air the scent rode on was as fresh and clean as anything Marcus had ever breathed. In a strange way it pained Marcus to feel something so pure while enduring an experience so miserable.

Thus, Marcus's stomach and lungs did much to calm the boy who started going through the mental checklist of what to do when lost. Besides finding food and water he remembered keeping a positive attitude was vital. "How am I supposed to keep a good attitude when the whole world is playing a twisted joke on me?" Marcus asked himself.

Like most inquisitive boys of fourteen Marcus had read enough fantastic books to have a few outlandish ideas as to what might have happened. The appearance of his surroundings made Marcus think he was in the same place but in a different time or perhaps some parallel universe version of Earth. Marcus also reasoned that the whole thing could be some elaborate joke or experiment someone was playing on him. With some trepidation he recognized that while time travel and parallel universes were common in science fiction books and movies, insanity was much more prevalent in the real world.

Marcus hoped sincerely he was not going crazy. As sane people often do, Marcus reasoned that since he was considering the idea that he might be crazy, he was probably not crazy but wasn't sure insanity was worse than being lost in time or space. The last possibility Marcus considered was that he was dreaming. Marcus preferred this possibility because it meant the end of the madness would be coming soon. Unfortunately, nothing about his surroundings or feelings felt dream-like. He went through the list of things dreamers do to wake up, nearly pinching himself sore but all to no avail. After eating the last bite of a small banana, he decided to go back to the cave. If the cave should prove a dead-end, he resolved to start exploring the surrounding areas.

Marcus walked back to the cave taking note of how much everything looked almost the way he remembered it from a couple hours earlier, but also different in some way. When Marcus entered the cave, he felt the same strong sense of foreboding, but the cave appeared as benign as any cave could be. Marcus tried to convince himself that whatever had transported him from his world might still be there. A detailed inspection of the cave walls yielded no clues as to any secret that might be hidden there. He tried walking through the cave in different ways trying to spot any glimpse of what resembled a heat mirage. After a thorough examination Marcus gave up wandering in circles in the cave.

"Please, I'd give anything to be home." Marcus said his prayer aloud to anyone who might be listening and reached out his hand once more for some hint of a way back but found nothing save stale cave air.

Marcus looked at his phone which read 01:15PM. The phone contained a wide array of games and information on it, including hundreds of books and an exhaustive encyclopedia. Though it caused him a sharp twinge of emotional pain, Marcus decided to shut it off, clearly separating himself from the connectedness of the 21st century. A small solar array built into the case would be able to charge it, but he knew it would take a day of sunlight just to regain a few minutes of function. Besides, Marcus couldn't think of anything he would use it for in the immediate future. Before he did turn it off, Marcus took a photograph of the cave. He thought taking a picture was the sanest thing a person could do, and he wanted to document everything as it happened in case he ever had the chance to explain it to someone at some future date. Though Marcus held only the slightest hope of some sort of rescue, he already feared no one would believe his story if indeed he was fortunate enough to return home.

After dutifully documenting his unbelievable situation Marcus resolved to start thinking pragmatically. "I have to treat this like I got lost camping," Marcus thought aloud. "All those times Dad made me prepare for getting lost, I was sure that only happened to idiots, but maybe I'm that idiot," he conceded. Marcus started by making a mental list of what he had.

"I've got a bunch of bananas, two mangoes, a papaya, a bag of lychee and Brazilian seasoning, which will be great after I find and kill a cow," he said to himself looking through the bag. "I've also got the stuff in my pockets."

In his pockets Marcus found a pocket knife which he had begun carrying in emulation of his father, but also because he imagined it gave him a dangerous persona that fourteen-year-old boys relish. He also had his wallet which contained a school identification card, plus a few notes in US and Brazilian money. Looking through the wallet he also found the number of a fairly attractive Brazilian girl who was impressed with his claimed ability to speak four languages, despite the fact he only spoke three. He pulled from his pocket a misshapen grey silicone ring that he now eyed accusingly, trying to remember where he had found it and how it had ended up in his pocket.

Marcus decided the best thing for the time being would be to look for water and food, as well as set up a base camp. He knew as long as he stayed occupied he would have less time to be afraid, angry, or depressed, which he admitted he was. Marcus reasoned it would be perfectly acceptable for anyone to be afraid but knew his father would not see it that way. He would ask Marcus if his fear would accomplish anything. Eventually Marcus would admit it would not. His father would then end the debate by saying, "You must not fear, Marcus." As he ended the theoretical conversation in his head to start the search for water, he realized the last voice he heard was not his father's, but the empty voice of the strange man at the market.

Marcus remembered crossing a stream when he had walked along the path and figured that direction was a good place to start. The trail from the main path towards the hill was gone, but he quickly found a much smaller trail in the same general area. The smaller trail appeared to have been created by small four-legged travelers and not the two-legged ones Marcus was looking for. It didn't take long on the meandering trail through the low brush for Marcus to wind up at a little stream. This one looked remarkably the same as the stream he had crossed what felt like days ago but was really only a few hours earlier. The stream wasn't much as far as streams go, but it did have flowing water which looked clear and potable. Marcus recalled stories of people drinking contaminated water from polluted streams before so he tried to be cautious and looked for dead or sick animals but found none. Despite no sign of any sick or dead animals Marcus knew he should do something to boil or filter the water through sand or charcoal. He didn't have any method to do either of those things, so he sat and watched the waters, hoping to see an animal or bird drink first.

The more Marcus watched the water the thirstier he became. However, he thought about how throwing up or getting diarrhea in a place where no one would be there to help him would be far worse than his present thirst. He thought about how he could very well die out in the middle of nowhere, which he reminded himself, looked exactly like it was about a fifteen-minute walk from his home despite there being no sign of civilization anywhere. The fear of sickness and death fighting against his thirst lasted until the moment his fear of dying of dehydration tilted the scales in favor of drinking the water. Despite knowing death from dehydration takes days, Marcus kneeled down and cupped the water to his mouth and was pleasantly surprised at how clean it tasted. Marcus thought about lying all the way down and lapping it up but remembered being told this was not the way men drink from a river. The water was not cool, but it was refreshing in a way only those who are very thirsty can appreciate. Cupping the water to his mouth was not especially efficient so satiating his thirst took longer than he anticipated. After the several hours Marcus spent debating about water and finally drinking, the day was almost over. Marcus reasoned the sun would set soon though he couldn't see it through the low clouds.

Starting a fire and finding food were both high on his priority list. In his short trek through the forest he hadn't seen any fruit trees he knew were native to this part of South America, nor had he seen anything he could catch and eat. He had seen a few birds, as well as spiders, ants and flies, which gave him a somewhat hollow reassurance he wasn't the only living thing where or whenever he was. Marcus tried in vain to start a fire but after a short time gave up and decided to eat some more of the fruit he had brought. Though he estimated it was only nine in the evening, Marcus felt exhausted. Without light there wasn't much else he could do, so he returned to the cave. As much as he loathed the place, Marcus hoped someone else might come through. Besides he couldn't think of anywhere better to sleep.

And so, Marcus spent his first night in a strange place with a nearly empty belly and no fire. A little cold and a tad hungry, a touch damp and very much alone--Marcus cried a bit and thought about his family a lot. He tried to convince himself they weren't even born yet, but that didn't help him miss them less. He often asked himself who was to blame. The list was long. Primarily he blamed the stranger at the market for toying with him. He also blamed his mother for sending him to the market when she could have gone herself. Marcus also decided his father was partially to blame because he had been the reason Marcus had been in a hurry and taken the short cut. Marcus even remembered to blame the fat man coming off the path for deceiving him as to the nature of the path. Most of all Marcus blamed whoever had created the earth and everything else. Obviously, Creation was a big responsibility and someone should make sure there were no holes in it. The first night in the cave Marcus kindled his anger at whatever Creator there might be and made sure to nurse that fire for a long time. As many who have known the coldness of sadness can attest, anger is sometimes a warm blanket.

It would be unfair to say anything happened whilst Marcus slept, because nothing he did in the cave the first night could honestly be called sleeping. Marcus's brief periods of rest were broken by sounds which at first sounded as frightening as the past twelve hours had been but were all just typical nighttime forest sounds.

Towards morning Marcus had the feeling that there was someone else with him. The words were not as much of a shock for Marcus to hear as he would have expected.

"Don't be afraid. It's only me. I don't want to hurt you," a voice said calmly.

"Who are you?" Marcus asked not sure if he was dreaming but glad for any company.

"I'm just another traveler in the wrong place." The voice sounded sad and a bit condescending, but any voice at this point was welcome.

"Me, too; I was on my way home... something happened in this cave and everything changed; all the people, everything is gone."

"Very strange... I was sent down here, thrown out of my home like a bent knife the owner couldn't use anymore."

"Where am I? Do you know what year it is?" Marcus inquired still lying down and becoming surer he was dreaming.

He wasn't able to get a good look at the source of the voice in the darkness, but he could tell a bit from the light of the moon. The speaker had reddish skin--redder even than his grandmother--and red hair that was long for a man. He looked to be a young man. While much older than Marcus, he was not at the point in life where the mere passing of time starts to make one old, but rather the age where life's trials make one old. Marcus couldn't help but think the man was blessed with an uncommon beauty. Nevertheless, his face was marked clearly by his emotions; primarily sadness and anger. He wore a robe which appeared to be ancient but remarkably beautiful and well made. The light of the moon was not bright, but the way it illuminated the stone and the speaker made the experience all the more surreal.

"You are in a cave on the land given to the red children," the stranger remarked annoyed that he should have to answer such a question. "But you are not a red child, at least not entirely." He continued looking Marcus over and sounding somewhat intrigued by this last observation. "As far as when it is, this is the third decade of the second millennium of man." The stranger concluded dismissively.

"Oh..." Marcus didn't know what the stranger was talking about, and his dreamlike dazed state only made his confusion worse.

"Are you sure you don't know how you got here? No one sent you?" the red haired, red skinned stranger asked accusingly.

"No, no I promise. I just want to get home. Can you help me get home, please?" Marcus asked, though he could tell the stranger was more interested in talking about his own troubles than any requests Marcus had.

Anger suddenly replaced the calm in the stranger's voice. "Can I help you!? What about me? Your being here is your fault, but I'm being punished for no reason. Of course, I can help you. I can do anything. But what's the point? You don't even know where you want to go. I should still be up there, none of this is fair. I have so much power, but here I am on this whole cursed rock and some silly boy who doesn't understand how time works wants me to be his personal genie."

When Marcus heard the stranger boast he could help him return home, Marcus's heart leapt, and he started to look for any way to gain the stranger's friendship. He hadn't been gone for a whole day, but Marcus had already had enough of this adventure. Since the man hadn't sounded interested in Marcus's plight, Marcus figured he would have to find some way to ingratiate himself to this stranger.

"Who are you? Why did you get stuck here?" Marcus asked.

"Around here they call me Ahsigna. You wouldn't be able to say my original name... as far as how I got here... He tricked me..." the stranger trailed off. "He tricked me. He said I would be able to do whatever I wanted... I didn't know what would happen. Nobody told me it would be like this... so empty, so cold... and I don't even know why everything has to be this way." The stranger was rambling but was also clearly glad to talk about his mistreatment.

"He told me I could choose my side, and with him I could do what I wanted... but he didn't tell me I would get banished! Sent down here! It's not fair... I don't know why this had to happen to me... no one can ever tell me why this had to happen to me... but at least I'm free." At the thought of his freedom the anger seemed to shift back to sorrow. "I'm free and all those fools will see what freedom can allow one to do... I'm going to show them all what happens when someone treats me this way!" He was now crying. Since Marcus had no idea what to do when a supernatural being cried, he defaulted to what his mother would have done and started to sit up to give the man a hug.

At this Ahsigna backed away. "NO! Leave me alone.... I don't need you, you don't care anyways. It doesn't matter, I'll get even. Nobody treats me this way..." As the red-haired stranger walked out of the cave, he gave a longing glance at the sky then was gone in a blur into the forest. His sudden departure left Marcus as alone and as confused as ever. The whole conversation felt like a dream to Marcus when he awoke the next morning.

The following day Marcus resolved to do more exploring. He first made a pile of stones at the top of the hill so that if anyone came, they would immediately see there had been recent human occupation. He wrote "HELP! STRANDED" as deep as a stick would carve the words into the dirt nearest the cave entrance, in case someone else came through. After these precautions were taken, Marcus went to find the trail that had taken him to the stream the previous day. Since he had not taken ill, Marcus again drank from the stream despite having some misgivings about the color of the water which had become less clear than the previous day. Marcus followed the trail a little further and was overjoyed to see what looked like a guava tree. It did not look exactly how Marcus remembered guava looking, but it was similar enough that he decided to give it a try. Marcus started with a small bite to see if it would make him sick; and after waiting less time than he should have, he had a few more. Marcus found a few more trees bearing food, but to his disappointment, no bananas. At one point he caught a grasshopper, which he ate only because he thought a survivalist should eat something strange on principle.

It only took three days before Marcus started to consider the cave his temporary home although he loathed using the word 'home' to describe it, even to himself. In his mind it was both the cause of his predicament and the most probable way to return home. He started his day there and in an ever-expanding loop around the cave and its hill, collected fruits and the driest wood he came across. Sometimes at night, most often during rains, mice would seek shelter in 'his' cave. The first one caused him an unreasonable panic, mostly because he was of the mindset that mice were unwanted vermin, but he quickly became accustomed to them and would simply shoo them with a stick.

While Marcus did his best to sleep on the fourth night of his involuntary adventure, he felt movement against his foot. He kicked at the intruder with his bare leg and felt the fur of a mouse. The thought of sharing his abode with mice still made his stomach turn a little. He thought about getting a stick to chase it out, but decided he was too tired to chase a mouse around in the dark. A few moments passed and again he felt something move against his leg. Although this time it felt different, he was still sure the intruder was a mouse so he kicked at it blindly. This time, however, his bare foot found something more solid and hairless. In a panic Marcus was suddenly wide awake, and he tried to push his body away from whatever he had felt as he sat up.

The moon had just enough light that Marcus could make out shapes, but not see clearly. Marcus searched for his phone in hopes of using the flashlight to illuminate and hopefully scare what he hoped was a mouse. Before his fingers gripped his phone, a silhouette came into a clearer view as the moonlight bounced off the scales of the largest snake Marcus had seen in the wild. The entire mouth of the cave appeared to be blocked by the snake's head which was raised off the ground enough to stare into the eyes of the terrified boy.

Marcus's heart nearly jumped into his throat as his stomach looked for another bodily exit. The sensation of blood throbbing in his arms and legs as all his muscles clenched tight made any movement impossible. The snake clearly saw him as well, and its inhuman eyes regarded Marcus coolly. Marcus had always heard that snakes were more afraid of people than people were of snakes, but this particular snake had no fear of Marcus.

The snake kept deathly quiet, but Marcus was sure the beating of his own heart was louder than any thunderstorm that had crossed South America. The snake eyes stared through him as it swayed a little from left to right, its yellow scales each illuminated by the paleness of the moon. Marcus watched the undulations of the head which housed the lifeless yellow eyes and duplicitous tongue, certain the reptile was toying with him before launching itself into a death bite directly on Marcus's neck. While no fangs were visible, in his imagination they were as long as his finger and dripping with life-ending green venom. Marcus wanted to stand up and run, but the fright kept him paralyzed. Certain any movement would result in his death he stared at the snake as he stretched the frozen moments with his fear. Marcus felt tears start to swell in his eyes when the snake's swaying slowed as it coiled back.

In a flash the snake launched itself forward, and if Marcus would have had time he would have thought that was his last second. The lack of teeth in his neck shocked Marcus as the snake's lunge missed him by a hair's breadth. The snake did not, in fact, miss but now had in its mouth Marcus's other unwelcomed house guest. The body of the mouse hung lifelessly by the time Marcus could see the two in the light of the moon. While Marcus felt a pang of sadness for the mouse, his relief that the snake's mouth was now occupied overwhelmed him. He spent the rest of the night between nightmares in which he was a mouse and pondering ideas to keep pests out of the cave.

Marcus spent the next three days sleeping in the cave, each night believing he would wake up at home. Marcus had been worried the temperature drop at night would be as severe as he remembered some nights south of the Amazon could be. Instead he was relieved to find the temperature drops to be just enough to be a welcomed break from the heat of the day. Marcus had started to fashion a few tools such as a toothbrush and a bit of a spear, which he put effort into every time he heard the far-off sounds of a jaguar roar. While the jaguar sounds did scare Marcus a bit, it also made him confident that there was meat around. He was definitely starting to grow tired of eating fruit three times a day. Marcus was also getting tired of doing nothing which would bring him closer to home. He spent a fair amount of time researching things on his phone about South America that might be useful. He studied what plants he could and could not eat. He learned about a spider who could cause an erection lasting for days, and about the bullet ant whose sting was supposed to be thirty times more painful than a bee sting. Marcus also believed he had identified the mouse-eating snake, jararacussu, which sounded as scary as it had looked. On the seventh day, after consulting a few more fire-starting instructions from the encyclopedia on his phone, Marcus decided to put a real effort into making fire, and that changed everything.

Marcus started his quest to make fire as soon as he had eaten a few fruits, aware it would take him a fair amount of time. During the previous few days Marcus had tried to gather the necessary dry wood, which was not an easy feat in a place of daily rain, and some grasses that were still dry enough to light. The last step was for Marcus to make a bow drill. Good sticks were plentiful, and he used the lace of his shoe as the string for the bow. The base he made from fallen bark that had managed to stay somewhat dry.

His knife was essential to making small kindling and shaping the base and the bow so it would function smoothly. His creation was not the most elaborate bow drill, however Marcus put several hours of work into it. Time was the thing he believed he had plenty of. When he finished, he felt a fair amount of pride in his work, though he still harbored doubts about his ability to start a fire without matches or a lighter.

Marcus hoped that starting a fire would be his dramatic conquest of nature. He envisioned himself as prehistoric man discovering fire-making in his cave, but since he hadn't needed the fire so far it didn't feel as important as he might have fancied. Marcus ran the bow drill until his arms ached before he saw any change. The bow would go back and forth for a while and either the tip would jump out of the hole as he became lax on applying pressure, or he would apply too much pressure causing it to collapse over. He thought about giving up several times but the discoloration on the wood caused by the heat of the drill inspired him to continue.

When he saw the first tiny plume of smoke and the first tiny flick of yellow and orange on the grass, Marcus wondered if they were only products of wishful thinking. A few more sparks of yellow and orange convinced him his progress was real. As difficult as getting the first sparks had been, Marcus almost reached a panick in his rush to keep the fresh embers supplied with fuel to grow. His heart swelled with pride when he saw the first marks of a fire.

Once he had a good smoldering pile of grass, he added the dried twigs and some branches as he had done on camping trips before with other fire-starting methods. It took a fair amount of time, and lots of huffing and puffing, but eventually he stood to see his creation of fire. Marcus dutifully added the larger dried wood until he had a respectable campfire. The fire gave off considerable heat, but even more smoke.

Looking out from the cave mouth the fire was impressive, but fear and excitement soon displaced Marcus's pride. From the multitude of uses man has devised for fire, Marcus had forgotten one of the earliest. The plume of smoke had brought the attention of six men standing a short distance off watching him and the fire. Marcus quickly learned that sometimes the only thing more frightening than thinking you are alone is finding out that you are not.

CHAPTER THREE - THE RED CHILDREN

"Manifest plainness,
Embrace simplicity,
Reduce selfishness,
Have few desires."
　　- Lao-Tzu, Tao Te Ching

Marcus wasn't sure what exactly to do when making contact with a new civilization so he tried to act natural and put up his right hand in a half wave, half salute. All the people watching him made a remarkably good imitation in returning the gesture. Marcus and the natives stood staring at each other for some time. Marcus kept hoping eventually one of them would walk up to introduce himself and establish contact, but several minutes crept by and the strange people did not do anything other than observe Marcus. As much as Marcus felt his whole adventure had been quite out of the ordinary, he also reasoned that having someone show up out of place and time was not something these people were accustomed to either. Marcus walked down to introduce himself, spurred by the fear that his visitors might leave if he did not.

These unfamiliar inhabitants appeared different than anyone else Marcus had ever seen. They wore nothing but a loincloth which in the heat didn't surprise Marcus very much. The dark redness of the natives' skin appeared unusual to Marcus. Even the indigenous people of South America he had seen before lacked this deep color of red. None of them showed any visible type of tattoo or piercing, nor wore any type of decoration. The men all bore sets of small scars on their right hands, though on the older ones the scars looked faded with time. The apparent fitness of the men immediately intimidated the lost boy; to Marcus they looked like an Olympic gymnastics team. Marcus had always been very athletic compared to his peers, but he imagined he looked pretty weak in the eyes of these athletes. Having spent the last week afraid of the unfamiliar world around him, Marcus had also been longing for comfort and companionship that only other humans provide. However, surrounded by intimidating strangers, he felt anxious they would harm him in some way. Their lack of weapons did little to allay Marcus's fear.

Marcus could feel chills on his skin as he cautiously walked toward the group. Several members stepped back away from him, so as Marcus approached it became clear with whom he would be interacting.

The one who did not walk away at Marcus's approach stood slightly taller than the others but nothing about his size or apparent strength made Marcus think he stood out. The man, like most members of the group, had a wide nose and full lips as well as jet black straight hair. The most identifying mark on the man before him was a burn which looked decades old on his left arm. To Marcus he looked more than forty years old, but a calmness in his eyes, more common in much older people, implied something ancient. This calmness and serenity in the man standing before him struck Marcus most. The man viewed Marcus without any of the excitement or awe Marcus expected. The group mirrored this balanced temperament, but the one nearest Marcus exuded it. The others constantly looked at the man, but he looked only at Marcus which made his leadership all the more evident. The man radiated vitality and a joy in life which sparkled from his deep-set eyes. No emotions played on the worn expressionless face which looked proud without arrogance.

"Hi," Marcus said, wishing he could think of something better, but growing uncomfortable in the silence. The red skinned man looked at him and nodded his head. After staring into Marcus's eyes long enough to make the boy uncomfortable, the red man turned his head and said something loud enough for those around him to hear.

"Mita, la Tavari," he said confirming something to those gathered around him. The language was clearly not English, Portuguese, Spanish, or Chinese, though Marcus had not been paying enough attention in Mandarin class to converse if they had been. The words were very measured and clear, and though Marcus had no idea what the man said, the others around him nodded in understanding. The man then took a step to Marcus's side and looked at Marcus's back which had been bare since his shirt became a pillow on the first night. With a nod the red skinned stranger then pointed at Marcus's right hand. With some confusion Marcus lifted the hand and presented it. Marcus thought perhaps these people feared he had some weapon. The man took hold of Marcus's hand and gave it a quick inspection.

"La Tavari, la Narwa," the red man confirmed to his companions.

Anticipation of the next step in a meeting between alien cultures excited Marcus, but to his disappointment his first contact merely turned around and started walking away. All those with him also began walking away as well. Marcus determinedly followed, though he knew it meant leaving behind his new fire. Marcus, as gently and as politely as he could, touched the man's shoulder to stop him.

"Marcus," he said touching his hand to his chest the way he had seen done many times before in movies. The man looked at him somewhat surprised, and Marcus couldn't help but feel it was the same look as Marcus would give a stranger who had walked into his home uninvited. The red man nodded his head as if learning something interesting, but not relevant to him. Then he resumed walking away again much to Marcus's distress. Marcus feared stopping him a second time might make him seem impertinent so he decided to follow for a while. When the group realized Marcus was following them, they all appeared a bit surprised. None of the primitive men said anything to Marcus, but they continued to exchange confused looks as the group continued on.

After about thirty minutes of walking Marcus started to wonder when they would come to a village or wherever the red people called home. Marcus imagined a fantastic prehistoric village with primitive structures and Stone Age tools. He pictured a pike outside the village with an enemy tribesman's head on it. Being set up as some kind of god when he showed them his knife or phone didn't seem outside the realm of possibility. Even if they didn't worship him, Marcus hoped they could tell him when or where he was, and how to get home.

The group broke up when they reached a clearing about the size of a soccer field, and each went his own way. Contrary to his expectations the camp was little more than a few areas worn by habitual sleeping and a pit used for cooking. Marcus had imagined the tribe would be close to a hundred people, but now he doubted there were more than a quarter of that. Marcus looked in vain to find where people's belongings might be, but he saw no weapons, no substantial tools, not much besides a few large branches they may have roasted food with recently. Even these didn't look as though any protracted effort or work had been put into them.

"Stone age savages," Marcus said under his breath, with an evident disdain for such primitive living conditions. Marcus immediately started to think of all the tribe lacked and how easy it would be for them to construct an easier life. Looking around at the lack of any conveniences, beds, weapons or tools, Marcus concluded that they lived barely more developed than animals. The tribe was not big, and the way they spread out, everyone had ample personal space. Distances between sets of worn sleeping spaces seemed to reasonably separate family units from each other.

Several members of the tribe gathered near the fire pit including an older man who Marcus thought must have been approaching seventy. The man who had inspected Marcus, who he would later know as Retap, motioned his way a few times while talking to a small group. Despite no knowledge of the language Marcus thought they sounded and looked a bit confused by the situation, however none appeared to be either pleased or displeased by the arrival of an alien in their camp. Marcus started to wonder if maybe visitors from the future or alternate realities were commonplace, and he hoped they all left as easily as they came. When the primitive tribe first arrived at his fire, Marcus feared that they might imprison or even eat him. His hope had been more along the lines of the tribe setting him up as some kind of deity. Instead, some looked at him with suspicion while most ignored the stranger in their midst.

Marcus saw several adults and four young children, plus a twin girl and boy about his age. The glow of health and happiness made the twins quite strikingly beautiful, although their features wouldn't have fit with the Southern California beauty standards of Marcus's recent past. Being a stranger in a strange land, Marcus thought for sure someone would want to communicate with him to at least find out where he was from and where he was going. After several long minutes of standing alone Marcus noticed that the boy his own age kept looking at him. Since the boy's smile was more of an invitation to talk than any of the adults offered, Marcus decided talking to someone his own age would be a good place for a second attempt at making friends.

"Hi. Marcus," he said placing his hand on his heart.

The boy grinned about as wide as any adolescent boy would grin at meeting an alien or time traveler. He kept grinning as he touched his own chest. "Roquen," he said. The youth looked muscular for a boy of only fourteen or fifteen as Marcus estimated. Roquen had the same broad nose and dark eyes as the rest of the tribe. The boy motioned to the rest of those gathered and with an unwavering smile said, "Narwa."

Finally making some progress pleased Marcus immensely. He thought about a million questions for Roquen and for the tribe, and the questions all centered on how Marcus might return home. To that, the mystery of where he was paled in comparison.

Young boys and girls upon meeting exciting strangers have a nearly inexhaustible energy to learn, and these three proved no different. The amount of knowledge that could be so rapidly learned from hand gestures amazed Marcus. Early in the interaction Marcus had tried to show his new friend both his knife and his phone, but the boy reacted by hurriedly trying to hide them both from the sight of others and himself. Marcus hastily put both away though he felt certain others from the tribe had seen. As much as meeting new people thrilled Marcus, it didn't compare to his thrill when a few young men came back caring what looked similar to a small pig. The creature was a peccary, which roam throughout South America. This one had a much flatter head than ones Marcus had seen, but as long as it tasted like meat, Marcus wanted to try it.

The Narwa, like most native cultures and indeed almost all true hunters, had a profound respect for the creatures they killed and ate. A young man stepped forward. Marcus concluded he must have been the one who killed the peccary, or at least delivered the final blow, because he said a few words and pointed a few times to the swine and forest. He didn't look sad but certainly spoke with a grave and serious tone. Marcus hoped at this point the tribe would want to make use of his knife to clean dinner, but they did all the preparation with surprising ease using the bones of other previous dinners. These also didn't appear to belong to anyone in particular but available for group use. The harvesting of the meal went expeditiously considering the rudimentary tools they used, and Marcus saw everyone fulfilling some role in the preparation of the meal.

Eventually the cooking started. Only one who has been ravenously hungry and smelled a cook fire can understand how good that fire smelled to Marcus. If he would have been standing next to the roasting peccary a week ago, he probably would have only smelled smoke. A lot had changed however, and now as Marcus stared at the barbeque which held the swine, he felt his stomach preparing itself. Marcus didn't do much other than observe, but his new friend and the rest of the tribe all took part in the preparation. The other children and Roquen's sister, Layen, came back from the forest a few times with various herbs, nuts and fruits Marcus correctly assumed would be used for the meal. They also brought back delicious berries the likes of which Marcus had never seen before.

While the tribe went through the necessary preparations for the meal, Marcus continued his education in the language of the tribe.

He pointed to the roasting animal looking at Roquen.

"Weech," Roquen said.

"Weech," Marcus imitated. The name of the animal being prepared by the tribe to eat sounded the same as the way the animal would squeal. Marcus found if anything made a sound, the tribe most likely used that sound as its name. This struck Marcus as remarkably sensible though it made the spoken language sound a bit funny.

Though not the largest peccary Marcus would see, it took quite a while for the animal to be cooked all the way through. Lacking plates everyone simply used a broad leaf to hold the food. The young children were given pieces first, and then the two oldest people. After them everyone else went by the roasted meat to take a portion.

Before anyone ate, all the tribe sat down in a circle. From what Marcus could tell seating was assigned from oldest to youngest. At first Marcus thought he might be left out of the circle, though he had already hungrily grabbed some food. Marcus wasn't sure if he would be invited to the meal but decided it would be better to beg forgiveness than ask permission. While looking for a place to sit, Marcus witnessed a quick discussion between the older man and Retap. They didn't appear to be arguing but rather trying to solve something as mundane as an arithmetic problem, a few times gesturing in the direction of the cave or towards Marcus. In the end Retap came by and escorted him to sit next to Roquen.

Marcus understood none of the prayer that was offered, but after the old man finished his words they went around the circle. Each person would say 'aguyje' and sometimes follow it with a few more words. When Marcus's turn came, he was determined that they not skip him so as soon as the person before him stopped, he promptly said 'aguyje' as well. The tribe greeted his gesture with nods of approval, and Marcus congratulated himself on making progress to fit in with the tribe. Marcus thought that he would need them if they could help him return home and probably need them even more if they could not. The final speaker was the smallest child, Coo, and after her words everyone ate. To say the food tasted delicious to the traveler would be an understatement, and it filled Marcus's belly with a contentment which allowed his first real night's sleep since arriving.

Marcus spent the next several weeks learning the language of the red people. The conversations initially consisted of little more than gestures, but rapidly progressed.

Gesturing to herself and her brother and then in all different directions Layen repeated, "Narwa, Narwa." Which Marcus had learned meant red children, the inhabitants of the land.

Roquen then gestured to himself, then his sister, and specifically to the tribe members nearby, "Piucca." He then produced a berry and pointing again repeated "Piucca."

"Piucca is the tribe's name, like the berry," Marcus said nodding in understanding before swiftly taking the berry and plopping it into his mouth with a smile.

Then Roquen pointed at Marcus "La Tavari, La Narwa, La Piucca," and shrugged his shoulders in confusion.

"Tavari?" Marcus asked, remembering the word from his initial encounter.

Both twins then made a series of gestures that took Marcus some time to understand. Marcus tried to draw images in the ground to help communicate, but the twins looked very uncomfortable with any drawings. As soon as they understood what Marcus was trying to communicate they would rub the marks out of existence.

"Tavari are like ghosts or angels or aliens or something I guess," Marcus said to himself. "La Tavari," he agreed. Roquen and Layen looked at him waiting for an additional answer, and Marcus noticed a few other Piucca observing the conversation from a distance.

"Lost," Marcus said pointing to himself. He made gestures to indicate he was searching and said "La Narwa."

His new friends nodded in understanding.

Marcus continually tried to make clear that he was very far from home and wanted to get back. This was always met with the same understanding nod followed by an expression Marcus would hear many times over "Mana indome indome." He understood it to translate roughly to "what will be will be" but also meant "it is what it is" and "what has happened has happened." The Narwa language's simplicity also made it somewhat vague.

While Marcus worked diligently to learn the language of the Narwa, Roquen and his sister, Layen, learned English from Marcus. It was the first time any of these Narwa had ever heard another language, and the two youths learned rapidly. Layen showed an affinity for learning which matched her brother's physical prowess. At first Marcus thought learning English would be a waste of time and energy on their part, but before too long the three of them had their own secret language. Marcus appreciated the irony of English being a secret language, and whenever the three would talk about Marcus's unique predicament they would almost always speak English.

Ancient rules of hospitality existed in the Narwa culture much as they have in all the world since mankind began. While many viewed Marcus's arrival as an omen, and some viewed his arrival as another mouth to feed, the majority viewed Marcus and his presence as simply a part of some grand plan, but one which did not concern them. The plan or God or the universe, Marcus could not tell if they differentiated, had brought Marcus to the Narwa land for some reason. The Piucca did not know the reason, but that did not bother them. Most felt it was not their part to understand every aspect of the grand plan, as long as they understood and accepted their own part.

Roquen's father, Roqued, spent a large portion of his day with his two children focused on their education, and Marcus attended as well, sometimes out of curiosity, sometimes out of boredom. While Narwa culture required little in the way of school, lacking a written language or advanced mathematics, there was much to learn. Roqued's teachings for the three of them focused on explaining, as best he could, the Narwa views on life. Roquen and Layen would educate Marcus on the plants and animals which could be eaten or should be avoided. They also showed him the best places to drink water and bathe. At fourteen in such a simple world there wasn't much they were unable to do. Still there were a few things they were not allowed to do; Marcus because he was not Narwa, and the twins because they were not officially adults yet.

The lack of basic rudimentary tools slowed many of the tasks that might have been done more efficiently. Despite this the smoothness with which daily chores were accomplished without hurry or fuss frequently surprised Marcus. All items such as tools or bowls the Narwa employed would be used only for a day or as a task required. Every few days, when they killed another animal, they harvested every part to make new bone tools as needed. Lacking cups or bottles, anytime someone wanted water they were forced to walk to the river for a drink. The Narwa did use a gourd as a bowl of sorts. Gourds were mostly utilized for making medicine, but also for some cooking employment. Since they could not hunt yet, Marcus and Roquen were often given the task of hollowing out the gourds. Marcus came to loathe this duty due to the texture and smell of the gourd's flesh. He made the task even worse for himself by constantly thinking it could be avoided if they kept wooden bowls.

To Marcus's disappointment no shaman or witch doctor lived with or near the tribe. A woman named Naa came closest to being a spiritual leader and healer. She had no children or mate, and Marcus suspected her role came from a refocused sense of motherhood. It pained Marcus to admit many treatments for headaches and cuts Naa made were superior to twenty-first century medicine. From Naa Marcus also learned more of the Narwa views of the cosmos and their spiritual beliefs. Narwa believed in many mythical beasts in addition to the gods, spirits, angels, and demons, which they referred to as Tavari.

The Narwa believed in the existence of many Tavari, and though the Narwa didn't view them as good or evil, there were two distinct divisions. On the one side were the Tavari who had chosen freedom. While this independence gave them liberty on Earth, it caused a separation from where they had been before. The Narwa believed the Tavari came from what they referred to as "Ohmfea" which vaguely meant a complete soul but sounded similar to heaven or afterlife to Marcus. The other Tavari were not free but still connected to, or at least serving, Ohmfea, and they customarily did not involve themselves with mankind directly. The two sides apparently kept a truce, which was by nature temporary and often violated in cases where mankind acted as proxies.

In general, the Narwa believed it was better to leave the Tavari alone in hopes of being left alone. Marcus learned the names and attributes of most of these Tavari, and was not surprised they resembled the Norse, Greek, and Roman gods he had learned of before. He told Naa of the visitor in the cave, but that he wasn't sure if it was real or a dream. Naa didn't think there was much difference when speaking to Tavari. They both agreed it would be better to not tell others of the event, which of course made certain Marcus told everything to Layen and Roquen.

The two oldest in the tribe were Evad and Paa. They were a couple, and Marcus would later learn the parents of a daughter who now lived with another tribe. Marcus often thought Evad acted more like a mascot than a leader. The man did have some fantastic stories which Marcus grew to enjoy. Evad loved to tell Marcus a story that involved a traveler who was also not Narwa, a monster, and magic that sounded absurd to Marcus. It wasn't much of a surprise to Marcus that the old man spent most of his time telling stories, the rest of which sounded much more believable. Most of the adult Narwa would leave the camp from time to time for a day or two, but Marcus never saw Evad leave.

Retap, as Marcus had suspected, was closer to being a tribal leader than anyone else. Marcus noticed Retap went to great pains to make sure that he never exerted any power over the group, but rather tried to lead by example and sound argument.

Lemor and Mii were a couple who did not take much interest in Marcus, and though they were not hostile to him, Marcus suspected they would not be disappointed when he left. Their adult children were Tahmi and Kahmi, two young men who were often responsible for the successful hunt. Tahmi and Kahmi had another brother, Lehmi, who had joined the tribe of the woman he had paired with. Roquen looked up to the three of them as sort of older brothers, though he was already nearly as strong and adept at tracking animals. Tahmi and Kahmi were also gone more often than most, and Layen told Marcus they were courting women at a nearby tribe.

Roqued and Enn were the parents of Layen and Roquen, Marcus's friends. Women often passed their names to the first-born daughter, and Marcus learned Layen's older sister, Enn, had died as an infant.

There were also Kirtep and Huo, who had no children, but were more interested in Marcus than the others, and often asked about the customs of where he had come.

Sivat and Dee were the parents of Sivdee and the younger Dee, who were eight and five. Marcus grew particularly fond of them as they frequently took the lead in cooking the meals.

Semaj and Yii, the youngest couple, were the parents of two girls, Yii and Coo, the youngest of the tribe at four and two.

The uncoupled women were Naa and Tooh, who were indispensable to the tribe because they helped with everyone else's children. Tooh's spouse had died from a fever at some point before having children, but Marcus never learned more. When all were present, which was rare, there were twenty-three members of the tribe, which with Marcus made twenty-four. Marcus tried to ask where the others went when they left the tribal camp, but his queries were always dismissed with a shrug or a vague gesture to the forest. This, of course, only made Marcus more curious.

Roqued explained to Marcus the shortness of the women names allowed for their inclusion in the names of their children which was seen as an honor to those who created life. Contrary to Marcus's initial expectations, no man dominated the tribe. If anything, women held more sway over decisions than men did, often reaching consensus amongst themselves while the men were hunting. The men on the other hand were normally content with what the women decided, though in truth there was not much to decide in such a simple life. When couples paired it was common for them to live with the smaller tribe, though it was not required to do so.

Once he grew familiar to the daily routine of Narwa life, Marcus observed the main functions of the tribe were to hunt, cook, and sit around the fire singing or telling stories. Marcus expected the Narwa would tell stories of wars between tribes, but the Narwa were adamant that the only violence came from those who had abandoned the Narwa way. These outcast Narwa would sometimes cause problems for villages near lands which had been set aside for the outcasts.

All members had a daily athletic regime which greatly impressed Marcus. Each morning the members of the tribe would start the day with a routine that to Marcus resembled a blend of yoga, tai-chi, and basic strength exercises. The routines themselves were not as impressive as the great effort each individual put into the routine. All the men were extremely well conditioned and generally the hunts were successful due to teamwork that allowed them to run the weech, or peccary as Marcus knew them, to exhaustion.

The tribe had a few of its own songs, routinely sung after meals, which were very simple and sounded to Marcus like chants more than songs. Even to himself Marcus was slow to admit how much he enjoyed the songs and stories of the tribe. Kirtep prodded Marcus to share the songs of his own tribe, and before long the Piucca tribe knew the words to Don McLean's 'American Pie.'

While everyone in the tribe had a purpose and things to do daily that kept them busy for short stretches of the day, Marcus settled into a despondent idleness. He was contemptuous of Narwa customs and beliefs as often as he was respectful. Marcus made a few attempts at showing the tribe things he thought would make their lives better, or at least easier, but these were always dismissed with a shaking of the head.

It didn't take long for Marcus to realize not only did the Narwa have no possessions; they were in fact forbidden. One day, lacking anything better to do, Marcus made a wooden fork and was quite proud he would no longer have to eat with his fingers like a savage. When Retap saw him use it a second time he made the boy throw it into the fire. A few days later Marcus constructed a very primitive shelter by collecting branches, but these were dispersed after the first night Marcus slept in it. Marcus saw the shelter was gone when he returned from getting water and knew Retap had done the demolition. He immediately sought the Narwa man out to ask why.

"Whime rucs koara? " Marcus demanded of Retap, trying his best to look both hurt and angry as well as show his growing ability to use the language.

"Marcus phaika?"

"Na!" Marcus replied, he was certainly angry. As much as the destruction of his shelter bothered him, Retap's questioning upset him further.

"Marcus an phaika, an lakiska, lek koero," Retap replied and he gave Marcus a nod as though he had done the boy a favor and then walked away.

Marcus stood confused for a few moments and tried to make sure he understood. He couldn't argue against Retap's correct assumption that he would probably be more upset to lose both of the things if he had been using them for a while and developed an attachment.

"That's not the point..." Marcus protested in English to Retap as he wandered off.

While both incidents initially upset Marcus, in a short time he found he did not need either cutlery or a shelter.

CHAPTER FOUR - MAKING FRIENDS

Friendship is the hardest thing in the world to explain. It's not something you learn in school. But if you haven't learned the meaning of friendship, you really haven't learned anything.

- Muhammad Ali

Marcus spent weeks at the Piucca camp not doing much other than eating the tribe's food, observing their routines, and being a bit of an annoyance. Eventually his curiosity about where the adults went when they left the village got the best of him. Convinced they did not need his help, Marcus watched idly as the twins helped the rest of the tribe clean the remains of the morning meal. He saw Retap talking to Evad and then clasp the old man's shoulder. This was usually done when one of the Narwa wouldn't see another for more than a day or so-- a long time for such a small communal group. As Retap headed into the forest, Marcus followed.

Unlike his follower Retap's decades of traveling through woods made travel second nature. At first Marcus kept up with relative ease. Marcus did his best to be quiet and stay out of sight and prided himself on the fact that Retap had not turned around at the sounds which Marcus inadvertently made. Ironically, not long after Marcus silently congratulated himself on his forest mastery, he realized he had lost sight of Retap. Certain that the man could only be a few paces out of view Marcus increased his pace.

A few more minutes passed, and Marcus still did not see Retap. Marcus stopped to listen for a sign of Retap but only heard the forest's eerie quietness; the wind's soft blowing and the beating of his own heart. Despite being a little unsettled Marcus decided to continue forward.

As soon as he began moving again Marcus felt a hand over his mouth as an arm wrapped around his neck. He struggled to pull his head free, but the arm around his neck tightened and restricting his breathing. Marcus tried to scream but could not make much more than a muffled cry against the hand which now felt like an iron clamp.

In a panic Marcus tried to elbow the midsection of his attacker. His frantic attempts barely made contact while the grip around his neck tightened. Each time Marcus made an attempt at breaking free or striking whoever held him, the arm squeezed tighter. The short moments felt like an eternity of struggle. Marcus had such trouble breathing that he started to see stars and the sounds of his struggle and the forest merged into one dull tone. Losing hope and consciousness Marcus tried to relax and regain his composure to breathe. As he did, he felt the arm freeing his throat enough to allow him to take in a deep gulp of air.

As soon as Marcus started to inhale and exhale regularly again, he felt a panicked need to get loose of the arm which held him captive. Surprised at how much his first struggle had exhausted him Marcus nonetheless tried to free himself again, this time by leaning forward in hopes he would pull his assailant off balance. The move backfired as his attacker's weight rested on Marcus, and the arm tightened around his neck, restricting his breathing again. Marcus tried to shake the unseen assailant but only succeeded in making himself dizzy and faint again.

It became painfully clear to Marcus that his struggling was in vain, and the boy nearly collapsed unable to continue. Immediately after he stopped fighting the arm let him loose, and he turned around to face his attacker. Marcus's injured sense of pride demanded he spring forward and retaliate on whoever had mishandled him so. However, when he turned around and saw Retap staring blankly at him, he realized any aggression on his part would probably end up with him back in an embarrassing and painful position. Retap stared into Marcus's eyes making the boy very uncomfortable.

"Marcus gaity Retap," Retap said accusingly. Marcus wondered how long Retap had known he was being followed.

Marcus nodded looking down. He began to speak and offer what apology he could, but Retap cut his words off.

"Gaity." This time the word sounded like an instruction to follow and not an accusation.

Retap started walking, and Marcus followed. For the next few minutes Marcus thought about making a run for it but knew he didn't have much of a chance against Retap's skills in the woods. Retap never turned his head towards the boy, but Marcus knew his presence was constantly being monitored.

After more than an hour of walking the two came out of the woods onto a rocky area, and Marcus could see they stood on the side of a substantial precipice. Retap walked to the edge, but Marcus hung back not sure of Retap's intentions. The cliff looked suspiciously like a good place from which to throw someone you never wanted to see again. Retap turned back towards Marcus, and Marcus imagined Retap weighing out the pros and cons of throwing a stranger to his death.

"Guapy," Retap said pointing to the ground. "La guat," he added. Even if Marcus would have not known a word of the Narwa language, he would have been certain Retap was telling him to sit and to not move. Marcus did as he was bidden, and Retap sat down beside him crossing his legs in the prayer or meditation position. Marcus huffed in protest and tried his best to look offended at having been spoken to like a dog.

For the next several minutes Marcus looked at Retap and then at the forest. The experience reminded Marcus of being in detention at school but with a cliff as a reminder to not misbehave. Retap didn't move and in truth barely appeared to be breathing. After about an hour Marcus thought maybe he had taken enough time in confinement and tried to stand up slowly to make his escape.

"Guapy," said Retap firmly, his eyes still closed.

Marcus stayed standing looking at the seated man.

Retap opened his eyes and looked at Marcus then at the side of the cliff. "Guapy," he repeated. Retap waited as Marcus deliberated between sitting or being thrown down the side of the cliff. As much as he didn't cherish the idea of spending his day sitting quietly doing nothing, he sat back down. Marcus wanted to tell Retap he had better things to do than waste his time staring at the sky, but he was certain Retap was not interested in conversation. Marcus also grudgingly admitted to himself he really didn't have much else to do.

To a body and a mind accustomed to constant stimulation a few quiet moments stretch forever. Marcus couldn't remember ever sitting still for so long without having his phone, a book, or someone or something to entertain him. The restless boy stared at Retap who sat still and silent as a monk. Marcus decided since he was there he would as well. He had tried mediation before at his father's behest, but to him meditation felt like doing nothing, and he preferred to be entertained, or at least amused, when doing nothing. He wondered at the irony that doing nothing in his previous world had been considered a vice or a punishment depending on the circumstances.

For the next several hours Marcus rotated among different sitting positions and alternated between having his eyes opened or closed. He tried to think about everything, and he tried to think about nothing. In the end he let his mind wander and found it came back to him more at peace. Marcus also saw Retap would alter between his cross-legged position in different states of deep mediation and lying on the side of the cliff staring at the land below or watching birds.

Marcus had thought about his family constantly since his arrival, but this was the first time he actually let himself stop and wonder what they were doing, and how they would react to his being missing. Whenever he had thought of them before he had always tried to stop his train of thought when the pain of sadness struck him. Sitting on the side of the cliff he allowed his thoughts to continue. The sadness Marcus felt was not solely from missing them, but also from knowing they would be devastated to lose him. He wondered how life would go on for them if he didn't make it back. Marcus feared that maybe they would blame him as much as he blamed himself. At the end of this thought process he realized that all he could do was continue to try to find a way home and remember all the good times. Everything else was an exercise in futility.

Time, like most thieves, made its move when Marcus stopped paying it any attention. Before he knew it, Marcus saw the shadows had grown long and the sky had turned shades of orange which herald the oncoming night. Marcus hoped they would leave or at least eat when darkness fell, but they did not. Instead the two kept alternating between observing the scenery and mediating, never speaking a word.

Marcus had prayed before but usually in a rushed few sentences before a meal. Other times Marcus's prayers were a desperate cry of need as they had been when he had realized he was lost. Now he took the time to sit and think of the things he would want to say to a god, the God, or whatever power held the universe together. Marcus started with his long list of grievances most of which were about being lost. He followed his complaints with a list of requests which he felt were reasonable. He also had a few questions he wanted to pose. Though Marcus didn't feel he received any answers from without, he found he already possessed many answers within and felt better for going through the thoughts with clarity.

During one of his more successful tries at deep meditation Marcus fell asleep. He awoke with a jolt thinking Retap might throw him over the cliff for napping. Instead when he awoke he saw his companion still sitting silently. Marcus stared at the sky for a while and tried to see if there were any notable differences from the sky he remembered at home. Eventually he fell back asleep.

When Marcus awoke to the first lights of dawn, he saw Retap going through the normal routine of morning exercises the Narwa followed. Marcus rose to join him. Retap nodded with approval. When they completed the movements, they sat down together to do the breathing routine, which Marcus still found as pointless as ever. Then Retap stood and gazed out over the cliff and the vegetation below. Marcus did as well and wondered how it still held a fresh beauty no matter how many times he had stared at it the day before.

"Gaity," Retap said this time with a nod and much gentler intonation. Marcus had prepared himself to be glad as soon as he could leave the scene of his imprisonment, but now he found he wasn't as happy as he thought he would be. He wondered how much his mind had changed in less than twenty-four hours.

On the walk back, Retap seemed more approachable than he had ever been before. Between his broken Narwa words and descriptive gestures Marcus tried to ask Retap if he normally went to the cliff when he left the camp.

Retap nodded in affirmation.

Marcus also asked if Retap would have thrown him off the cliff if he had tried to leave. This Retap affirmed with a serious nod.

Marcus tried several times to ask Retap what he mediated on or what he prayed for. While Retap avoided the question, Marcus persisted. Finally, when Marcus was sure he had formulated the question correctly, Retap stopped and looked at the boy.

"Mana Retap hyam," Marcus asked again.

"Marcus," Retap answered looking into Marcus's eyes much as he had done at their first meeting.

The two continued back to the tribe in silence.

After his day with Retap, Marcus did become a better guest and made an effort to contribute as well as respect the way of life and culture of the tribe. Helping out still left plenty of free time, and Marcus and Roquen would often take walks through the forest. Roquen would pretend to hunt peccary, large birds, or a jaguar, and Marcus tried to learn as much as he could from his friend about moving silently through the jungle. Sometimes they would come upon some sign of an animal and try to track it as best they could. The first few times Marcus thought his friend was following his imagination pointing out trivial minute details as a joke. After a few weeks of close attention, though, Marcus also began to notice little things in nature which each told a tale. He could tell how the areas around the camp and stream all were disturbed by human presence while further out every little change in the twigs and leaves held some story. In the past the forest had all just appeared to be a bunch of trees and brush, but soon Marcus came to appreciate the detail in nature.

The mock hunt one day started the same as usual trekking through the trees. They continued on a trail Roquen believed had been made by a jaguar. They followed for a short time until surprisingly the two were sure they heard voices. Staying close together the boys stealthily tracked the whispers which sounded very out of place so deep in the forest. When they finally saw the source of the sounds, both boys recognized Kirtep and Huo. Marcus thought it would be fun to follow and spy on them, and though Roquen at first disagreed, teenage boys tend to be better at mischief than resisting peer pressure.

The boys followed the couple for a brief time and saw them come to a tree apparently familiar to the pair. Kirtep held some herbs that must have been recently gathered, and Huo reached into the hollow of the tree and pulled out a simple wooden bowl. Marcus thought it was the most mundane thing he could have possibly spied people doing, but his friend's expression made him reconsider. A look both shocked and solemn had replaced Roquen's eternal smile. Kirtep placed the herbs in the bowl and began grinding them. The whole process struck Marcus as quite ordinary. Roquen's eyes in stark contrast looked filled with torment as he tugged Marcus's arm to go which surprised Marcus. Even tracking jaguar, he had never seen Roquen move with such care to not make a sound.

After walking away in strict silence for half an hour, Roquen and Marcus came to a part of the stream where they would often watch the water, sometimes for hours at a time. Marcus tried to ask Roquen why seeing two people with a bowl upset him, but his friend stopped him, and answered only in English.

"Keep bowl against Narwa," Roquen said.

"But it's just a stupid wooden bowl," Marcus insisted. "Honestly, it makes more sense than cleaning a gourd every time. Besides, what if one time you can't find a gourd, and you need a bowl."

"No. Narwa way. Narwa are free. Not own not be own." Roquen's voice sounded very unhappy and bordered on angry. Marcus often thought the Narwa were remarkably dispassionate, and he had tried to attribute it to a lack of emotional development. He often thought of them as happy imbeciles, a belief that made Marcus feel better about his own melancholy state. Roquen at this point was far from emotionless, and Marcus could perceive the frustration emanating from his friend.

"Let's pretend we didn't see anything and forget this whole situation. We don't have to do anything about it."

Roquen contemplated that option, though Marcus could tell he didn't take delight in it. Marcus couldn't tell if Roquen was angrier at Kirtep and Huo for having the bowl, or himself for knowing about it.

"Roquen panta," Roquen sighed.

"No, you are not guilty. It's not like you own a stupid bowl anyways, besides no one is going to know."

"Roquen know. Trees and weech know. Stream know. Sun and sky know. Pano know. Fea know."

Marcus was confused and surprised at how much his friend's strict morality upset him. "Listen if you feel so bad about it, just say you're sorry to the trees and everything else and move on. Trust me I'll have forgotten some stupid bowl by dinner time, and you should too."

"Roquen say is sorry? If Roquen is true sorry Roquen do what is right. If no right, Roquen no forget. Roquen always panta."

"Yes; Roquen guilty, and Roquen know, and Layen know," spoke a feminine voice behind them. Marcus didn't have any doubt who the voice belonged to and felt sorely disappointed by her arrival. He thought Roquen would be more upset since her arrival limited his options further. On the contrary, Roquen's returning smile showed his joy at seeing his sister.

"This is ridiculous," Marcus said exasperated with the primitive view of right and wrong.

"They break, you know, and no do, then you break," Layen continued, not speaking to Marcus but only her brother. She spoke in her best English as well, and Marcus felt relieved they were not speaking Narwa lest anyone else overhear.

"But we didn't mean to find out, and we don't want to start problems," Marcus insisted.

"Marcus no do nothing. Marcus no see Narwa. No understand. Roquen see Narwa way Roquen know," Layen continued. The dogmatic sound of her normally rational voice surprised Marcus. Layen was usually the more rebellious of the two, and Marcus didn't understand her adherence to a seemingly trivial rule.

"Roquen knows. Et," replied Roquen looking downcast but more resolute.

"Roquen no have choice. If no, Roquen Et. Roquen no Ohtat, no hunt with tribe. No to Ingole. Roquen lose all for another hucha." Layen tried to console her brother, her earlier harsh tone absent. She knew what her brother must do, and she knew how much it would hurt him. Though Marcus didn't understand all that 'Et' referred to, he could tell it made an impact on Roquen.

"Roquen tell Evad before next sun go down. Hanta Layen," Roquen said. It was clear in his voice the huge burden had been lifted by his commitment.

Marcus shook his head; he could not imagine how a society stayed together when everyone was responsible for everyone else's transgressions. He didn't understand exactly all the rules of the Narwa, but he did understand that to have possessions was forbidden and violation of that rule meant banishment. Marcus didn't think banishment sounded so bad, considering the Narwa didn't live much better than animals in some ways. As the three of them sat in silence, Marcus thought hopefully all the silly business about a bowl would be forgotten. Moreover, he hoped whatever did come of it would not involve him.

CHAPTER FIVE - GROWING UP

Excerpt from **If**

If you can make one heap of all your winnings
And risk it on one turn of pitch-and-toss,
And lose, and start again at your beginnings
And never breathe a word about your loss;
If you can force your heart and nerve and sinew
To serve your turn long after they are gone,
And so hold on when there is nothing in you
Except the Will which says to them: 'Hold on!'
   - Rudyard Kipling

D uring the four months following the meeting of the Piucca tribe outside his cave Marcus became more accustomed to the Narwa way of life. He would still routinely return to the cave; partly in hopes some change would allow him to return home, partly because it was as close as he felt he could physically get to home, and partly because he wanted at times to be alone. Marcus was starting to appreciate how much more accepting Narwa culture was of spending time alone than the world he came from. Me marveled that neither he, nor most of the people he knew had ever spend an entire day without hearing or seeing another person.

On one of his trips to the cave Roquen and Layen came with him. Marcus would sometimes power up the phone and look at pictures of his family or read. Often, he spent hours trying to find some bit of information that even if it would not help him return home, would help him understand where or, more importantly, when he was. The more he read, the more convinced he became that he somehow had been transported to some forgotten time in South America's ancient past. It was impossible to tell when exactly because in Marcus's time some tribes in the Amazon still lived life only slightly more technologically advanced than the Narwa.

Marcus's companions were amazed as he scrolled through pictures. Eventually he came to one of his whole family at Christmas. He remembered his father holding him so tightly when Marcus gave him the painting which his mother assured Marcus his father would cherish. He could smell the roasting turkey and the baby smell of the newborn. He could taste the morning treats, and his heart broke. Marcus hadn't cried much since meeting the tribe and felt ashamed to do so in front of his friends, who Marcus often thought were free from such emotional displays. Both of his friends embraced him.

"Roquen Man test Ohtat. Roquen Marcus Ingole talk," Roquen said as he looked his friend in the eyes to comfort him.

For the past several weeks Roquen's excitement at the coming manhood initiation had been evident.

"Marcus will take the man test also," Marcus said resolutely, thinking that was the reason Roquen has brought up the subject.

"No. Narwa test Narwa man," Roquen said shaking his head. He stated this more as a fact, than to exclude Marcus.

"So, I can't take the man test because I wasn't born here? I don't ever get to be a man?" The restriction on his ability to truly join the tribe disappointed Marcus more than he could have imagined four months ago mostly because the idea that he may be stuck with the Narwa forever stayed present in the back of his mind, but partly because he chafed at being excluded by people he still felt superior to.

"You cannot be Ohtat, because you are not Narwa," Layen chimed in. Her grasp of English progressed so rapidly Marcus had gone from being impressed to being annoyed. Her brother, who relied more on physical strength than linguistic ability or knowledge, probably would have preferred she didn't speak at all though he loved her as only brothers can.

"La Narwa," Roquen said as he picked up Marcus's hand and held it next to his own heavily scarred hand.

"I have to be initiated before I can become a man?" Marcus asked more to himself than to anyone in particular. The cause of the scars on the hands of the male Narwa was never made explicitly clear to Marcus. He only knew they came from the initiation to the tribe.

"When do you take the tests?"

"Must wait for... ten." Roquen held up ten fingers as he tried to remember the English number correctly. "Then be full Narwa."

"After fifteen," Layen accentuated the number knowing her brother didn't count that high in English, "then a Narwa boy can become Ohtat, if he can prove worthy. This year both of us will take our tests."

Marcus learned the Narwa women also underwent a far more secretive induction. The women were always present for the testing of the men, but the men were not privy to what the woman test consisted of. Layen wouldn't say anything about the women's trial, but Marcus asked Roquen what he knew.

"Bla bla bla kinsa ara," said Roquen, meaning the woman test was to talk for three days straight. He laughed at his own joke as his sister rolled her eyes. Marcus noted that it must be a universal gesture, especially among siblings.

"What is the initiation for the male Narwa?" Marcus asked.

"Naicele," the two answered almost in unison. Marcus knew the word. It was one of the first he had learned: Pain.

When Marcus and his friends returned, they found the tribe all gathered around the fire pit. The grave faces and stern voices Marcus heard made clear the gravity of the event. Roquen and Layen looked at each other, and Marcus saw the apprehension on their faces. Roquen mouthed "Hosta," and Layen nodded in agreement. Marcus at first thought they would be excluded from the meeting on account of youth, but when one of the adults saw them the three were escorted forward where they could see what transpired. The tribe stood gathered around Kirtep and Huo who sat next to a wooden bowl. Marcus recognized the bowl immediately.

Kirtep pleaded with the tribe to stay. He blamed Huo who looked more angry than repentant. Marcus feared they would find out his role in the situation and turn on him, but no one paid him any attention. Enn, the mother of the twins, made sure her son and daughter paid close attention. The three watched in rapt silence held by the knowledge of the part they had played in bringing about the event. The younger children also stood nearby, their parents hoping they would learn from the mistakes of others.

The situation upset the whole tribe immensely. None of the Piucca disliked the couple, however, the law superseded any desire for leniency. Evad took hold of a branch from a tree that Kahmi pulled from the fire. The old man's whole body visibly trembled as he dipped the glowing red end of the branch in a dark thick liquid in front of the couple. At his nod they each held out their left hands. The branch shook with Evad's unsteady hand as he touched the now searing hot paste to the back of the outstretched hands. Marcus knew the touch of the embers on the tree limb must have caused immense pain, but neither of the two made a noticeable reaction. Kirtep only looked more distraught while Huo looked more angry.

"Et Narwa," Evad pronounced sadly.

With that they both stood up, Huo taking the bowl. All members of the tribe turned their backs to the couple, and a path through the bodies formed for them to exit. Not being Narwa, Marcus didn't feel compelled to turn aside. When Huo glanced back her dark eyes locked with Marcus's for a moment, and Marcus feared she knew the part the boys played in her undoing. He watched the two of them walk away; one still angry, the other still heartbroken.

Less than a month later the preparation for the initiations began. As the event drew near, Layen and Roquen agreed Marcus should tell the tribe of his desire to be initiated. His announcement drew immediate discussion. Marcus feared disagreements over whether his joining the Narwa could be allowed, but the conversation following Marcus's declaration sounded nothing like a disagreement. The Narwa respect for each other often precluded outright argument. In this case, as in all cases, men and women discussed the subject objectively. While individuals often took sides, they would just as often switch sides or offer reasons that supported the other side. The Narwa appeared to thoroughly enjoy debate, perhaps because they didn't look for who was wrong but rather what was right.

The Piucca had never come into contact with anyone not Narwa. They knew of other people, or other children as they called them, beyond the great waters. Why or how a boy from one of these people would be sent to them was beyond any of their reckoning. The law stated that no one who had been banished from another tribe could take the test. Marcus assured them he had not been banished, and that his tribe wanted him back. Marcus also had to promise that if he joined the Narwa he would remain one forever. At this Marcus hesitated since his goal remained to return home, but the tribe agreed that all Narwa possessed the right, and even the duty, to go where they believed they should.

At fifteen (Marcus's birthday had slipped by in June) Marcus would be the oldest taking the initiation. The boys were allowed to take it at ten, but most waited until twelve or thirteen. The only other requirement being that males take it before the Ohtat, the test for full manhood. Failing the adult test, like breaking the laws of the Narwa, led to banishment. Marcus tried to ask what happened to those who failed the tribal induction test, but his friends avoided answering. Marcus started to think the initiation might be so easy that nobody ever failed it.

Later he found Naa and questioned her about it. He asked her how many had failed last year.

"Kinsa," Naa answered with profound respect for those three. Marcus asked where these three were now. The woman answered by pointing at the ground and then pointing at the sky, Marcus had seen the gesture before and assumed it was the Narwa way of avoiding the word 'death.'

"First the tests, then Ingole, then home," Marcus said to himself aloud.

Naa nodded as though she understood, though Marcus convinced himself she couldn't have.

The last days leading up to the initiation went by quickly for Marcus. He didn't always turn on the phone anymore when he went back to the cave and often would simply sit and think. A short time before he underwent the trial, however, he did turn it on once more. He couldn't believe that it was already mid-September, and a month had passed without looking at pictures of his family. A wave of guilt swept over Marcus. He wondered if by not thinking of his family as much, he might be in some way giving up on going home. Marcus asked himself if he was abandoning them and knew that wherever his parents were, they would be searching frantically for him. Marcus couldn't imagine the pain they suffered, and he felt at fault; his stupidity and carelessness had destroyed the family. With each passing day he grew more certain he would never see any of them again. The thoughts caused a wave of wretchedness that mixed comfortably with his guilt.

Marcus cursed the cave, cursed whoever had created such a stupid fault in time, and cursed himself. With each utterance the sick feeling in his stomach grew like a monster that would consume him in a blue-green ball of guilt and grief. Marcus tried to think of happier thoughts of his home, but each one felt tainted by the belief that such things would never-- and could never-- happen again. As the whole of his previous identity faded, he wondered if his family did as well. He placed his hand on his face and felt the warmth of tears as he asked 'why' again and again to no one in particular. Marcus's self-reproach and sorrow seemed to know no end, but it would be the last time he cried in the cave.

Marcus wondered who would stay to watch the camp when they traveled to the ceremonial grounds and then laughed at the idea. The Piucca had nothing to steal, unless a person wanted old bones and charred rock. In fact, the only possessions were Marcus's knife, wallet, phone and ring, all of which Layen and Roquen convinced him not to take. With little fanfare Marcus wrapped them in the plastic bag from the market and buried them near the cave.

"But what if there is some cute girl at the ceremony, how will I get her number?" Marcus asked, and as usual only he laughed at his joke.

"No Ohtat No woman," replied his wonderfully concise best friend. Marcus knew Narwa didn't begin dating until after passing all the trials of the culture.

"I'm sure I'll pass the initiations," Marcus said.

"Did your tribe teach you many things about pain before you left?" Layen asked, always eager for more information about Marcus's world.

"No... I guess not. When we have pain, we eat or drink something to make it stop."

"Aykiy," Roquen stated solidly. He may not have mastered spoken English, but he understood well.

"I suppose it is an escape," Marcus said, "but why wouldn't someone want to escape from pain?"

"Marcus, sometimes it seems you know nothing. Maybe because you did not grow up Narwa. Narwa know pain is a teacher. Pain tells you things. Change is pain. Growth is pain. Pain is not mysterious or evil. Pain is only a message, and a person who runs away from the message of himself only has one escape," Layen said.

"But no one wants to be in pain. That's a fundamental truth, isn't it?" Marcus asked.

"Are you sure no one wants to be in pain? You go back to the cave and look at your family even though it hurts."

"I need to do that... you don't understand," Marcus said to himself as much as to her.

"Does anyone understand anyone else pain?" she asked.

"Marcus know Narwa hand pain tomorrow," Roquen added with a little laugh. As much as he didn't enjoy talking, he did enjoy making jokes.

"No matter how bad it gets, don't choose the escape," Layen added with a touch of concern.

Marcus just rolled his eyes convinced that anything a stone age ten-year-old could do, he would have no trouble with.

Two days before the initiation the whole of the tribe woke up early and instead of the gymnastic routines and morning activities, they all set out at once. The tribe walked the whole day and traveled for most of the next before they came to a large open area where many other Narwa had already gathered. Marcus learned these gatherings happened twice a year always on the full moon following the equinoxes. The initiations were a big part of the festival; there were also marriages and reunions among family members who had married into other tribes. Each of the tribes had an area where they would set up the same sort of temporary camp. Six other tribes, Laurenque, Drimea, Nyaro, Laique, Hyalma, and Ohte, made up the gathering. Most names related to where their camps were, though they all identified as Narwa. Marcus learned the Narwa were composed of hundreds of tribes.

"There are tribes that cover all the Narwa land, except the areas where the outcast, Et Narwa, are," Layen explained. "After the day and night are equal, four to ten tribes gather, but seven is the number that Narwa prefer."

"But this is not Ingole, right?" Marcus asked.

"No, Ingole is sacred land. When we pass the test, we will wait until the longest day. Then we go to Ingole, and each Narwa can ask a question or make a request of the Ingole."

"Is Ingole a person or the place?" Marcus asked still confused.

"Ingole is a place, but the place is Ingole because of what is there. The power of the Fea of many who have left this world often remains at Ingole, as well as the power of those who prepared the world before the Narwa," Layen explained.

"So, it's like going to a magician who gives you one wish or answers one question?" Marcus asked skeptically.

"Ingole see Pano. Help Narwa see," Roquen said, a bit annoyed by his friend's doubts.

"You think magic is where you do something and magic gives you something. But for the Narwa that isn't magic. Magic is everywhere inside all of us. If you use it right, you can do anything. Those at Ingole are closer to a bigger magic, and they use it to see where some of us fit in the Plan, or to help those who are in need." Layen's explanation of the magic of Ingole disappointed Marcus who harbored a little hope that someone could make a supernatural time portal for him to return home.

"Is there a king at Ingole, or a chief of all the tribes, all the Narwa?" Marcus asked.

"No, of course not. No one can tell everyone what to do. How would they know what is best for someone else?"

The idea of losing personal freedom went against the Narwa way of life, but Marcus could not believe that the Narwa had no leadership, nor some type of mutual peace or security commitment.

"So, everyone always can do whatever they want?" Marcus asked. To him such freedom sounded like it would dissolve into anarchy.

"To live with the Narwa, to be Narwa, one must follow Narwa law, other than that everyone must decide what is right for themselves. At Ingole many of the most respected will gather to discuss problems, and give guidance, but they don't tell anyone what he has to do or can't do."

On the walk to the gathering Marcus wondered if he would stick out and cause problems either for himself or the Piucca. He would have been surprised a few months ago to see how much he now fit in. Marcus's skin was not nearly as red as the Narwa, and other physical features made him distinguishable even from a distance. However, he had adopted wearing the same loincloth as the children did. The pants he wore to the market ages ago were not comfortable in the heat and the active routine of primitive life. When given the cloth by Naa, Marcus learned that there were some minor variations in the wear of the cloth amongst the three groups; uninitiated children, initiated members of the tribe, and fully recognized adults. Marcus was the oldest wearing a children's garment, but he hoped he would change that soon.

Despite all Marcus's trepidation as more and more Narwa arrived, most of them treated him with the same respectful indifference as the Piucca during the first meeting. A few were concerned that he might be a Tavari; but once those fears were allayed, they viewed the presence of the foreigner as something that was outside the ordinary but didn't concern them. Word spread quickly of a boy with skin lighter than the Narwa, but the biggest reaction came from children who simply wanted to get a glimpse of something or someone different.

The night before the test Marcus, and most of the initiates, spent some time alone. He tried to sleep but found himself unable to do so. He thought sleeping on the ground for the last few months would have prepared him for sleeping on the ground anywhere, but the evasion of sleep was not due to his body protesting as much as his mind. Marcus had spent many nights and endless hours in the grip of the guilt over losing his family and the sadness at the separation, and tomorrow for the first time he would finally take action. He considered he might die here, so far from his family without being able to say goodbye. He knew there may not be anything at Ingole other than the superstitions of a primitive people, but then again there might be something; and to get to Ingole the first thing he needed to do was pass the initiation.

When the sun started coming up, Marcus decided to take a look at what the upcoming trial involved. Before the sun rose completely, women started making gloves out of leaves and fibers. As Marcus understood it, he only had to put his hand in the gloves and withstand the pain. If the pain became unbearable he could choose the escape. As Marcus walked around he also saw the escape being made. The ingredients consisted of berries and flowers which Naa used to make medicine or cautioned him to avoid. Marcus saw a few other boys nervously walking around. He also saw some of the older women rounding up the younger girls for their induction. He would not see them again for three days. Not long after the women walked into the forest, a few of the men returned carrying sticks between them with mounds of dirt hanging from the sticks. As Marcus got closer, he saw the dirt had been taken from an ant hill and teamed with ants--bullet ants.

Less than an hour later Marcus sat cross-legged in front of a glove teeming with the pain inflicting insects. Marcus stared at the thick liquid smeared on a leaf next to him which he knew would allow him to escape the pain. Escape was an understatement; the paste would free him from pain but also end his life and any chance of getting home. The instructions given to Marcus were clear; once he put his hand in the glove, he must not make a sound or stand up. The glove would remain on for a time and then be replaced. Each time the initiate would have to put his own hand back into a new glove with new freshly angered bullet ants. As far as Marcus understood, this would go on for about twelve hours.

Before the ceremony started, one of the elders of another tribe came up and spoke. Marcus now knew enough of the Narwa language to understand the elder's words which he translated to himself.

"You are children, but you must become Narwa, for this is the land of the Narwa. The Narwa have no possessions except their minds and their bodies. Do you forsake all possessions?"

"Nahto," the boys answered affirmatively in unison.

"You must take possession of your mind and your body. Pain is the way your body and mind will talk to you. You must not escape pain. Either you will master pain, or pain will master you. Will you master pain?"

"Nahto!" the boys answered again, their voices strong and any sense of fear well hidden.

The elder continued in Narwa, "Then take the pain. Do not run from it. Do not hide from it. Do not imagine escapes. Respect your pain and be one with it. Embrace it until only you remain. Begin."

Marcus looked at the glove. Thoughts went rushing through his mind. He wondered if he might die from the pain or an allergic reaction to the sting. Maybe he would succumb to taking the toxic pain-killing drug. Marcus tried to reassure himself he would never choose the escape, but how could he know for sure? What if he went through all this and never made it home anyways, he wondered. With all these fears and more dancing thought his head, Marcus reminded himself of what he must do. Marcus put on the glove.

He had seen the ants moving around and felt one of the enormous bodies pressed against his skin. For a short moment that stretched in Marcus's mind he wondered if perhaps they were not going to sting him after all. Then Marcus felt the most searing pain shoot into his wrist. Marcus expected that the sting's pain would be an ache, but the pain felt more like a burn. That burn seemingly fired every pain receptor on the spot at once. He imagined the stinger piercing through his hand like a lance that ran all the way up into the sky and down into the depths of the earth. An entire skyscraper of pain stacked up on his wrist funneled burning pain into every cell and every synapse of his hand and forearm. A second sting followed the first with several more just behind. In his agony Marcus imagined the nerves in his arm turning into burning lava scorching the intensity of the anguish into his mind. The pain quickly became so intense Marcus believed he would vomit.

Marcus longed to scream, despite the instructions that all the boys sit in silence for the duration of the initiation. When the thirteen initiates first gathered, Marcus imagined the rite would be a sort of bonding experience. However, the pain in his hand prevented Marcus from feeling a kinship with anyone or anything besides pain which would redouble and come crashing back on him before he noticed it had receded at all.

Marcus, as everyone does in suffering, went through the typical stages. At first, he tried to think of something else. He tried to think about his family and remember various happy memories they had shared, but each time the pain would shoot through shattering whatever scenario Marcus replayed in his mind. Marcus tried to think of more exciting things: the biggest wave he ever surfed, the time he jumped from the roof into the pool, and the time a car hit him while he rode his bike. Again, the pain came crashing through much larger and more real than any memory. Sometimes between waves of pain Marcus would be engulfed in a sea of nausea, not due to any poison but rather his body's inability to deal with the agony.

Marcus then tried to ignore the pain. In his mind Marcus tried to erect a barrier and block out the pain. In the past Marcus had experienced success with this technique. He remembered when he burned his hand trying to work the barbeque, and when he cut his leg on glass at the beach. On both occasions Marcus had been able to 'tough it out.' Unfortunately, neither of those instances prepared Marcus for the intensity of the bullet ant stings, or for the way in which the agony would recede and then come crashing back onto him.

Marcus tried to convince himself that hours had passed since putting on the glove, but when he opened his eyes, his shadow had not move perceptibly. He still didn't know when exactly the ritual ended, and now he understood uncertainty added to the difficulty of the trial.

The nearby mixture of pain-killing, life-ending elixir continued to catch Marcus's eye and play in his mind. Marcus's conscious mind was faltering against the pain and he looked for an excuse to choose failure. "I wonder if maybe these ancient people have a different way of feeling pain. Maybe I'm just more advanced, and I feel pain more than they do. There is no way all of them have gone through this before. No one could take this much pain for a whole day. Roquen has always been way different than me." His belief in any real physiological difference dissolved in his memories of just how alike he and his friend were. Having solidified an excuse to fail, his thoughts shifted to convincing himself the escape wouldn't really be failure.

"This whole test can't be real anyways. Only a lunatic would believe in time travel and this supernatural crazy stuff. I'm really back home in a hospital having a dream. I just need to take that medicine and I'll wake up. Mom will be there holding my hand and telling me how brave I was to fight through my dream." Only the pain in his hand overwhelmingly convinced Marcus of the undeniable authenticity of his situation. Marcus heard a sound and glanced up. A new glove lay in front of him, and the bullet ants swarmed angrily.

Marcus remembered the instructions with clarity. He shook the glove off his hand and stared at the fresh glove in front of him. Marcus thought again about the escape. He thought about home. He thought about the unfairness of his situation. Marcus looked over at the escape, just a mound of paste which would end this and all his pain. As he did, he saw the Narwa; the boys taking the test with him and the ones observing. Marcus was in too much physical pain to reflect on the society they had created in the forest but came to the realization that the Narwa society seemed to be nearly free from emotional pain. He thought about the times he spent crying in the cave and longing for his family and home. In comparison the pain in his hand while more intense was in some ways preferable to the depths of sadness that came with missing home. The reminder of home strengthened his resolve, and he put away the thoughts of escape. Instead he put on the glove.

Before long, exhaustion consumed Marcus. He never imagined just being in pain would be so physically and mentally taxing. He wondered if he would faint from the stress and hoped that he would, but he didn't want to fail the test after having endured so much pain already. Marcus also wondered if they would administer some drug to him if he lost consciousness, either to make him wake up or never wake up. Nothing Marcus tried to fight the pain succeeded. His thoughts were broken by continuous waves of anguish that would come crashing down on him shattering his thoughts like broken glass.

When Retap brought the next glove to Marcus, the man saw a young boy shaking with convulsions of pain and silent tears streaming down his face.

"La qurriy. La nakuy. La pakay. Naicele Marcus Er. " Marcus heard Retap's voice speak softly.

Through the fog of pain Marcus repeated it back to himself silently, "Don't run, don't fight, don't escape. Pain and Marcus are one."

Marcus concentrated on the pain furthest up his arm. He forced his mind to focus deeply on the agonizing sensation. With each breath Marcus tried to let the sting hurt worse. Part of him hoped that if the pain overwhelmed him, he would go numb or pass out. As he went deeper and deeper into the pain, the clarity and intensity grew. He imagined he could feel the exact spot, and each nerve receptor sent pain and fire to his brain. He focused intently on all that he had tried to block out before. Marcus finally controlled his breathing and tried with each breath to go deeper into that pain.

As Marcus focused intently on the pain, he became conscious of the most amazing thing: the pain was not deep. The pain was only intense and overwhelming on the surface. There was no fighting or ignoring it; it was too strong and real, but here within the sting he found only the truth that he had been stung. At once Marcus marveled that he still felt the pain but was no longer suffering. Unfortunately, this revelation took his full concentration off the stings and his hand, and all his mental efforts fell apart. Marcus immediately returned his focus back into the stinging and subsequent pain, determined this time to not be pulled out or distracted by anything.

The act of embracing his pain over the next several hours had varying degrees of success. Marcus was often unsuccessful in removing the suffering for very long, but the fight was no longer against the pain. Now he struggled with his own mental discipline to accept pain and be present. He donned five more of the gloves, but each time the fear decreased as the pain became more known to him. In truth the end of the initiation surprised Marcus as he had lost count of gloves and sense of time. When he heard footsteps and looked up for the next glove he saw the sky had fallen completely dark. His body felt more worn than he ever imagined it could be. He closed his eyes again for another moment of inner reflection. Finally, he felt the last glove being pulled off his hand and opened his eyes. Roquen pulled his friend up into a knowing embrace. Retap stood behind Marcus's friend with a smile in his eyes, if not on his mouth.

As Marcus rose to his feet, he saw many of the other initiates standing as well. Two did not; they lay slumped over with a glove still on. Before Marcus started the ceremony, he imagined that after it ended he would have disdain for anyone who took the easy way out. He couldn't have felt more differently. He now knew what they experienced and understood how alluring it could be to end life and end pain. Many came by to view the bodies, but no one touched them. Indeed, there didn't seem to be mourning over those who were now dead, but only respect. Marcus started to wonder if they were indeed dead, but the paling of the skin soon convinced him of the seriousness of the completed trial. The vibrant red skin of the collapsed Narwa appeared to be hiding behind a fog of death. After his ordeal Marcus sensed a deeper kinship with all the Narwa, and the scars on the hands of the men now held meaning for him. Seeing the scars on the hands of Narwa men told Marcus that they also had endured a pain worthy of his respect. He hoped his own scars would say the same to others.

The next day would be the Ohtat initiation and Roquen could barely hide his anticipation. The manhood trial was simple; go into the jungle naked and come back with the head of a jaguar or not at all. Roquen had told Marcus his plan; make a spear as soon as he entered the forest, find a peccary and use it to bait the dangerous cat. Roquen was among the youngest of the men taking the test, but he had constantly questioned the older men who went hunting though he was not yet allowed to go. While Roquen had spent the last five years preparing, Marcus hadn't the foggiest idea how long it would take him to find and kill a jaguar. For better or worse Marcus was told he would not be able to take the test of Ohtat with his friend. The council had agreed no one should take both tests in the same gathering.

Roquen was the one who told him he could not join the Ohtat test the next day.

"Why didn't you tell me on the way here that I might not be able to take the test with you?" Marcus asked, feeling misled.

"Roquen think it no matter," Roquen shrugged with a mischievous smile.

"Why wouldn't it matter? I went through the initiation to take the Ohtat test and be a man like you."

"Marcus fail today, Ohtat no matter."

"You thought I would fail the pain test?" Marcus tried to look hurt.

"Marcus, Roquen go Ingole. Roquen Ohtat," his friend replied seemingly avoiding the question but smiling.

"There isn't much point in going if I can't ask my question."

"Some time answer come with no question."

Marcus thought about that for a moment.

"You were right, I know the Narwa hand pain now," Marcus said with a laugh, and Roquen laughed even louder clapping his friend on the back.

"I bet Retap couldn't wait to bring me another glove each time," Marcus said shaking his head.

Roquen looked at Marcus curiously.

"I mean I know he doesn't want me here..." Marcus said with some disappointment.

Roquen shook his head. "Bring naicele is honor. Tatya bring for Roquen. One who bring feel also. Retap hurt for Marcus be Narwa."

"I hadn't thought of it like that," Marcus replied with uncharacteristic humility. "It's probably better I don't take Ohtat tomorrow... I don't think I've ever been so tired, and I still don't know hardly anything about hunting. If I failed then I'd never get to Ingole."

Roquen nodded. "That what Retap say."

Very early the next morning Roquen rose from his sleep to present himself naked to the elders and begin the hunt.

Marcus's feelings were mixed between devastation and relief. He knew after the bullet ant ordeal he was not prepared to spend three or four days hunting anything. In fact, less than six months ago the closest he had come to a jaguar was his friend's dad's six-cylinder sports car. He also believed that Ingole, whether it was a bunch of savage's superstition or real magic, was the key to making progress home, or at least knowing for sure he could not go home. Marcus still refused to accept he would never see his parents or home again. The Ingole meeting of the tribes would be in three months to coincide with the solstice. If he waited six months for the next Ohtat opportunity it would be more than a year before he could ask his question at Ingole. The question burned at Marcus every day, "How do I get home?"

Roquen was among the first to return with a jaguar's head. The other initiates also returned over the next two days, and the ceremony ended in the same solemn private way it began. Only one did not return, and Marcus heard no debate as to whether he had left the Narwa or died. Perhaps it didn't much matter in the Narwa view of the world. The Narwa showed immense respect for the felines whose lives were sacrificed so that boys would become men. During the rest of the year killing of the jaguar was strictly forbidden, except in self-defense. Marcus realized the hunting of the beautiful creature might be a necessity, but the Narwa never celebrated the killing of any creature nor did they mourn them. Rather they strove to respect each part of the circle of life.

After the Ohtat test ended and Layen and the women finished their secretive trials, the tribes held a feast and many discussions. After spending much of the previous days gathering information,

Evad held a small meeting about rumors gleaned from some of the other tribes. There were rumors that the outcasts had taken up ways of life even more contrary to Narwa beliefs. The new more disturbing tales were that these 'Et Narwa' had recently become aggressive and driven Narwa tribes from traditional lands. None of the Piucca expressed alarm, and Marcus learned the lands of the outcast were several days travel from the Piucca. Most thought these developments would not affect them, at least not for a long time. Retap alone sounded concerned about the outcasts and advised they learn more at Ingole in a few months.

CHAPTER SIX - INTO A BIGGER WORLD

"Man can believe the impossible, but can never believe the improbable."
    -Oscar Wilde

Marcus didn't realize it then, but the next three months would be some of the happiest of his life. Everyone considered him part of the tribe. Though he thought of his family often he no longer felt the pain of their absence to be consuming. The Narwa life was simple, and most of the day was spent attending to daily needs which did take a considerable amount of time in primitive conditions. Still, there seemed plenty of time every day for the Narwa to spend in contemplation or in the easy but simple conversations which the Narwa language allowed. Marcus wondered if the language was simple by design to keep the people simple and happy, or if a happy, simple people just had no need for complicated words. Marcus, after six months, understood the language, but not the culture. He wondered if the contrast between Narwa and modern American views on life precluded him from ever assimilating entirely.

"Tell us more about your old home," Layen said one day while the three sat and watched the stream as they often did. They always spoke English when discussing Marcus's past life, partly because it allowed them privacy but mostly because the Narwa language lacked words to describe the twenty-first century.

"Well, for one, people don't usually spend hours watching a stream," Marcus casually replied.

"What they do to think?" Roquen asked, deep in thought himself.

"I don't know. I guess people never stop to think back there. They are so busy rushing from place to place to make money or spend it," Marcus answered as best he could but with a tinge of sadness.

"Why do they need to rush so much?" Layen asked. "I thought life where you came from was easier. Didn't you say all the food was in one place, and the water comes to you?"

Marcus turned to look at her and sighed, "Yeah, but food and water are only small things. There are lots of other things people want. There are cars to take you places, and lots of clothes, and other stuff that you need to get money to buy. Or maybe you keep the money to go travel somewhere. It's also important to save some money ..." Marcus trailed off trying to remember what exactly the American economy was based on.

"Why more than one clothes?" Roquen asked confused as to why one body would need more than one piece of clothing. To him all of Marcus's previous life seemed silly, and Marcus slowly started to understand why.

"Well, for one it is colder there than here," Marcus said, glad to finally give a sound answer. "But also, people want to look good and successful; kind of like a good hunter here." He hoped the hunting reference would appeal to his friend.

"Many clothes person best hunters?" his friend asked, intrigued.

Marcus sighed and stifled a laugh, "No, not really.... A lot of society is based on illusion and deception I guess."

"Lula?" The Narwa word encompassed all serious falsehood including lies and illusions. It was one of the most negative words in their language. "No Et?" Roquen sounded alarmed that a society accepted such behavior.

"No, we don't banish people for lying... we don't even usually put them in jail," he said though he knew his friend would not understand 'jail.' For a people so accustomed to freedom, jail would be worse than death for most Narwa and for Roquen in particular. He thought about trying to explain a monetary fine to two young people who didn't really understand money, despite his repeated explanations.

"Humm..." Roquen did not look comfortable with the explanation.

"Some people work really hard and help the world, and these people sometimes have the best clothes and best food also." As Marcus said it, he knew that while it could be true, it often wasn't.

"Alli Fea better. Better than best clothes, best food, best spear," Roquen said with certainty, though Marcus suspected there might be times when Roquen would prefer a permanent spear.

"I think you are right; a good soul is better than all the fancy clothes, expensive phones, trips to the Bahamas, or sushi dinners."

"Alli Fea is the reason," Roquen concluded.

Marcus didn't necessarily disagree that developing a strong soul was a good driving force for life but felt compelled to defend the last two thousand years of Western Society. "But what if you had a really great spear, one which was sharper than any other, and straighter than any other? One that was smooth to the touch and perfectly fit your hand?" Marcus continued with a smile emphatically describing what he thought his friend would most desire.

"Yes, Roquen had good spear," Roquen's mind cast back to a recent spear he had made for a hunt.

"No. I mean this spear was perfect; always went straight, never missed or broke," Marcus continued trying to charm his listener. "Wouldn't you want that?"

"Yes, good spears I like." Roquen sounded as though he might be interested in such a spear, but Marcus could tell it would not become an obsession the way material goods become to so many.

"So, wouldn't you want to keep it, to use it every time? A spear that someone else wouldn't take? You wouldn't share your spear." Marcus tried to think of something that the twins could relate to not sharing. "...just like you wouldn't share a wife." Marcus tried to finish with a deep emotional appeal.

Roquen thought in silence for a moment but then shook his head 'no' with a force that seemed to be physically shaking the temptations from his mind. Finally, Layen answered for her brother.

"The better the spear the more he would not want to lose it, but then he would worry about keeping it. Worried hunting to not lose it. Worried at night that someone else takes it. When we go places not hunting what can we do with it? If he has a spear always, someone else would also, and what if that one was even better?"

"Roquen keeps no spear. No spear keeps Roquen," his friend concluded, reminding Marcus of the incident with the wooden bowl. Marcus thought about all the things he had owned, wondering how many of them had indeed owned him.

"Now that I have nothing really, it doesn't bother me. But when I had things I always wanted more. It's like everyone there is judging you on what you have... I just never felt like I had the things to prove to people I was good enough."

"Good enough for what?" Layen asked.

"Good enough to be accepted I guess."

"The people you cared about didn't accept you?"

"I guess that's the worst part... The people who cared about me did accept me... always. Sometimes I just wanted to be accepted by everyone. I know it sounds crazy now."

Both Layen and Roquen nodded in polite agreement.

The three sat in a comfortable silence for a while until Roquen's ears pricked up. Quickly he went from lounging to sitting up.

Marcus looked at his friend unsure of what he had heard. Marcus listened but only heard what sounded similar to a bird's wings flapping slowly.

As they stood up, Layen and Roquen glanced at each other with a bit of alarm but also excitement. Marcus wondered if some giant bird was getting nearer as the sound of the wings' beating intensified at the same slow pace.

Roquen and Layen were looking around in the sky frantically when Layen's eyes lit up and a gasp escaped her lips. She didn't point a finger; Marcus and Roquen followed her gaze.

The sight took Marcus's breath away. Marcus would have claimed that after seeing movies and huge moving sculptures, the real thing wouldn't have been a shock to him, but it was. A dinosaur flying through the air made even the largest condors Marcus had ever seen look paltry. The creature did not resemble the flying dinosaurs Marcus remembered seeing pictures of. The immense size and obvious weight of the creature made its flight look impossible, but the huge wings proved powerful enough to lift the behemoth from the ground. Despite the great distance Marcus saw the remarkable musculature of the dinosaur mocking gravity with its strength. The sky-blue color of the beast surprised Marcus as well. The three stood in awe of the creature and the sounds that the beating wings made almost effortlessly.

"Wow." It was all Marcus could say as he looked at the other two witnesses.

"Amlug," Roquen breathed. His wide eyes sparkled as an excited laugh escaped.

"I can't believe we saw it," Layen said.

"So big! So strong! Could eat Roquen in one bite," Roquen said almost unable to form words in his excitement.

Marcus agreed, though not sure why his friend chose such a graphic description.

"They are all gone in my time, but my parents took me to see giant concrete statues of them on a trip through the desert when I was a little kid. They always looked so unbelievably large and powerful."

"Evad says no one has seen Amlug since before he was a boy." Layen was beside herself with glee at having experienced such a rare event.

"I used to love anything to do with dinosaurs. I would watch all the movies and read all the books about them, but I have no idea what type we just saw. It looked like the body of a big grazing one, but with wings... and the head looked like a meat eater. How can anything so big exist?"

"They are almost gone now. Tatya says any still alive are from another time," Layen said still in amazement. "Only their magic keeps them here."

Shrugging his shoulders Marcus said nothing. The magnificence of the flight of such an amazing animal was truly awe inspiring, but he did not believe dinosaurs had anything to do with magic.

When the trio returned to the camp, Marcus wondered if they would be believed, but several others had heard the beast, though no one else had managed as clear a view as Marcus and the twins. Everyone in the tribe listened attentively to Layen recount each detail of the creature. Evad said her description sounded the same as the one described to him as a child. Narwa, in general, were not excitable, but the sighting led to much discussion, only Retap seemed disconcerted about the event.

Some in the tribe wondered if the arrivals of Marcus and the creature were in any way related. Evad claimed Amlug had been there all along and was probably simply sleeping. To be sure, two very extraordinary visitors in one year made many uncomfortable. For his part Marcus assured them he had nothing to do with any giant creatures, and they did not exist where he was from. Roquen mentioned how amazing it would be to see such power up close, to which Retap shook his head.

From the discussion Marcus learned the Narwa believed the beasts to possess incredible magic and knowledge. They were also undeniably dangerous. Marcus had no problem believing dinosaurs were dangerous, but remained skeptical of their having magic, knowledge, or spoken language. From all the dinosaur movies he remembered, they were simply dumb brutes. Talking, magical, blue dinosaurs sounded more like a good story for a three-year-old.

Roquen mentioned that the creature didn't look very far away, and it may be possible to find. Both Roqued and Retap looked unhappy with such a plan.

Evad said nothing good ever came of looking for Amlug, as he exchanged a quick glance with Retap.

Roquen reluctantly agreed that looking for trouble was not wise, no matter how alluring.

"Mandu mita, mandu uywa, mandu lum," Retap noted at the end of the night's discussion. A very grave expression covered his face as he reflected on the strange boy, strange times and strange creature. Retap paused and looked toward that boy with a very slight smile. Marcus was surprised at just how much the smile meant to him.

Marcus didn't go back to the cave as much after becoming a member of the tribe. He also didn't dig up his phone, wallet, ring, or his knife; and he left his old clothes tucked away wrapped in leaves. The seasonings which shared the blame for starting his whole adventure he had shared with the Piucca, to mixed response. Marcus knew the oath to forsake possessions was important to the tribe, to his friends, and especially to Retap, none of whom he wanted to disappoint. Marcus was surprised when he also realized he wanted to keep the promise to himself. The longer he went without the phone and the knife, the more he realized he didn't need either of them, he certainly didn't need his wallet or a misshapen rubber ring. He missed reading the books, but the Narwa told good stories, even if the language didn't lend itself to great works of literature.

Traditionally the tribe would send four representatives to Ingole. Two of which would be Layen and Roquen who would go to ask a question or make a request at Ingole. The other two the group determined by consensus. When the tribe sat around the fire to make the decision, Marcus started to dread that he would not be chosen to go. Still, he recognized that he was not a full Narwa man yet, and not a good representative of the tribe.

Evad spoke first saying that Retap should go. In a leaderless tribe Retap often showed the most leadership skills and this time showed humility and initiative again by saying that Evad should go if he wanted. Sivat mentioned Lemor could go from the men if it would give him a chance to see his son. Lemor declined and said he would rather wait until next year when he thought Tahmi and Kahmi would both have spouses. All the men agreed Evad was the best ambassador of the tribe.

Evad replied with a laugh that he did not wish to go. He did not look forward to the traveling and preferred to stay and pick berries with his wife, which elicited sly laughter from the tribe. Two years ago, Evad had been on the elder council which met at Ingole, and he clearly did not desire to repeat the process. Evad commented on the news of attacks by outcasts and wanted Retap to go since they all trusted his judgement in investigating the rumors.

Paa said that she would nominate Naa to go. The other women quickly agreed Naa would be a good choice to represent the tribe. Naa said that she had wanted to go back to Ingole for some time for reasons she did not elaborate.

After the tribe confirmed Naa would go, Evad became very serious. He started by saying the arrival of Marcus, as well as

Amlug implied the tribe may have a part to play in things they did not understand. Ingole, he continued, is the place for things Narwa do not understand. The tribe should seek answers about what, if anything, it should do in this unique situation. All again agreed.

Evad spoke once more, after glancing at his wife. He explained Marcus could go but not as a man or a member of the tribe, but as a guest of the Narwa. Retap would go and present Marcus at Ingole and see if anyone knew why a stranger or ancient creature would be in the land. All the women simultaneously agreed before any of the men could argue. Marcus didn't like being presented as an outsider now that he considered himself part of the tribe but accepted the wisdom and utility of the decision. As the meeting broke up, Naa gave Marcus a smile he suspected held some hidden but benevolent meaning.

The next day Marcus and Roquen went to look for berries with Layen before the feast. Following a successful hunt, a huge roasting peccary awaited them for dinner. Before Ohtat Roquen hated looking for berries, but now that he wasn't obligated to, he often enjoyed it.

"You don't really believe in this magic stuff, do you?" Marcus asked the two while they picked at a heavily berried bush.

"Believe?" Layen asked.

"Yeah, you don't think it's real. I mean no one can tell the future. No one can just make stuff appear or disappear. Zapping people or making them float with strange words... reading someone's mind or fortune and all that. It is only make believe. There is no magic where I come from," Marcus said with certainty.

His companions looked at him astonished. "The first time we saw your phone we thought it was magic," Layen said.

"Marcus disappear from home, appear to Narwa. Sound like magic," Roquen added almost condescendingly.

"There are perfectly reasonable explanations for both of those things. I could explain to you how the phone works, it would just take a very long time." Marcus knew it was not true but doubted they would call his bluff. "And I am sure there is a perfectly good scientific explanation for how I got here."

"Because you know how it works doesn't mean it's not magic. Narwa know the power of the Fea. Fea is the power in each of us. It is everything. Ingole uses this power..." Layen sounded as though despite her unwavering belief she didn't fully understand how magic or Ingole worked. "Not knowing how something works doesn't make it less real and knowing how something works doesn't make it less magic," she concluded.

"The idea that anyone can do anything supernatural through some unseen power doesn't make sense; it violates the fundamental laws of science." He thought of the things in his world which would have seemed magical; from cars and airplanes to phones and televisions not to mention guns or the atomic bomb. "There is an explanation for everything, and most of it is just smoke and mirrors."

Marcus felt proud at having stood up for science against the archaic superstitions of a people who didn't even have a written language, but his thoughts drifted to the strange man at the market on the day his life was turned upside down.

The trip to Ingole took five days of travel by Narwa reckoning. Narwa didn't walk slowly; in fact, they often would take up a quick trot for hours at a time. Nine months ago, such exertion would have probably worn Marcus out in less than an hour. Now after months of running with Roquen the pace did not bother him at all. Naa was the slowest and jokingly lamented coming the year in which no one older would be going. At dark on the first night they found a place as good as any other in the forest and made a small fire.

On the first night of travel the three youths did little to constrain their curiosity about their destination. Out of respect they would not ask either of the elder Narwa direct questions, but

Naa sensed their curiosity, and they eagerly listened to her experiences at Ingole.

Before starting her story Naa looked at Layen and noted how much the young woman reminded her of herself at the same age. At that time all she thought about was being a woman for a man and a mother for a child. She had gone to Ingole and like many young women met a man. Following tradition, they each had lived with the tribe of the other for one lunar cycle to get to know each other and let the members of the tribes get to know the person who may be joining them. After both tribes agreed the couple were compatible with each other and with either tribe, Naa and her man married and joined the Piucca tribe.

Until the point of marriage the telling of her story brought joy to Naa's face. Now her mood changed to be deeply reflective. Retap remembered the events as well, though he said he was about Roquen's age when it occurred. Naa expected to become pregnant immediately the way most healthy young girls do when first coupled, but it was not to be. Marcus listened to her recount the three frustrating years she and her man tried, but never conceived a child.

The Narwa tradition held that a couple who did not conceive could ask a man to help them. If that failed to work, the couple could ask a woman to help as a partner. In Naa's case when the woman became pregnant, Naa's husband left her in violation of tradition but within his rights. Naa went to Ingole the following year in hopes she would find a reason for her life not going according to her plans. Naa cautiously noted these events occurred the same year in which Retap's father left the tribe. Retap said nothing but only stared into the fire at the mention of his father. The elders at Ingole that year told her to wait; she would be a mother at the right time. Since then thirty years had passed, and now the woman was returning for a third time.

Naa told the group how much she loved the tribe, but she had always wanted someone to care for. With sadness she admitted creating a life was now, at her age, very unlikely to ever occur.

Retap asked if Naa would ask to be Ingole; to join those who lived there year-round.

Naa nodded her head yes; if she would have no children, she would prefer to be a guide in other ways.

"Ingole rondo?" Retap asked not looking directly at Naa.

Naa nodded her head and shrugged with indifference. She noticed Marcus's confused look and explained that Ingole rondo was the cave which held the power of Ingole. Those who choose that life would enter the cave to experience the magic contained within. Many never returned.

"Mana imi rondo?" Marcus asked what was in the cave though he expected that none of them knew.

"Hakay merne," Retap answered staring again into the fire.

"Whatever I want?" Marcus said to himself. "I know exactly what I want but I doubt it's in that cave"

The group made good time again the next day. Marcus, Roquen, and Layen didn't know it but the trek and timing to make it to Ingole early enough was based on traveling with aged members who would not keep the pace which even Naa kept. At the end of the third day Retap said that they would be at Ingole the next morning, an entire day before they had planned. That night around the campfire they recounted Marcus's meeting the Narwa and Retap's inspection of him.

Marcus learned the Piucca had been aware of his presence from the first day he arrived. At first the tribe thought he might be a Tavari because he appeared out of nowhere. Narwa avoided the super natural beings as best they could, so they intended to leave the strange boy alone. As Retap said, Tavari were not the concern of the Narwa, and when the Narwa were the concern of the Tavari ill usually came of it. When they saw Marcus go without a shirt they thought he likely was not Tavari. None of the tribe had seen one but believed Tavari had wings or scars on their backs from where wings had been. Marcus's making of the fire confirmed he was human, since only man had need for a fire. Retap spoke of his concern with Marcus's arrival, and how strange events usually did not bode well for anyone. He referred to the rapidly growing rumors of the trouble with the outcasts and the sighting of Amlug, both of which he thought would bring trouble for the tribe eventually.

Marcus asked Retap if maybe strange events could also be an opportunity or good omen.

At the suggestion Retap shook his head. The tribe had food, he said, and they had clean water. They were healthy. The rains came and went, as did the sun. In his view wanting more would only lead to trouble. Marcus found it harder and harder to argue with this contented and simple way of life.

Marcus asked Retap if he had been upset when Marcus followed them back the day they met. Retap looked at the boy before nodding yes.

Retap said the tribe was his first priority. Retap admitted he initially believed that Marcus might have been banished from his tribe for being so sad and angry. Marcus listened with a stifled guilty laugh. As the months passed, Retap watched Marcus learn the Narwa ways. Retap was confident that the Narwa ways were best for the world they lived it. He expressed concern that the Piucca would learn Marcus's old ways and become sad and angry as well.

A bit hurt Marcus asked Retap why it wouldn't be good to learn the ways of the other children and of the future. Retap nodded and started a tale.

According to the Narwa tradition in the beginning of the age of man there were seven brothers. They were formed out of their father who came from the great eternal and perfect Ohmfea. For a time, the brothers worked together to make amazing things, but the peace did not last as the brothers could not agree on the best ways to live. The caretakers, the ones who prepared the world for men, were still in the world then but only in small numbers. They agreed to take the children to different places where they would no longer fight.

The care takers took the red brother to the land that is now for the Narwa. Each of the brothers needed wives, and some took wives from Tavari who had become human, and some took wives from the caretakers. The red brother took a wife from the caretakers. As part of her dowry she brought with her words and the craftsmanship of the caretakers, but the first red child was wise. He saw that the caretakers fought amongst themselves and were never at peace. And so, he sent back the crafts and half of the words, trusting the land created for him would provide, and his soul would speak clearer than his tongue. The caretakers were at first offended but after reflecting on the ages of war and strife they themselves had endured, saw that he showed wisdom in his refusal. For this reason, the caretakers separated the land of the red children from his brothers so they would not take advantage of their brother's simple ways.

The other children all had chosen another way of life. They made things from the trees and from the earth. They tried to control where the plants grew and where the streams went. Still, they were not happy. No matter how many things they made, or lands they spread to, nothing was ever enough, and so they took to killing each other. The red children, however, were happy, and so the Narwa have kept the laws of the first red child.

Marcus understood why the tribe and Retap were cautious of him and his ways. The story of the Narwa was certainly at least part fiction, he was sure, but he also couldn't argue with the part about the troubles of a complicated life. He wondered if knowledge of the impending arrival of Spanish and Portuguese explorers would change their minds.

CHAPTER SEVEN - A CAVE AND A QUESTION

"Judge a man by his questions rather than his answers."
- *Voltaire*

Nothing could have prepared Marcus and his friends for their arrival at Ingole. Though Marcus's opinion of the Piucca camp had changed a great deal over the past several months, it was in essence still just a sleeping area with a campfire. The location where the seven tribes gathered for the initiations and feast was only a larger version of the Piucca camp. Marcus had expected that Ingole would only be an incremental improvement over the other Narwa locations.

One look at Ingole proved that assumption wrong. Once Marcus and his traveling companions came out of the wild forest, they entered a clearing from which they saw a living construction beyond anything Marcus imagined. The walls and corridors of Ingole consisted of a thicket of shrubs blended into a grove of enormous trees. All the plant life had been grown to fit a pattern and also act as a wall around the encampment. By simply walking through the grove Marcus could not make out the design, which he imagined could only be seen from above. The effect of thick rows of plant life reminded Marcus of hedge mazes he had seen in Europe but on a much grander scale and with huge ancient trees. The amazing variety of plants which comprised the structure of Ingole contrasted the uniformity of the small green mazes which had impressed him then. The whole location, Marcus felt, was part monastery, part fort. Adjacent to the grove rested a small mountain, and Marcus imagined one would be able to see the design of the trees and other plants from there.

The mountain was far larger than the hill that held the cave which threw Marcus's life into disarray, but still small in comparison to the mountains Marcus had seen in North America. Though small bushes and grasses grew on it, the mountainside was also far rockier than the area around it, and the chaos of the rocks made a stark contrast to the order of the living village of Ingole.

Retap said that they would first go present themselves to the Ingole elders who lived at the location year-round. Marcus, Layen, and Roquen looked around in awe the whole way to the meeting. The trees' branches having been pruned to form walls in places made it feel as though one walked through the corridors of a living building. A lush thick coat of moss covered the ground which felt similar to expensive carpet beneath Marcus's bare feet. Marcus marveled at how long it must have taken teams of gardeners to persuade all the plants to grow exactly where and how they intended. The thickness of the trees made Marcus think they must be hundreds of years old if not older. The openings in the canopy overhead allowed light in similar to skylights but also kept the area mostly covered, protecting it from the reoccurring rains of South America.

As the five traveled through the grove of Ingole, Marcus saw varieties of herbs growing that he had never seen before and a few which he knew were very rare and hard to find. As they continued on, the abundance and beauty of the flora astonished Marcus. He had been to a few botanical gardens before but had never seen such beauty and harmony that spoke of a near-mastery of plant life. Everything grew naturally but with such great order. It was clear intense planning dictated the placement of every branch and leaf on the site. The minute details of every living plant appeared to grow under the guidance of some architect botanist.

The three who were seeing Ingole for the first time continued looking around in awe as they entered the hollow trunk of a tree wide enough across for the seven Ingole elders seated within it. Naa introduced herself first as the oldest. She also told them of her intention to enter the cave and remain at Ingole. The elders nodded at the seriousness of her proposal but showed no emotional reaction. Retap introduced himself as the representative of the Piucca who passed their respect to all Narwa. Layen and Roquen then introduced themselves as having come as adults before Retap at last presented Marcus.

Retap told those gathered there of how the tribe had found Marcus and of his passing of the Narwa initiation. Marcus's heart swelled with pride as Retap referred to him with gentle praise, saying the boy had learned and begun to accept much of the Narwa ways despite his not being a red child. Retap then passed on Evad's concern that the arrival of a stranger and of Amlug may portend further changes. Marcus then stepped forward, introduced himself and turned to leave with his companions.

"Suyay..." a woman to Marcus's right spoke softly. Marcus looked at her hoping the command to stop had not been for him alone but for the group. She dressed as plainly as all the Narwa women, but Marcus could feel a heaviness around her that contrasted to the light sparkle of her eyes. The woman nodded for him to come closer. Marcus did mostly out of fear of what might happen if he resisted. Marcus wasn't sure what made it so difficult to look the woman in the eye, but when she motioned him forward with a beckoning hand he shuffled along staring at the ground. Marcus stopped nearer the woman than he intended. The woman's old and frail appearance belied the power Marcus felt she somehow held over him.

"Ingole Rondo?" the woman softly asked Marcus her eyes still glittering.

Surprised, Marcus lifted his head and was caught in the woman's gaze. Undoubtedly, Marcus had no intention of going into any more magical caves for the rest of his life unless it was one which led directly back to his family. He felt the word "la" forming on his lips as he tried to look away from the woman's eyes. Marcus could feel the sound gradually sinking back into his mouth. Marcus felt he was in some sort of mental free fall as his conscious thought slid back, and he merely observed his mouth's response. He wondered if someone else were speaking for him when he heard the words come from his own lips.

"Ingole Rondo," Marcus's voice confirmed, drawing surprised glances from all members of his group.

The next day the ceremony of Ingole started in earnest. To Marcus it felt like a music festival, albeit with no musical instruments, combined with a religious retreat. The young adults spent most of their time generally being social and looking for mates. The older representatives sought out long established friends and mostly discussed events going on in the lands of the different tribes. Retap and Naa said during normal years most of the adult discussion focused on any changes that might affect the animals they hunted. This year was far different and every discussion eventually lead to the problems with the outcast Narwa. The raids and attacks they had learned of at the equinox's gathering represented only a fraction of the troubles. In just the past three months the outcasts had been using weapons to not only drive out peaceful Narwa, but also take many captives. The Et Narwa had also taken up worshiping the sun and making sacrifices to it.

Sun worship sounded more along the lines of what Marcus remembered about South American native culture.

During the discussion of the sun worshippers, Layen sounded especially upset with the situation. "Why would anyone worship the sun? It does the same thing every day no matter what any of us do."

"Want more sun," her brother replied with his typical half joking smile.

"But they can't have more sun, no matter how many tribes they drive out or how many people they sacrifice," Layen pronounced.

Marcus thought to mention that if the earth was a little closer to the sun it would overheat, loose orbit, crash and be burned up, but figured planetary physics would be lost on his audience. "They sacrifice people?" Marcus asked, a little concerned though he had heard of the custom before.

"They sacrifice people to the sun and call themselves Urinhyame, sun worshipers." Layen confirmed having been busily collecting rumors since their arrival. "Maybe they think sacrifice of another makes up for self-sacrifice they run away from."

"Well, I can tell you that a life without possessions isn't for everyone," Marcus replied.

Roquen and Layen both looked at him in a way that made it certain they disagreed. "Life without possessions is not foundation of Narwa life. Respect and trust is foundation. Narwa keep nothing because we respect and trust that all will be provided. Narwa respect sun, it gives warmth, it gives life, it keeps the time for doing things and going places. We show respect to the sun by giving thanks for all we receive. We don't sacrifice to it, and we don't pray to it. Urin does the actions of Urin because it is Urin. Narwa must do actions of Narwa because we are Narwa."

"I agree that the sun doesn't want or need our prayers," Marcus added, glad that at least in this instance science and the Narwa views on life were in agreement.

"Tavari want prayers," Roquen added in at his sister's pause.

"Do you think this could have something to do with the Tavari I dreamt about when I first arrived?" Marcus asked with some concern, forgetting his doubts about the existence of Tavari.

"Some of the old stories say that Tavari will get involved with affairs of men, especially if men want them to," Layen replied.

"Why would angels, gods, or aliens or whatever they are want to get involved here?" Marcus asked himself aloud still doubting their existence.

"There are problems with outcasts, strangers from the future, and Amlug. I don't think anyone really knows what is going on, but if it is something important there might be Tavari involved," Layen concluded.

By midafternoon all those who had traveled to Ingole gathered in a large open area. This area was uncovered but enclosed on all sides by the trees whose limbs grew together forming walls. The Narwa attending all sat in concentric circles facing in. When they were all seated an older man walked forward to the center of the circle and welcomed the group. He led them through a single Narwa chant and then they all began the Narwa breathing exercises.

The Narwa breathing exercises, by this time, were familiar to Marcus. He had tried to do them a few times with Roquen or when the Piucca tribe would do them together. The most effort he had put into the breathing routine had been with Retap on the cliff but even on that occasion it had made little impression on him. For the most part the routine was very simple. One person would direct them to breathe in and out together for twenty-four breaths. The length of time for the inhale, exhale and hold would all grow gradually longer over those breaths. After that they would breathe in and out together for thirty-three more breaths and attempt to remain unbreathing as long as possible after the thirty third exhale. When they couldn't wait any longer, they would inhale and focus until the facilitator would instruct them all to exhale together. They would then repeat the process for thirty-three more breaths. At the end they would take twelve more deep breaths concentrating on cleansing the body.

Every one of his previous iterations of breathing exercises left Marcus feeling such exertions were a waste of time. To his credit Marcus tried to approach the exercise at Ingole with an open mind. Marcus breathed in and out with the group on que, but after a short time he started to feel that he no longer totally controlled his own breathing. With each breath he felt himself becoming part of the group which was forcing the air in and out of his lungs. He felt each inhale filling up his whole body with tingling sensations electrifying each cell. He then felt each exhale leaving his lungs purging negativity and fear. Marcus felt pins and needles throughout his body when the facilitator called on the listeners to exhale completely. Marcus confidently and forcefully pushed the air out of his lungs. Most times Marcus could not hold his breath anywhere near as long as the Narwa who grew up doing these exercises their whole lives. This time felt different. After the deep breathing and forceful exhalation, he felt his body no longer needed air.

As the seconds slipped by, he could feel the tingling continue to spread all over his body and intensify. Marcus lost track of time and wondered if he would know when to breathe again. When he did, he felt an amazing rush of euphoria to his brain. The exercise was repeated as it had been when Marcus practiced with the tribe, but now Marcus felt he was going so much deeper. Finally, after exhaling the last time the chanting began.

The man leading the traditional chants started chanting "Nar" calling for a fire. The crowd around him, and soon Marcus as well, chanted "Nar... Nar... Nar." Marcus was caught up in the intensity but stole a glance at his friend and saw Roquen even more caught up in the spell which everyone seemed to be under. In contrast to her brother, he could see Layen stealing glances around at others in her normal inquisitive fashion. Abruptly the speaker raised up his hands to silence the crowd. The silence was deafening and Marcus wondered if everyone else could hear his pulse which thundered in his ears.

Flames suddenly engulfed the speaker. Marcus could not believe his eyes. At first, he wanted to believe it was some optical illusion or mental trick, but he could feel the heat. The Ingole leader appeared to be consumed in flames, and yet Marcus could see the man was neither damaged nor in pain. For the first time in his life, Marcus had no doubts as to the reality of magic. In fact, he felt part of the magic of this fire. The group resumed the chants and continued for another hour or so around a fire that was part man, part magic. Marcus could feel the magic of Ingole coursing through his body the whole time. He knew then his going into the Ingole cave would be an essential next step in his journey, and he began to look forward to it.

Eventually the ceremony came to an end. The group dispersed silently, each tribe to the area where they would sleep. Marcus and the rest of his traveling companions found the same spot they had stayed the night before and lay down to sleep. Part of Marcus wanted to talk about the day's experience with anyone and everyone, but another part of him felt that only silence could honor the essence of the event. While no words were spoken, Marcus's thoughts focused in a clear and vibrant way that amazed him. What he did not realize-- but may have amazed him even more-- was that for the first time since his arrival, he fell asleep and did not wish to be any other place or time.

The new adults' introduction to Ingole and the opportunity to ask a question or make a request began the next morning. Marcus imagined there would be a line outside of some fortune teller's office, but in fact there was no line, and not really any waiting. While Roquen and Layen ate in the morning with Marcus, they observed an adult who looked very serious come and take another with him. Naa said that each time after talking to a supplicant, the

Ingole would send that person to find the next. She said that eventually the twins would be fetched by someone when the time came for them to ask their questions or make their requests. All three of them wanted to ask Naa or Retap about their first time at Ingole and what they had said and heard there, but knew the experience was private. They doubted Retap would ever divulge his experience, but Naa could sympathize with the curiosity of the young adults.

Smiling at their inquisitiveness, Naa confirmed that she had asked for a child to care for. Marcus could tell she was conflicted between her faith in Ingole and the seeming failure of her request being fulfilled. When Marcus asked if maybe some requests couldn't be granted, Retap shook his head. Naa agreed; the power at Ingole would fulfil any request, the only exceptions being that they could not interfere with the lives and free will of others.

With a touch of pain in his voice, Retap reminded them that the requests were always honored, but not always in the way one intended. The way Retap spoke made Marcus wonder if Retap's own request had not been answered as he envisioned it would be.

Roquen told the group he believed making requests to be foolish, and to prevent a request from being fulfilled in an unforeseen way, it was better to ask a question and then fulfill your heart's desire.

Marcus didn't disagree, but he was certain he didn't have the power to return home. He was also concerned that the way home was impossible, or maybe he would be told to wait several hundred years.

At that time an Ingole elder walked over and made eye contact with Naa.

"Gaity," she said, and Naa stood immediately.

Marcus felt they should say something like "good luck" or "good bye" but neither translated well into the Narwa language. He knew that the way to honor Naa before her journey would be simply to smile at her, and not watch her as she walked away.

A short time later a girl slightly older than the twins came and made eye contact with Roquen in a way that made them all certain it was his time to go. The other youth appeared immensely serious, and though Roquen tried to hide his eternal smile, his excitement showed. Marcus knew Roquen would much rather be out hunting, and that his friend preferred the simplicity of physical challenges to the nebulous challenges of the mind and soul. Still, Roquen had been looking forward to this day for many months, and Marcus wondered what his straightforward friend would ask.

This left Marcus and Layen alone with Retap. Almost immediately after Roquen left, a woman who Retap evidently knew came over and gave Retap a smile the likes of which has made so many men leave conversations with friends. Marcus expected Layen would use this opportunity to practice English and expound on her knowledge of Ingole. She didn't disappoint him.

"They say that caretakers built Ingole before the Narwa came to be. When they left they entrusted the Narwa with what had been their home." Layen said looking around at the magnificence of the natural creation. "They taught the first red child and the Narwa how to care for it and how to care for the land. Now that I know so many words in another language, I can't help but wonder about the words the first red child sent back."

Marcus laughed to himself at this and wondered if Layen would hold a grudge against anyone who would deny her more words. "Well lots of words have caused lots of problems in my world," he observed, then paused. "I don't know if more words cause more misunderstanding or less. The problem is people often only hear what they want to hear."

Layen nodded in agreement. "Ingole is beyond words; it speaks past the mind and into the soul. Sometimes the misunderstanding is there between the minds of those who cannot connect. Or do not want to."

Marcus looked at her and the amazing setting of Ingole. "In my world if people could ask a magic genie for one request, most of them would ask for money, power, or fame. Maybe a few would ask for love, or for a certain spouse, or to be more beautiful. Here the Narwa have no possessions to ask for, and no one has much more status than anyone else. If I didn't want to go home, I'm not sure what I would wish for or ask."

Layen smiled. "Your world has so much and yet everyone wants more; it seems madness. There is always something every heart wants and every mind wants to know." She paused a moment, deep in thought. "And even if you can't use magic to control a person, I think you can use it to control yourself, which is more important."

Marcus couldn't argue with her logic. He would have accused Layen of being a philosopher if he would have met her in California, but the Narwa education consisted almost exclusively of survival and philosophy. Marcus wondered at his own education and thought that while knowing who sailed across the ocean blue in 1492 might be useful now, it was not as useful as the wisdom necessary to lead a happy life. He didn't ponder much longer as an older man came and gave Marcus a look that beckoned him to follow. As he rose to go, Layen gave him a smile, though he thought he could see a bit of fear in her eyes. Several hours had passed since Naa's leaving and Marcus worried about her continued absence. Marcus tried to gather his thoughts as he followed the Narwa out of the communal area.

Marcus followed his guide outside of the beautifully manicured trees toward the mountain. The unremitting lifelessness of the mountain contrasted to the vibrant welcoming life of the grove. The mountain also carried a heavy weight; its grey rock reminding the world that while the trees represented life, the rock would endure long after. Marcus came to a path where the man stopped. An Ingole elder sat outside the cave in deep mediation. The one who led him to the cave embraced him which was very rare for Narwa to do with strangers, but since Marcus knew so many did not return from the cave, he considered it a nice gesture.

Marcus stared into the cave with that intoxicating mix of fear and excitement which precedes the start of so many great changes. He tried to tell himself it was reasonable to be apprehensive of a cave since another one had recently disrupted his life. The two caves, however, bore almost no similarity. The former was barely more than a hollow spot in the hill while the cave he stared into now looked much more deep, dark and foreboding. Marcus could feel the magic emanating from inside, and the intensity of the power in the mountain mixed with his own intense feelings. When he first felt the energy, he thought it held a darkness, but in truth he knew it was neither evil nor good by nature. The power in the cave was simply a force and a tool as indifferent to Marcus's fate as its own use. Marcus's fears grew as he approached, but he believed if he did not enter the cave, he would lose all hope of seeing his family again. A slight breeze brushed across the hairs standing up on Marcus's arms as he descended down the smooth worn steps of the Ingole Rondo.

The cave interior was not smooth stone like the one Marcus spent nights upon his arrival. This cave was overgrown with plant life. Marcus saw insects and spiders crawling around the floor and his calloused bare feet. Old mindsets are slow to die, and Marcus feared being bitten by some rare spider, especially the one he had read about on his arrival. For better or worse Marcus's focus on the possibilities in the cave rapidly displaced concerns of spiders.

Journeying deeper into the cave and losing sight of the entrance, Marcus expected to smell the dank reek of decay, but instead he started to smell the most inviting thing he could have imagined: barbeque. Marcus wondered as to why there would be such an exquisite smell in a cave, but soon found all his thoughts in a state of confusion. The heightened thrill of entering the cave rapidly gave way to the sensation one feels upon awakening before shaking off sleep's stupor.

As Marcus walked deeper into the cave, the plant life and rock of the cave gave way to the paved floor patio of his house in California. He saw his grandmother tending the barbeque where the choicest pieces of meat sizzled. Next to her a few delicious pieces awaited hungry mouths. The meat looked and smelled delectable and the grilled vegetables begged to be consumed. Marcus's mouth watered. As he walked closer, he could see car keys on the counter sitting next to the food. The golden keychain had "MARCUS" engraved on both sides. The attached key was emblazoned with the linked rings of the Audi emblem. He intuitively knew it fit an all-black Audi R8 he had always wanted; he pictured the expensive car sparkling clean and new in the driveway.

Marcus glanced down at his clothes, and no longer saw the fibrous plant wrap thong of the Narwa but brand new fitted designer clothes. The material felt so new and expensive he knew all his friends would be envious, and he would never have to worry about looking poor or out of place again. His left pocket bulged with the newest phone, and his right pocket overflowed with cash.

Instinctively Marcus felt the eyes of someone watching him, and he turned to see the smile of a girl a year ahead of him in school named Mary. Marcus had always thought she was the most beautiful girl in all of California. As gorgeous as she looked she smelled even better, and the mix of her perfume and the barbeque fit perfectly. His brother and sister smiled at him from the table where they had meat and vegetables from the grill piled high on their plates. Mary, who he knew was only sixteen, but now looked every bit of a woman, walked up and curled her arms around Marcus's neck. "Stay," she whispered into his ear with a sweetness that made Marcus's skin tingle.

Finally home, everything was even better than he had imagined. Sleeping on the dirt floor and drinking from a stream like an animal faded into a past dream with this new paradise being the true reality. He wondered how many hours he had wasted staring at trees and water when he should have been home taking in all the excess the modern world had to offer. *What have I been doing this whole time?* Marcus asked himself.

Marcus looked around in his haze of happiness to take in the wonderful homecoming and saw his mother leaning against the wall, nodding in approval. It had been a long time since Marcus could remember his mother being proud of him. Now she looked pleased that Marcus should have the newest phone and nicest car. Her vacant smile applauded the expensive clothing and salacious girl in a way Marcus was sure she never would. He fought against the confusion that clouded all his thoughts to remember what his mother had told him would make her proud.

Struggling, Marcus broke free of Mary's embrace to walk to his mother. "Am I a good man now?" Marcus asked. His mother just smiled blankly.

"Stay," she said in a pleading voice he could not remember his mother ever using.

Every limb on Marcus's body started to feel heavy. The seat next to where Mary sat implored his heavy mind and body to sit down. His mother's smile looked as warm as it did false.

"Tell me I've become a good man!" Marcus pleaded. He ached to hear his mother--for anyone--to say, 'yes,' but he knew no amount of money, fine cars, flashy clothes or pretty girls could make it true. His mother would be proud of him learning the ways of a culture which had already started to make him grow into a better man. His father would have been proud of him for entering a cave, despite his fear that it could have held his death. Suddenly Marcus remembered he was in the cave, and not anywhere near his parents. It was not a beast, not a trap door above a spiked floor, nor a giant stone ball rolling over him that meant to doom Marcus, but rather his own desire for all the things he feared would be denied him.

Desperately trying to clear his head, Marcus took a step away from the inviting illusion of food and his family.

"Stay," his mother called after him.

Marcus hesitated; everything he wanted was there. Why should he leave? Didn't he deserve these things? What could be ahead in the cave or outside should he ever emerge that would be better than this? Marcus's head felt full of confusion, but he knew he must keep moving deeper into the cave. Stumbling, he managed a few more steps distancing himself from the temptation. Marcus willed himself forward and deeper into the cave, past the facsimile of his family and home. As the smell of perfume and grilled meat faded, feeling and life returned to his arms and legs. His head began to clear.

A little further into the cave Marcus saw a glow. There the object of his task awaited him; the magic of Ingole Rondo. He came to a pool in the cave, and Marcus could see light emanating from it. As he drew closer Marcus saw the light came from the seven faces of a brilliantly glowing crystal of the whitest white he had ever seen. All the water around the crystal glowed with its energy. Marcus walked up to the water and knelt down.

Marcus felt a huge sense of accomplishment sitting at the pool and staring into the brilliance of the crystal. So many of life's achievements always felt so empty; from youth sports to elementary school graduations. Even his trial with the ants, his biggest triumph thus far, Marcus had known almost all Narwa passed. Kneeling in front of the water, Marcus finally knew he had done something in his life that most people would never and could never do. Marcus had often observed in his own time such opportunities to be rare or simply non-existent. After the encounter with the apparition of his family, a part of Marcus wished they could witness his passing through the cave, but Marcus knew this was an accomplishment meant to be savored alone. The pride he felt in himself sufficed, and for the first time he didn't need confirmation from anyone.

A stone cup rested next to the pool, and Marcus used it to scoop up some of the water which continued to glow. As Marcus drank it in, he could feel the crystal's power in the water coursing through his body, the way the chill of a cold drink does on a hot day. A sense of euphoria washed over him. Similar to the feeling he experienced during the chant on the second day at Ingole, but less transient; it reinvigorated his body and mind. After drinking a few times more and savoring the stillness and peace of the sanctum, Marcus walked back toward the opening of the cave. As he passed the area of the barbeque, the scene now appeared to be nothing more than props from movies; only as real as Marcus wanted to believe.

Marcus exited the cave into a world brighter and more alive than before. The Ingole elder meditating outside the cave noted Marcus's return with only a slight nod. Marcus would have previously been upset at the man's indifference to Marcus's survival in the cave, but now a sense of understanding pervaded Marcus's thoughts. He heard no words, but a picture of a middle-aged man suddenly appeared to Marcus, and Marcus knew him to be the next acolyte for the cave.

Marcus found the man quickly despite the crowd in the gathering area. It seemed as though he was drawn to this man by some spiritual magnetism. Marcus made eye contact with this next aspirant for the cave and the look returned reminded Marcus of how strange, yet simple and clear, the process had been from the other side of the exchange. He led the man to the cave and embraced him, not knowing if they would see each other again. They would not, but as Marcus would learn, most who entered the cave did not return in the flesh. Marcus could not concern himself with the man's story but rather went to find a place to be alone with his thoughts and decide what would be the next step for him to take on his own journey.

As it grew dark, he became aware of someone near him standing patiently at a respectful distance. At first, he thought it might be Layen, but the woman was much older. Marcus stood to follow her. When she stopped, Marcus found himself inside a hollow tree; this one much smaller than the one where the introduction to the spiritual guides at Ingole had been made. Marcus wasn't sure how he and the guide had arrived at the tree but knew it must be located deep within the carefully planned grove.

::Come in,:: Marcus heard. The sound of English caught Marcus off guard, but then he realized he heard neither English nor the language spoken by the Narwa. It felt as if the words were spoken into his head, and he realized he had experienced the sensation before with the strange visitor during his first night in the cave.

Marcus at first wanted to ask about the cave, but he realized he didn't have any questions about the cave. It had been a test and a trap. The bait being everything he thought he wanted, and the test being his ability to walk past it for something greater. Marcus wondered if the illusions and the confusion were caused by magic or by some natural phenomena within the cave.

::Sometimes there is no difference,:: the woman spoke into his head.

"You can read my thoughts! Can I read yours?" Marcus asked, now aloud, both alarmed and amazed.

::Sharing thoughts is the simplest magic. Before your birth you did this with very simple thoughts all the time, but we all forget the power we have,:: she answered with a little laugh.

"Can you know everything in my mind?" Marcus asked aloud, a bit concerned.

::I can hear what you want me to hear, and you can hear what I want you to hear, but if we wish to hide we can. Reach out with your thoughts, don't concentrate on the words, but on the meanings::

::Could I do this before? Or is it from drinking the magic water in the cave?:: Marcus replied without making a sound.

::Everyone can; the power at Ingole simply enhances and focuses the power that is already within every one of us.::

::What else can I do?:: Marcus asked with excitement.

The woman only smiled at his enthusiasm. ::I asked you to come here to give you the opportunity to ask a question or make a request.::

Marcus heart leapt inside his chest. He thought to tell her he had not become an adult and would be back next year, but somehow, he knew there would be no next year at Ingole for him. He likewise knew that for those at Ingole passing the test of the cave meant adulthood. Narwa were conditioned to want little, and so the test was more difficult for those whose heart longed for something or someone. He doubted that Naa had been able to walk away from having a child to care for.

::Do you have a question or will you make a request?::

Marcus had a request, which was to be back home with his family. He thought of how easy it would be to simply ask to be back home. He thought about how he would word the request to leave no room for error or tricks as he remembered devils play on petitioners in so many stories. Marcus recalled the words he had carefully rehearsed 'I want to be back home with everything the way it was before I went into the cave.' He heard the words in his mind. Nine months ago, the words would have become solid in his mouth as well, but now he doubted them. He was no longer the same person as who had entered the cave, and therefore things could never be as they were before. He knew he wouldn't want it anyway. It would be no different than trying to put his grown calloused foot into last year's shoes.

Marcus wondered at how much of his reasoning the wizened woman could hear, and he did not attempt to hide any of it. Marcus thought he would simply ask how to return home. It would be a fair request, and he would deal with the consequences of having disappeared and changed. Whenever he thought of going home he always heard a familiar sad voice asking, 'Why did this have to happen to me?' It came to him often in the voice of his guest the first night in the cave. Marcus knew he didn't want that voice to be his own.

"Why did this have to happen to me?" the voice repeated, but Marcus demanded of himself that he be a stronger person. The strength Marcus had gained in his time with the Narwa enhanced by his experience in the cave battled against the weakness inherent in all mankind reinforced by a lifetime of fear. Marcus's sadness at the things he felt he had lost weighed against the respect for the things he had found; things he knew he would never have found without the radical intervention in his normal life.

Marcus repeated the question to himself anew 'Why did this happen?' He tried to ask with the same respect Narwa held for the plan. He wasn't asking the method of life's interruption happening though he knew that would be of great interest. Now he asked as part of a whole; as a small part of a bigger plan. He wanted to know what part he needed to play that involved being torn out of time and away from his family and being placed into a time and a culture opposed to his entire life's world view.

"Why did this happen?" Marcus now addressed his question aloud. He spoke not to the woman who he realized was simply an intermediary, but to a greater power which he felt part of.

The woman smiled.   As she did the world around Marcus went dark, and while his body may have been standing in an ancient hollow tree, his consciousness suddenly felt far away. A voice spoke into his consciousness, but he knew it was not the woman's.

"You must save humanity."

Marcus had dealt with a lot over the last few months. He probably would have bragged that nothing would surprise him after traveling through time by accident, being stung by ants on purpose, and walking through a hallucination of all he previously thought he wanted. However, this did more than surprise him. He had hoped the answer would be something simple like 'learn humility' or 'appreciate what you have.' Even 'gain a deeper understanding of the universe' would have been an acceptable answer. Almost as if in response to Marcus's skepticism the surrounding darkness gave way to a view of the entire Milky Way but with ten times as many stars. His vision narrowed as countless planets and stars screamed by, and he started to recognize his own solar system as it grew from a tiny dot to a sun encircled by planets. Marcus marveled at how spread out everything was; how much emptiness the universe encompassed.

As Marcus's consciousness approached his solar system, he could see Earth; a tiny blue and green marble. Time sped up, and he could see Earth was no longer safely spinning around the sun. Earth was getting closer to it. Soon the white disappeared, then the green did as well. The blistered brown Earth continued to spin closer and closer to the sun like a marble circling a drain. As it did, Marcus could see it growing hotter and hotter, and he was certain it could no longer support much life, and certainly not human life. Eventually it crashed into the sun, though with much less fanfare than Marcus felt his home deserved. Marcus stared out at the endless other stars, each a sun to its own array of planets, some of which he instinctively felt supported life, and many of which could support humanity. Marcus had always believed man should one day overcome that vast void to find other homes, but from what he had seen, it was not to be.

As easily as Marcus had been pulled out of his body, he returned to standing in front of a woman with some connection to a far greater power than Marcus previously imagined.

CHAPTER EIGHT – WHAT TO DO

There is always enough time to do what is important,
but never enough to do what is not.
–Narwa Proverb

F ollowing the revelation given to him at Ingole, Marcus pondered the experience and lost track of time while he started to find himself.

After more than nine months Marcus was a complete believer in the Narwa custom of solitude when contemplation was required. With so much going on in his head Marcus decided to go for a walk. The top of the mountain which the grove butted up against looked like a good place to try to sort out not just the past few hours, but also how they related to the past few months. Marcus couldn't help but think what a great view the summit would provide. He quickly decided a walk to the top of the mountain would be good to put things in perspective, especially after his journey below it

It didn't take more than two hours for Marcus to make it up the mountain to a point which provided a nice view while still hiding his presence from those below. From above Marcus could discern the structure the trees, bushes, and all other plant life formed. He knew the Narwa had no written language, but whoever designed the grove ages ago clearly made a symbol of it. To Marcus it looked similar to the letter 'H' or more specifically the symbol on Honda products. Marcus wondered what meaning the symbol held to those who had dedicated so much effort to preserving it.

Out of habit Marcus wondered what was going on below at Ingole, and if he was missing something. A sense of peace reminded him of his own important journey and to focus on his own path. He sat down and started to ask himself how he was going to save the world.

"I would give anything to know how exactly how a lost fifteen-year-old is supposed to save humanity," Marcus said out loud with a little laugh. The idea wasn't any more outlandish than time travel or magic caves and dinosaurs but was still daunting.

"There has to be someone else to help me... or hopefully someone who has a plan already and I can help them... I guess that creepy guy from the market was right; pretty important journey. How am I going to save everyone, when I don't even know where I am...?"

The stretch of plants below offered no advice, nor did the wind in the trees. As he watched the sun set, it pained Marcus to think something so beautiful would be the doom of the planet someday.

::How amazingly unfair,:: he heard a voice say. Marcus first thought it came from behind him, then realized it came from within his head. Still, he turned around to make sure and saw the stranger from his first night in the cave.

Ahsigna appeared remarkably the same to Marcus as he had at the first meeting. Perhaps because Marcus's whole life had changed, he expected some change would occur in everyone else. Without knowing why, he somehow sensed this particular stranger's appearance might change, but he would never have to age.

::Absolutely unreasonable to ask a boy of just fifteen years to save the world!:: Ahsigna walked up and sat next to Marcus. He looked as though Marcus's plight weighed heavily on him. ::Things have been unfair for me as well, but I won't just stand by and let it be. Someone has to stand up and say that we can't be treated like this.::

The stranger's pity earned him Marcus's attention. The boy could hear his own words in the stranger's dialogue and wondered if he weren't some figment of his imagination who came when he was feeling lost or confused.

::I am certainly not a figment of your imagination!:: Ahsigna declared, not without some indignation. ::If anything, you would be a figment of mine.::

"So, what should I do?" Marcus asked; the Tavari's sour mood already infecting him.

::You shouldn't do anything!:: Ahsigna replied with exasperation at Marcus's simplicity. ::Why should you do anything? Did you ask to be pulled into this mess? There are forces at play here which you can't begin to understand. You'll only get yourself and everyone you care about killed.::

"But I can't do nothing; I'm already here," Marcus protested. "If I do whatever it is I need to do, then maybe I can go home." At the mention of home, Marcus's pain reflected in his voice.

::I promise you this; even if you do whatever it is that whoever brought you here to do, they don't care about you or sending you home. You are a tool, a means to some ends, and at that end, disposable. Like I was.::

Marcus thought about this for a while. The idea of abandoning any imposed responsibility and doing nothing appealed to a part of him which he had been trying to bury but was not yet dead.

::And I can get you home... To your real home, not some false illusion like that silly cave these savages think is magic. Your family misses you. They need you, Marcus. Let someone else worry about saving humanity. You weren't made for this. You were born to have a fun and simple life on the beaches, and I can get you there.:: Marcus could feel Ahsigna digging deeper into his thoughts, but Marcus did not resist it.

"You can send me home... really?"

::Trust me, Marcus. I just need you to do something small for me first.::

"Can you send me back to right before I went into the damn cave so I can warn myself not to get involved in this whole mess?"

At the suggestion Ahsigna became a little annoyed, ::Of course not... your soul can't be in two places in the same time. No one can do that, but I can send you back to the moment after you left.::

"Really?" Marcus asked. He wanted to believe, but he felt as afraid of believing he could go home as he did of being tasked to save the Earth. He felt warm tears start to stream down his face. The emotional roller coaster of the past twenty-four hours left Marcus drained. A part of him wanted to believe he could be part of a plan to save humanity, but that responsibility also scared him. Marcus did not believe himself to be the type to save anyone. His life had been filled with fear, not heroism; selfishness, not sacrifice. As each tear fell down his face two more replaced it, and soon he was sobbing. "Really? Home?" Marcus asked again.

Ahsigna nodded.

"But what about saving the Earth from falling into the sun?"

::Should your parents lose a son? Should your future wife lose the man of her dreams? Should all your friends, and brother and sister, be left lonely? Just so some cosmic powers can use you as a pawn? If Earth really needs to be saved why doesn't 'God' or whoever just do it themselves? With the crystal I could have you back home in no time.::

Marcus was sobbing but didn't have a reply.

::Let me help you,:: Ahsigna whispered as he leaned over and took Marcus's hand.

A crack of thunder pierced the quiet of the mountain.

::TRAITOR!::

Marcus looked around trying to find where the noise came from, but suddenly he felt a blast of lightning strike him and Ahsigna. As he felt every muscle clench in a locked spasm, the white glow of the lightning surrounded him. The sudden searing pain of the high voltage coursed through his body in an instant that stretched without end as the pain made all Ahsigna's words suddenly seem a distant memory. Marcus felt certain such energy would kill him. Instead the pain stayed with him as the world went dark, and pain gave him assurance he was still alive.

The blast knocked him briefly unconscious as he collapsed into the dirt. The attack left Ahsigna a little fazed, but Marcus clearly saw a dark anger on the beautiful face. As the dazed Tavari staggered to his feet, a figure came flying down seemingly out of nowhere, fist first, and caught Ahsigna solidly on the side of the face. Absorbing the full impact of the blow, Ahsigna went down limp into the dirt. When he fell, it sounded more like a car falling out of a two-story window than a man getting knocked down. Ahsigna appeared unconscious, but the huge new comer looked ready to strike again. He had skin the same color as Ahsigna's but his hair was much lighter, though also long. He stood at least a head taller and weighed twice as much as his relative crumpled on the ground. He wore a long tunic of leather that exposed his muscular arms and legs.

::You are fair game now, deceiver!:: the newcomer's declaration resounded in the thunder with authority.

Marcus stared at the two astonished. After experiencing the strength of Ahsigna's opponent, and the burn of the lightning, Marcus was determined not to do anything to interfere with either of the demi-gods. The hulking Tavari also wielded a club that Marcus thought probably weighed more than he did. Marcus concluded the combination of the enormous club and the lightning could only belong to Potek, the Tavari of Lightning and Thunder.

Ahsigna still didn't appear to be moving and the club-wielder turned to look at Marcus. ::This traitor brought you here to wreak havoc with the Plan.:: His voice boomed with the rumble in the heavens.

Marcus shook his head trying to regain his senses after being nearly electrocuted to death.

"No, I'm just Marcus. I have to save the world," Marcus stammered meekly, he couldn't think of any better reason for someone to spare his life. Marcus thought he should add something about being from another time or world but didn't know how such a claim would come across.

::Lies! From a servant of the Servant of Lies!:: Potek shouted. His voice was a thunder deafening and painful to Marcus's mind and ears. ::For service to the Fallen One, I now sentence you to death!:: With those words another bolt of lightning erupted from his club toward the dazed traveler.

It would be hard to explain why Marcus was certain he would not die there. Maybe he had finally begun to believe that there really was a reason he had been torn from his world. Maybe he was unwilling to believe he was going to die over a misunderstanding. Perhaps it was his youthful belief in his own immortality. In any case the impact from the blast of lightning threw Marcus and his new-found confidence in life flying back several paces. Marcus landed on his back with a thud. He lost consciousness only for a few brief seconds before he woke up staring into the sky. As he gazed up at the heavens, he couldn't help but marvel at the beauty in the blueness of the firmament and the simple heavy strength of the single storm cloud. Marcus's disoriented mind hoped his participation in the violence was over, and he could enjoy the view of the peacefully passing clouds for a while.

Potek turned to look for Ahsigna. ::Where are you?:: he continued thundering. Marcus realized that this stranger not only spoke into his mind, but that his voice was actually the violent cacophony in the atmosphere.

"He's gone," Marcus tried to sound pleasant and helpful in hopes the giant would stop shouting.

Potek turned around amazed that Marcus was still alive.

::Impossible!:: Potek thundered, and the sky thundered with him. He leapt into the air and brought the full weight of his club coursing with more lightning than Marcus would have thought possible down on the boy's chest. Not surprisingly Marcus remembered nothing after the giant club's impact. If he would have remained conscious, he would have seen the most perplexed look on the face of Potek.

When Marcus regained consciousness, he was lying on a bed of fragrant herbs. The smell emanating from below him engulfed his body and his senses, but unlike most heavy smells, the experience felt clean and fresh. To Marcus the fragrance of the plants somehow made the air more breathable and invigorating. He opened his eyes and saw blue sky sneaking small peeks through the leaves of trees towering over him. Marcus knew he must be somewhere at Ingole, maybe in a type of healing or recovery room.

"Lore," he heard a voice telling him to sleep. He knew the voice belonged to Naa and felt relieved she had not been lost to the cave. A less optimistic part of Marcus then wondered if perhaps they might be dead together. "Lore," she repeated. He wanted to tell her that he didn't need any more sleep, but it seemed his tongue was pretty tired after all. His mind weakly protested the sleep his body needed only for a moment, and soon he fell deep asleep again.

Marcus slept for almost two full days, and in that time, he only had one dream. Unfortunately for his young consciousness it replayed itself over and over. Each time the dream was the same; Earth collapsing into the sun. Sometimes in his dream he was able to will the earth away from the sun, but this only caused it to lose orbit and freeze in the emptiness of space. No matter what he did, he failed to save it and humanity. Time in dreams and time in waking don't flow the same, and Marcus would never know how many times he tried and failed to save the earth. As the earth spun from orbit one more time he heard a woman's voice saying "That's not for you to do. That's not for you to do."

"That's not for you to do," Marcus heard Layen saying to Roquen. Roquen stood over Marcus with some crushed herbs, the smell of which awoke Marcus from his extensive slumber.

A giant smile on his friend's face greeted Marcus's return to the realm of consciousness. Layen tried to hide her smile at seeing Marcus awake.

"I tried to tell him Naa was tending you, and she would know when to wake you, but listening is the only thing he does worse than speaking." Layen sounded exasperated with her brother, who grinned at his friend's apparent recovery.

"Marcus hungry. Mereth." Roquen knew Marcus would be hungry, but Marcus didn't think anyone could know how hungry. Marcus knew his friend referred to the feast at the end of the Ingole gathering. If the feast was anything like the rest of life at Ingole, he knew it would be amazing. Marcus didn't know how close to death he had come, but he felt like he would die if he didn't eat soon. As he sat up, he saw his chest. A pretty substantial burn marked where the electricity and club almost ended his life. He realized the last thing he remembered was getting beaten within inches of his life by the Tavari of Thunder.

"What happened... how long was I out?" He looked at Layen and Roquen, then up at Naa as she walked in.

"Big story. Lots to talking." Roquen nodded sideways at his sister and smiled "Layen love lots to talking." Roquen laughed at his own joke. "After Mereth." He added seriously.

"Mereth," Naa agreed with a nod, and the three of them helped Marcus to his feet.

As he stood up he realized the loin wrap he had been using since his time with the Narwa had been replaced. The cloth was not only new, but Ohtat clothing. Marcus instantly felt guilty for asserting an unearned status.

Roquen recognized Marcus's confusion immediately and laughed. "Marcus Ohtat." he said with pride. Then with a laugh he added, "For sleep one year."

Layen rolled her eyes and elaborated, "If five adults confirm a youth has done something surpassing the Ohtat test, they can make him Ohtat."

A huge smile covered Marcus face at the knowledge of being recognized as a full Narwa. "What did I do?"

"Marcus nakuy Tavari. Tavari raxi guar. " Roquen said with obvious awe that his friend had not only 'fought' a Tavari, but had survived.

Marcus realized no one had witnessed his 'battle' with the Tavari but only knew that despite being beaten, he lived through the encounter. Marcus understood his survival surprised them as much as it did him. "Yeah, Tavari raxi for sure," Marcus confirmed.

He could walk with difficulty, but they still assisted him toward the area where the Narwa had gathered before and now smelled of the most delicious barbeque. Genuine delicious barbeque, Marcus noted reflecting on the illusion from the cave. On the short walk from his bed of healing to the feast Marcus was sure he would faint from hunger and only the smell itself propelled him on. As they approached the largest weech he had ever seen, Marcus wondered if he was visibly drooling. Even if he had been, he probably wouldn't have done much about it.

They all sat down to eat, and between bites Marcus and Roquen agreed they had never tasted anything better. Everyone else at Ingole enjoyed the food as well, though the mood was far more somber than the first night of the gathering. The delicious meal made Marcus regret sleeping through the past two days. Evidently rumors of his encounter with the Tavari had spread and many of the Narwa stole wondering glances at him.

Retap joined them to eat. He seemed preoccupied with the rumors of the sun-worshippers but tried to reassure everyone the attacks were far from the Piucca tribe's location and had no reason to bother with them. Naa didn't seem convinced, and Marcus wondered if she heard different rumors, or if she interpreted them differently. Perhaps she just worried more.

Marcus understood that Retap and the Piucca would all be leaving first thing in the morning. Retap planned to take a less direct route and travel with two other tribes, one of which was on the way. By doing this they would be less susceptible to attack from sun-worshipers and also could discuss with some other tribes the growing threat. Marcus didn't want to talk about it yet but knew he needed to tell the others that he wouldn't be going back to the Piucca camp.

Marcus shook his head "La."

He didn't want to look at Retap, who he had grown so attached to, and tell him that he would not return to the Piucca camp. Marcus didn't know how to tell Retap everything which had occurred, but he knew he owed him and the rest of the Piucca an explanation. He knew Roquen and Layen would understand, but Retap had a more grounded view of such things.

"Marcus la guat, Marcus bapo." Marcus said softly, sad that he would not return with the others, but remembering his task.

Retap looked at him understandingly. Marcus thought Retap would ask about the task, which Marcus dreaded, or would protest in some way. Retap simply nodded and put his hand on Marcus's shoulder.

"Retap yachay Marcus bapo rehtie Amar," Retap said looking at Marcus as though it were not any bigger burden to save the world than to gather berries for the meal.

Layen explained Retap had come in while Marcus was sleeping and asked what Marcus said in his dreams. She told Marcus he had been ranting deliriously about saving Earth since his encounter on the mountain.

Marcus knew there was much for the three to talk about but refused to break his focus on the meat and fruits in front of him. Roquen also believed eating to be the priority and looked annoyed each time some discussion pulled him from his assault on the pile of food he had amassed.

Layen finished her food first and did little to hide the fact that she couldn't wait to talk about the events of the last few days. Marcus couldn't be sure but he wondered if Roquen ate a little bit slower and maybe a little bit more in response. Layen became more exasperated each time one of the boys rose from the table to get more of the delicious pork. After Marcus made up for not eating the previous two days, and Roquen could not eat a single bite more, despite how much he enjoyed teasing his sister, the two sat back contented. By that time Retap and Naa had left to investigate some commotion where many of the Narwa had been gathering.

"So?" Layen asked. Marcus noted that not only had she now mastered English, she had even picked up on many of his mannerisms in less than a year.

Marcus started by telling them about the cave and tried not to sound too emotional about his family. Marcus then told the twins about his question to the Ingole elder. He knew they would appreciate his struggle between wanting to know how to return home and finding out why he had been taken from home in the first place. He knew all Narwa felt the desire to understand one's part in the grand plan. He tried to explain the solar system collapsing but wasn't sure he could do too much other than tell them everything on the Earth would die if it came too close to the sun. Roquen didn't seem to care about the arrangement of the solar system, but Layen surprised Marcus by not asking for more details. The fact that everything was going to be destroyed impacted them both, though Marcus had trouble explaining just how many people the planet included. Marcus also told them about his dreams of alternating destructions for Earth.

"I don't have any idea how I'm going to save Earth..." Marcus's voice didn't sound as defeated as in earlier times, but rather just confused and a bit overwhelmed. "Besides I don't know why I am here to save Earth; it doesn't look like it crashes into the sun for a long time. I don't know when the end comes, but as I watched I could somehow see the people on Earth and know that there is almost a thousand years left from my time, not from now... besides I don't know how to get there, or then. I don't even know how I got here."

As Marcus stopped talking the twins took a knowing glance at each other. Marcus was sure they had some secret twin conversation just in one glance.

Layen made the smile she reserved for the times she knew something that someone else wanted to know. "I know how you got here."

Marcus stared at her in disbelief.

Layen looked rather animated, and Marcus could tell she was excited to share some bit of information burning inside her. Based on Roquen's expression he had heard it before, and it must have been quite a tale, because he only looked a little annoyed at the prospect of hearing it again.

"How do you know... how could you possibly know how I got here?" Marcus asked in amazement.

"Ingole," Roquen answered certain it would be the last word he could get in for a while.

Looking at Layen, Marcus realized his friend had asked the question he previously wanted answered. He had believed that he sacrificed the 'how' of his adventure for the 'why' and had lost it forever. Now he couldn't wait to find out how the whole mess started.

Layen picked up a long leaf from among the ones at their feet and tore it into a thin strip. "Imagine this leaf is like the path of time," she began. "The further along the leaf the further in time."

Marcus nodded. The idea of time as linear was straightforward and thinking of the flow of time as a three-dimensional object helped him visualize traveling in time.

"The entire story of Earth is on this leaf," she continued, "but nothing is lost and everything is re-used. When the end comes, everything is destroyed and used to begin again." Marcus took hold of the leaf from Layen and touched the ends of the leaf together creating a loop. "So, the end becomes the beginning, and time goes on, around in circles forever," Marcus said with a bit of awe.

"Not exactly," she continued as she took the leaf back. "Nothing is wasted by nature; she uses both sides of the leaf." Now she took the touching ends and twisted one. It still formed a loop, but one without a constant inside or outside; the outside twisted into the inside and vice versa.

Marcus stared at the loop of leaf, and imagined an ant walking around it endlessly.

"I've seen that design before... It's called a Möbius loop. The cave must have taken me from one part of the loop to another, right?" Marcus asked.

"No, somehow a hole formed in the loop. You came through that hole; say here," Layen explained as she poked a small hole through the leaf, "and now we've passed the hole." She said this with a bit of sadness as she knew Marcus would be disappointed to hear he could not return the same way he had entered.

"That makes sense, I guess." Marcus stared at the leaf and imagined himself as an ant accidentally crawling through and finding himself on the wrong part of the leaf.

"The loop was beautiful when I saw it," Layen reassured him and crumpled the leaf as punishment for being such a poor representation of something which clearly left a deep impression on her.

"I'm sorry we can't get you home," she said with a bit of a guilt.

Marcus assumed she blamed herself for not asking how he could return home. Marcus felt humbled that someone with such a strong thirst for knowledge had used her chance to know anything imaginable to find out something for him. He knew he could never repay her, and that made the gift even more important to him. He tried to think of some way to make her understand his gratitude, but more importantly he didn't want her to blame herself for not asking a different question.

"I don't need to go home," Marcus said. "Evidently I have to save Earth from crashing into the sun."

"I also saw the earth crash into the sun as the loop went into the part where things are destroyed and reborn. I didn't know it could be stopped. I thought it was the natural cycle of things."

Marcus shook his head. "I was told I have to save humanity."

Roquen looked at them both for a moment "Urin hyame Urin hammat"

Marcus stopped at the thought. Sun worship, sun destruction; maybe it was not a coincidence. "The outcasts who worship the sun god, do you think maybe they are what cause the catastrophe?" Marcus asked.

Layen nodded again as she pointed out, "They don't worship the sun god, they worship the sun." As she said it, Marcus could tell the idea was absurd to her.

"Okay, but still... could they use magic now, maybe the magic here and human sacrifice to cause the earth to crash into the sun a few thousand years later?" Marcus continued in excitement hoping maybe he had found the first piece to his puzzle.

"You still haven't told us how you got beat up by a lightning bolt, or who brought you back to Ingole," Layen interjected, somewhat changing the subject.

Layen told Marcus what they already knew. They heard thunder from the mountain on a clear day which implied some supernatural event, but they didn't know then that Marcus was up there. Naa had told Layen that a giant man who didn't speak at all brought Marcus to her. Layen said that when she first saw Marcus, she was sure he was dead because of how badly burned and beaten he was. The old man had left some medicine with Naa, which worked too effectively to not be magic, but didn't seem at all related to Ingole. The medicine had worked wonders, and now Marcus could see all that remained of his injuries was a scar on his chest no bigger than his fist. Marcus wouldn't want to admit it, but since he had survived a fight with, or rather a beating from, a Tavari, he thought he should have something to show for it.

Marcus told them of his trek up the side of the mountain and meeting Ahsigna. He continued about how the Tavari from his first night had advised him to stay out of any type of quest. Marcus felt there wasn't much else to the story except for Potek trying to kill him three different times. Marcus suspected that it had actually been Potek who took him down the mountain, but he didn't know why. While Marcus also didn't know how he had managed to survive the beating he took, he did know Potek had been equally surprised at his survival.

The three sat in silence for a long-time digesting both the information and the food from the feast. Marcus felt in over his head with saving anything or anyone other than himself. He looked at the rest of the Narwa, none of them were still eating, but almost all of them were still talking or gathered around the commotion which Retap and Naa had left to investigate. Regardless of the situation, they all carried a sense of peace Marcus still lacked. Marcus wondered if the outcast sun worshipers, or Urinhyame, were not a threat or if the Narwa were just able to maintain serenity in the face of impending danger. The sense of tranquility at Ingole made the place feel timeless, but Marcus reasoned that since it didn't exist in his time, it must perish at some point.

Retap and Naa came back together looking very grave. Layen wanted to tell them about all that had transpired, but Roquen protested. Marcus thought it would bring unwanted attention, and he had had enough of that already. Eventually they agreed that in the interest of honesty they owed an explanation to the two, especially since they thought Marcus's arrival could be linked to the Urinhyame threat. Layen happily recounted all the events including Marcus's first interaction with the Tavari in the cave when he arrived.

After Layen exhausted the story, Retap and Naa sat in silence for a while. Retap spoke first and told them that while they were eating, a survivor had arrived from a village which had been attacked by the Urinhyame. The survivor reported the Urinhyame had sacrificed everyone is his village but set him free to tell the others at Ingole. Many of the Narwa, including Retap, believed the outcasts would seek to attack Ingole soon. Marcus could hear a heaviness in his voice. Retap's struggle to not give in to sadness or anger was mirrored in many of the Narwa. The conversation about a course of action was discussed simultaneously in many small groups with similar gravity. The news of such violence shocked Marcus, but he was perplexed that none of the Narwa were alarmed or panicked. He wondered what type of pandemonium would ensue in Los Angeles if there were ever an advancing army coming to sacrifice her inhabitants.

Retap explained they would go back to the Piucca village as planned but would return with men who would fight. There had been much discussion about bringing the women and children to Ingole. The tribes which were near the attacks would bring their women and children. Those tribes who were less threatened would keep theirs at their camps with one or two men. There was simply not enough room or food at Ingole for even a fraction of the Narwa nation to stay long. Retap planned to leave first thing in the morning, and Marcus agreed to go as well and return with the fighting men. Naa also would be returning with the group and Marcus learned with some surprise she had not gone into Ingole Rondo after all.

Naa explained to Marcus, Roquen, and Layen, that the elder at Ingole had told her she could enter the cave, but she would lose the promise of children given to her when she became a woman. This confused the three who were all fairly certain Naa was well beyond the years of having a child to care for. However, after having seen the power there Marcus did not want to argue about what Ingole might have said or her interpretation of it.

Following dinner all the Narwa at Ingole went to the open air gathering location where Marcus had witnessed the Ingole elder in flames. Marcus couldn't tell if the mood of all the Narwa had grown solemn or if he felt the weight of all the troubles only in his own mind. The routine of the previous day repeated itself with the songs and chanting. What a few days ago had bewildered him now carried less spectacle. He wondered what good being able to start a magical fire would do if Ingole were attacked. Marcus also wondered what role he had to play in the upcoming conflict. Marcus didn't know much about the outcasts, but if they sacrificed human beings, he imagined they must at least be somewhat ferocious. The Narwa, by contrast, were not a culture ready for war. The Narwa men were all adept at using the spear to kill swine, birds or even jaguar, but Marcus knew killing a person who fought back would be different. Marcus remembered the Narwa didn't have any stories of past wars except those that involved the Tavari and wondered if he would witness the spread of that terrible habit of mankind to these peaceful people.

Eventually the energy of the group and the power of the chant overwhelmed Marcus's worries, and for that he was thankful. He tried to let go of the looming struggle and let the magic of Ingole take hold, and soon it did. After a few hours the night came to an end, and Marcus managed to make it back to the spot where he had been sleeping when he first arrived at Ingole what felt like years ago. Marcus fell asleep quickly, but his dreams did not allow him much rest, and again Earth alternated between fiery and icy dooms.

CHAPTER NINE - LONG ROAD HOME

"What can you do to promote world peace? Go home and love your family."

-Mother Teresa

E arly the next morning Naa, Retap, Marcus, Layen, and Roquen met up with four members of the Drimea tribe whose camp they would pass on their way to the Piucca camp. Before leaving, four members from the Hyalma tribe also joined them. The group of thirteen would not be able to move as quickly as when there had been only the five, as two of the four travelers from the Hyalma tribe were significantly older and slower than Naa. Retap expected to reach the first camp on the second day and reach the Piucca tribe camp at the end of the seventh or early on the eighth day. It would take two more full days to reach the last camp, but Marcus and his friends did not plan on continuing.

The travelers reached the Drimea camp without trouble. Marcus could tell they pushed the daily traveling time longer to compensate for the slower pace. Each night they did not stop until the darkness prevented travel, and even then, they usually didn't eat more than what they gathered along the way. Marcus couldn't help but note how convenient the forest made travel when you knew where to look for food. Insects were not a normal part of the Narwa diet but were eaten in greater quantity when traveling. Marcus was surprised to see how much energy and strength he gained from only eating fruits and creatures he previously would have smashed with a shoe and disposed of with a paper towel.

The nine continuing travelers spent little time with the Drimea. Retap wanted to return to the Piucca camp as soon as possible so they could begin gathering any who would fight. The Drimea returning from Ingole did not need any help explaining the gravity of the situation to their tribe. Marcus noticed Roquen only spent a few minutes at the camp before a girl, one or two years younger than he, made continual efforts to talk to him. Marcus observed she always found some excuse for talking to whomever Roquen was near, and Layen evidently noticed it as well.

As they left Marcus asked his friend, "Do you have a girlfriend in every village, or just this one?"

Marcus thought Layen would join in on teasing her brother, but she did not. Roquen also did not respond except to shake his head, leaving Marcus to wonder if something about dating was taboo for Narwa to discuss or if the subject just upset Roquen.

Following a short snack and drink of water the group pressed on through the forest. Marcus heard the sound of a jaguar at one point and mentioned it to Roquen who nodded in agreement. They also saw markings of a peccary trail, which Roquen would have liked to follow under different circumstance. The jungle went about its normal business of growing fruit and feeding animals which in turn fed on other animals. Each tree, bush, insect and mammal continued going about its business unaware or unconcerned of the coming conflict which weighed heavily on the minds of the nine running through it.

Near dusk on the seventh day they were close enough that Marcus recognized the first signs of the Piucca tribe camp. The travelers would have stopped for the night already if they had not been so close. Retap, walking at the front of the group as usual, stopped suddenly. He held up his hand in the universal motion for the others to stop as well. The forest became quiet, and Marcus strained his ears for any sound which did not belong in the forest.

Marcus would remember that moment of listening for a long time. The light from the waning moon was already visible with the sun's retreat nearly final. For months he would recall the greenness of the dancing leaf he watched in the silence of the forest as he focused on sounds. In a split second he saw the expression on the other travelers' faces become ashen, as did his own when he heard cries of children calling for help. Immediately the group's normal traveling trot was forgotten, and a sprint toward the village ensued. What Marcus saw changed him forever in many ways.

The cries of the four children came from a pit deep enough the little ones were not able to climb out. Around the pit laid several slain Piucca. Tahmi and Kahmi looked as though they had been killed where they slept, probably waking up to the attack. From what Marcus saw Lemor had probably been the only one who managed to put up a fight. His fists were bloodied, but his dead body bore the deep marks left by several weapons. Semaj's body rested not far from the pit containing the children; he died refusing to leave them. Evad had been killed near the fire by the Urinhyame to make a statement to the rest of the tribe. Tooh's dead body marked the sole woman victim.

Marcus had seen dead men before, but not people intentionally killed. The attack had been a surprise; the Piucca were caught sleeping and with no weapons. Marcus looked at the ground and marveled that people had so much blood in them. Describing the scene of human beings who have been killed is an exercise in futility to those who have never seen it, and an exercise in torment for those who have. Needless to say, none of the Narwa there had ever seen anything as horrid.

Expecting a wave of emotion to come over him at such an awful sight, Marcus tried to mentally brace himself. He thought any moment he would start crying or be thrown into a fit of rage at such a waste of life and mistreatment of the innocent. In fact, none of those things happened. Marcus wondered how he could feel so emotionally blank. As he surveyed the scene with the others he felt like a giant brass vault took the place of his heart transforming him into a machine going through programmed motions. Marcus was made all the more aware of his emotional barrenness by the tears streaming down Layen's face. He never thought he would see such emotional outpour from her, but he also never imagined she would experience such tragedy.

The nine travelers immediately knew who were responsible for the deaths of the fallen and the disappearance of the rest of the tribe. To dispel any doubts, a crude drawing of a sun marked the ground.

Marcus looked at the faces of Layen and Roquen, then at Retap and Naa. Nobody said anything. Their Hyalma companions exchanged shocked and worried looks among themselves.

When Marcus looked back over at Layen, he saw her sitting down with her face still wet from her tears. Her brother walked over and stood beside her expressionless. Marcus made certain the mother and father of the twins were not among the dead, but he doubted it made the situation any better. Marcus wanted to do something to ease the anguish they felt but didn't know where to start. He thought of all the times they had sat beside him as he thought of his family, and Marcus correctly decided just being next to them was probably the best he could do.

When the initial shock of the scene wore off, Retap spoke first. He said he would follow the trail left by the Urinhyame and do what he could to rescue the rest of his tribe before they too were sacrificed to the sun. Without hesitation Roquen said that he would go as well. Marcus knew Retap wanted to go alone, but as Ohtat Roquen had as much right, and duty, to go as Retap himself did. Marcus looked over at Layen and Naa who were tending to the children. The children had calmed as much as could be expected after witnessing such horror. Marcus thought exposing children to such violence was as much a sin as any other the outcasts had committed.

The four members of the Hyalma tribe were at a loss as well and began looking around the area in vain for any other survivors. Marcus wasn't sure if they really thought there may be others in the woods or if they simply didn't want to be near the bodies. Either way he wouldn't have blamed them for not wanting to remain near the bloodshed. Marcus helped Roquen and Retap inspect the bodies. The wounds appeared noticeably different than any they inflicted on animals hunting. Retap said the wounds were not caused by spears, but by the weapons which the Urinhyame crafted for battle.

It didn't take Marcus long to decide to go with Roquen and Retap to rescue the other members of the tribe, get revenge, or die in the process. His task of saving the Earth now paled in comparison to the immediacy of helping those who had become his surrogate family. The words he heard at Ingole echoed in his head, but that grand commission felt unreal in contrast to the very real horror he saw now. He refused to believe that abandoning friends in need could be part of any plan fate would assign him.

"Marcus Lennaye," Marcus said, meaning he intended to go as well.

Retap pulled his eyes from the bodies and walked over to Marcus. Retap stared into Marcus's eyes the same way he had when they met and when they had spent the day in meditation at the cliff. For the first time the boy did not feel compelled to hide from the stare. Marcus thought Retap would protest the addition, since Marcus was not as strong or as accustomed to the woods as the other two. Retap said nothing but embraced Marcus solidly. When Retap released Marcus from his embrace, he merely nodded his head. Retap walked off and stood alone with his grief leaving the three to debate their plans.

The four members of the Hyalma were now anxious to continue the journey to their camp. They appreciated the enormity of the tragedy, but concern for their own family and friends preoccupied them.

"We will not stay here tonight," Layen said emptily voicing the words both Marcus and Roquen already knew.

"Roquen and Marcus follow Urinhyame with Retap." Roquen told his sister, though Marcus knew she would not like the idea.

Layen's eyes met those of her brother and then went to Marcus.

"I don't want to lose my brother or friend trying to save my parents," Layen's voice sounded resolute despite the pain behind it.

"I always believed that no one in this forest had it worse than me. Now I feel bad for complaining, I can't imagine the grief you feel now... I'm... I'm sorry." Marcus said trying to help his friends in their anguish.

Layen stared at the ground and exhaled deeply before speaking, "I am sad, but I won't stay sad. This is the plan. I respected it when my life was full of berries and fun with the tribe. I must respect it now." Layen rapidly regained her composure, and Marcus could see his friend willing herself back together.

"You can't just choose not to be sad, Layen," Marcus said with exasperation.

"Roquen choose. Roquen choose action, no fear, no sad. Respect, act." Roquen was clearly in agreeance with his sister.

Layen asked Marcus, "Are you sure you will go also? This is between the tribes, maybe it's not what you are here for, maybe this isn't your problem."

Marcus looked at the scars that covered his hand and at Layen and Roquen, then at Naa. "Yes, I do have a few problems, and maybe this isn't one of them. But you all helped me when I felt sad and lost. Because of you, I joined this tribe and learned this way of life. Layen, you sacrificed your gift with Ingole for me. Naa literally saved my life. When I felt alone and lost Roquen was willing to be my friend. It's true I wasn't born Narwa. But I've lived the ways of the Narwa and seen the power of Ingole. You are my family, this is my tribe, these are my people, and so maybe this is my problem after all. If people in this world aren't willing to help each other, then it isn't a world worth saving."

Layen nodded her head in agreement but sat uncharacteristically silent. When Retap returned, he told the group that he would be leaving as soon as he disbanded the camp and sharpened a spear. Roquen went to do the same. Marcus asked Roquen to make one for him also, knowing his friend could make one better and quicker. He told Roquen he would be back in a short time. Retap would take some time to ceremoniously disband the camp by scattering the stones from cooking. The few things that marked tribes' camp he put into the pit they had found the children in.

Knowing that Naa and Layen would leave before he returned, he said his goodbyes, and promised to meet them back at Ingole, hopefully with the rest of the tribe. Naa and Layen agreed to take the children and travel with the Hyalma tribesmen. Retap assured them the rest of the Piucca would join them soon.

Marcus nodded at Naa tending to the children and getting them ready to leave, "Ingole chika." He recognized the unfortunate fulfillment of a promise from Ingole decades old.

"Ingole chika." she replied. Naa may not have become a mother in the traditional sense, but the orphaned children's immediate need for her fulfilled an old promise. Though the heaviness of the loss of life rested on her, Marcus could see that the weight of an unfulfilled life had been lifted. Marcus regretted that Naa's prophecy at Ingole could not have been come true in a happier way. After saying goodbye to the Hyalma, he headed into the forest.

Marcus figured he had just enough time to do what he needed and set off running into the jungle alone. It didn't take long before Marcus came to the cave, and even in the darkness he easily located his knife, phone, wallet and ring. After the trial to become Narwa, Marcus resolved only to retrieve these things if he knew he was going home. He could only imagine the confusion they would cause the primitive who found them, or worse, a paleontologist or an archaeologist. He kept them all wrapped in the bag and was surprised that the phone still held most of a full charge, but less surprised that there were no missed calls. Marcus solemnly promised himself that as soon as he stopped using them he would dispose of them in keeping with the Narwa way of using tools.

Marcus stared at the cave with a mixture of emotions. Every previous visit back to the cave he had investigated inside just in case a doorway to his home awaited him He told himself nothing had changed in the cave but a little doubt remained. Marcus knew he could run there and check, and it would take no time at all. Marcus also knew that even if there were a door back to his time, he didn't want to enter. It would be a long time before Marcus saw the cave again, but for once he walked away regardless of what it might or might not hold.

Though his retrieval of the wallet, knife, ring and phone went quickly, the group heading to the other village did indeed leave before Marcus returned. Retap and Roquen had both rubbed dirt on their skin and put black dust from the charcoal under their eyes. It transformed the appearance of both of them, and somehow made the whole idea of chasing after Urinhyame seem more real. Marcus did the same.

"Where Marcus go?" Roquen asked quietly.

"To get a tool," Marcus replied without looking at his friend.

Roquen handed Marcus the spear that he had quickly made for his friend. Retap nodded at the two, and the three of them entered the forest they had always known to be benevolent but now felt full of danger.

"How far ahead of us do you think the Urinhyame are?" Marcus asked Roquen.

"Childs say Urinhyame come at night do bad in the dark, then leave for all day."

"We must be less than a day behind them then."

"Urinhyame take Piucca, go slow. We catch them easy. Maybe two day. Then..." Roquen nodded but did not continue the sentence, he didn't need to.

When they set out the rescue party was still full of adrenaline from the sight of their home being destroyed and half their tribe killed. No one felt any inclination to sleep. However, it was agreed that they should before long in order to renew their strength for the events which lay ahead. Rested, they would move more quickly during the day and both Retap and Roquen agreed that the trail would also be easier and faster to follow in daylight. After an hour of movement to put distance between themselves and what remained of the Piucca camp, they decided to sleep as best as they could.

As soon as the first light came, Retap roused the two others, and they began the tracking in earnest. Roquen took lead, but the trail was so obvious Marcus could have followed it. Retap watched the trail for a trap or ambush, though they doubted they stood much chance against the larger group they were following. The first day they were sure that they made up time, despite not seeing any of the captives or the Urinhyame. They did come upon the Urinhyame campfire from the night before however. What remained of the fire implied that at least a half dozen Urinhyame had eaten there, and all agreed they would have their hands full if it came to a direct confrontation.

Not far from the fire they found the bodies of two of the Piucca women. Retap discovered Paa's body near the campsite, and Marcus wondered if she might have died from exhaustion as she bore no wound marks on her. Roquen found Yii a little further away. Retap said he believed the mother of the two youngest tribe members had desperately tried to escape to get back to her children but only succeeded in orphaning them. Marcus could feel his blood boil at such disrespect for innocent life.

"They're murderers!   They have to pay for this!" Marcus shouted to no one in particular.   "She was just an innocent woman."

"Mana indome, indome." Roquen replied to his friend. Retap looked at the bodies solemnly but in silence.

"How can you say that?! Don't you care?!"

"Marcus tears bring back Piucca?" Roquen asked.

"No... of course not."

"Marcus tears feel good?"

"No... I just can't stand to see this happening."

"Help Piucca make Marcus feel better?" Roquen asked again.

"Yes."

Roquen smiled, but this smile was conspicuously absent of his usual mirth. "Then we go now. "

Retap nodded at the conversations concluded, and Marcus wondered at how much his mentor understood.

The three of them continued on at a rapid pace the next day. The forest stayed unusually quiet.

"So quiet in the forest here," Marcus remarked to Roquen

"Forest know bad things going on here," Roquen agreed. "No one want to see bad things."

Less than two hours after this exchange as the sun was beginning to set, they came upon the Urinhyame band.

Roquen put his hand up to halt the group and call for silence when he heard the first noise. Marcus could see the masked joy in his friend's eyes and knew that Roquen's parents were near. In a flash Marcus also felt a surge of joy and pride at having found their friends and family, but the feelings quickly subsided as he focused on the huge task of freeing them. Marcus saw this same resolution mirrored in Retap's expressionless face. Though he made no show of it, Marcus knew Retap felt relief at finding the people he felt responsible for.

Roquen motioned the other two forward so they could see and hear as well. Marcus and Retap got close enough they could hear the Urinhyame speaking around a quickly made campfire. As far as they could tell there were eight outcasts and five Piucca, three of which were women. None of the Urinhyame stood guard as far as they could tell, which struck Marcus as odd. Marcus had expected them to hear cries of the captives before seeing them. Instead the prisoners sat stoically in contrast to their grumbling captors.

The first fat person Marcus saw on his adventure whined about how far they had traveled to attack the village when other villages were less than one day of travel away. Another one, much thinner, answered him that their job wasn't to make plans but to follow orders now, and he had better not complain when they arrived back with the others. The two talked about the impending deaths and sounded genuinely sad the sun demanded so much human life.

A third voice which sounded high pitched for a man entered the conversation. He reminded them that great things require great sacrifices, and if they wanted to be one with the sun, they would either have to be the sacrifice or make the sacrifice. At this all agreed they would rather kill than die.

The third voice, who Marcus started to think of as a tenor from the little he knew of opera, reminded them that these captives were the ones who had already 'killed' the Urinhyame through exile and banishment. He claimed it was the sun's decision that these should die, and so they were absolved of any guilt. Marcus was thinking how cowardly that sounded when he felt the sharp tip of a spear pressed to his back.

Marcus, Retap, and Roquen soon found themselves bound next to the others who were unhappy to see their tribesmen sharing the same dire predicament, but also bore that sense of relief which shared misery often brings. Roquen looked so pleased to see his mother and father that one would have forgotten he was being tied up. Retap only stared at the Urinhyame leader who refused to return his look. Marcus felt more disappointed in himself for not having acted on his suspicion there would be Urinhyame men around the camp looking for someone following them. Marcus assumed the three of them would be taken back to where ever the rest of the captives were going, but soon learned his fate would be much more immediate. A sacrificial fire was being prepared as the voice of the sun had specifically sent the Urinhyame to sacrifice the one without red skin.

"Limbe! Limbe!" the tenor voiced leader shouted at the others; his voice continuing to crack in his shouts.

"Kapakocha la Narwa" the high-pitched voice taunted Marcus. "Limbe!" Between demands that they move faster, and threatening Marcus with burning, the tenor continued to remind the other Urinhyame all the voice of the sun promised had come true, and more bloodshed was required.

The one who spoke first, whose voice sounded exceptionally deep in contrast to his boss, argued that it was not his job to do sacrifices but that the voice of the sun should do it.

"La Urin... la kapakocha," the owner of the deep voice said mostly to himself. Marcus could tell he wanted nothing to do with any further killing, even as he moved the three to the middle of the woodpile built to consume them in flames.

As Urinhyame moved the three, Marcus tried to use every opportunity to reach the knife tucked near his hip. All of the captives' hands were bound behind their backs and crossed which made reaching his own hip impossible.

Marcus kept visualizing his knife carefully tucked next to his hip, but no matter how much he focused his thoughts, his hands just weren't in the right position. The fiber rope was strong, but Marcus knew it would be cut through in seconds if he could only reach the blade he could see in his mind's eye.

Marcus's astonishment at hearing a female voice broke his concentration on reaching the knife. His surprise grew as he heard her volunteer to light the fire. The voice talked about revenge as Marcus heard its owner walk around the fire. As the face came into view, Marcus remembered where he knew the voice from. Huo glared at him and Roquen with a sense of satisfaction only revenge can bring. Out of the corner of his eye Marcus could barely see Roquen who inexplicably appeared to be suppressing a smile of his own. Soon the flicker of a newly lit sacrificial fire reflected in Huo's eyes, and he could see the same rage she had shown while being exiled with her spouse.

The idea something happening to him could just be a bad dream had proven false to Marcus so many times in the past nine months that now it didn't even cross his mind. It did cross his mind that neither Roquen nor Retap seemed very concerned with the fact that in a few moments they would be consumed by fire. Roquen had been wiggling before but had stopped straining against his bonds. Retap also stopped straining as well and just stared at the outcast tenor as he had since being captured.

For his part Marcus refused to believe he had traveled through time to die as a sacrifice to what Marcus understood to merely be a giant ball of hydrogen gas undergoing nuclear fusion. As the fire grew slowly, Marcus closed his eyes from the sting of the smoke and started to wonder if perhaps his death would somehow appease the sun and prevent Earth from being destroyed. Such a solution did not work for him personally, but to his credit if being burned alive would save humanity, Marcus would nearly have accepted it. Nearly. What he would not accept was being spit on.

When he felt spit again, he opened his eyes expecting Huo but saw no one near enough to be spitting on him. Instead, he saw the Urinhyame look very concerned. Marcus was also concerned because a wind had rapidly risen and fanned the flames nearing them. As the heat and flames grew, Marcus became aware that what he thought was spit was not actually spit, but rain. At first not enough rain to put out the fire, but the precipitation rapidly grew in intensity. The storm came out of nowhere to the surprise of both the Piucca villagers and their Urinhyame captors.

Before the fire had a chance to grow strong enough to start burning any of those to be sacrificed, the rain turned into a torrential downpour. The leader of the Urinhyame realized death by sacrificial fire would not be an option that night and grabbed a tomahawk, intent on carrying out his orders. He walked over at first unsure of himself but gained speed and confidence as he screamed in a shrill for his companions to come help him. Marcus couldn't believe that after this extraordinary stroke of luck in the weather he would be killed anyways, but as the man raised his weapon, a crack of lightning struck him instantly dead. Marcus couldn't help proudly thinking he had survived two much larger bolts.

At the sound of the thunder Marcus realized that it was not luck on his side, but a different power already familiar to him. A second lightning bolt stuck nearby ending another life; Kirtep would avoid the shame and humiliation of facing his former companions. Two deaths by lightning strikes convinced most of the outcasts not dead that if they wished to remain so, they would need to evacuate the area. The overweight Urinhyame, however, returned to grab a prisoner and paid for the decision with his life. This finally convinced all but one of the remaining Et Narwa to flee the camp.

The fleeing of their captors, the rain and the lightning bolt were all welcomed by Marcus, but he still didn't know how he could get loose of his restraints. Roquen stood up unbound answering the question. The vines used to tie him fell to the ground, somehow cut neatly. Marcus struggled against his own bonds only to find them cut as well, and quickly set to removing those from his feet. Roquen unbound Retap who rose to his feet and walked over to the last remaining Urinhyame. Roquen then freed his parents and the Piucca who were still bound. By the light of stars and waning moon Marcus could see Huo facing Retap in the rain. Retap and Huo stood staring at each other as the thunder cracked and the lightning illuminated a face of bitter rage squared against a face of stoic resolution. As Marcus wondered what Retap would do to someone who had betrayed his tribe at the cost of so many lives, the question became moot.

A tomahawk left behind by one of the dead Urinhyame plunged into Huo's head from behind driven by the hand of Mii. Marcus had always thought of Mii as being the essence of tranquility, but the loss of her spouse and two of her children had affected her deeply. Even killing the woman who had caused her such loss, Mii didn't appear angry. As the body fell to the floor Mii payed it no mind and instead looked up to the heavens as the rain began to wash away both blood and pain.

The wind, rain, and lightning ceased as quickly as they came, and soon the present remaining members of the recently liberated Piucca tribe held council on what should happen next. Sivat told Retap that while being transported, they heard the captors talking about an attack on Ingole before the new moon which meant they had less than two weeks. Sivat and Dee were most concerned with their children, and relieved that they had been taken to the nearby Hyalma camp. They were understandably anxious to start the journey to be reunited with their children.

The fact the Urinhyame used tomahawks did not surprise anyone but made clear the Urinhyame were preparing for a larger war. Retap, Sivat, and Roqued agreed that preparation would give the Urinhyame a clear advantage over the Narwa who only prepared spears when needed. Spears were effective for hunting pigs, but a tomahawk made a far better weapon for fighting, and most of the Narwa knew that. The Narwa gathered at Ingole knew what they were facing from reports of earlier Urinhyame raids, but Retap wanted the elders there to be informed that the Urinhyame had specifically targeted the Piucca camp looking for Marcus.

Certain it held the key to either the next step of his quest or return home, Marcus volunteered to go to Ingole immediately. He assured Retap that he would relay to the Narwa there all that occurred at the Piucca village, though he didn't mention he had no idea how to get to Ingole from wherever they were.

Retap agreed the three of them should return to Ingole to warn those there and prepare to fight. The others would go to the Hyalma camp to reunite with the children, Layen and Naa. Retap urged the men to then follow him to Ingole to prepare for the Urinhyame impending attack.

While the Narwa were involved in the discussion, Marcus saw someone watching them from the forest. He feared an Urinhyame may have returned, but before shouting for the others he paused. No man had a body of such size.

::We must talk,:: Marcus heard without words, and so he slipped from the group.

::There was a misunderstanding. I apologize for the harm I caused you,:: Potek spoke plainly. Marcus could tell apologies were not his forte.

"You saved my life and the lives of my friends, so I guess we are even," Marcus replied, though he still bore a bit of a grudge to match his scar.

::War is coming to the red children. Will you join it?:: Potek asked him gravely.

"Yes, these are my people now. We need your help." Marcus could only imagine what having a thunder god on your side in a war of spears and tomahawks would do.

::It is not my place. This is a war of men, and my role is to oppose my fallen brothers and protect the plan.::

"Ahsigna is one of your fallen brothers?" Marcus asked.

Ignoring the question Potek simply stated, ::Return to your new people, Marcus. I have a message for you, but you do not want it now,:: and with those words Potek disappeared. Marcus stared at the forest and wondered what that message could be. He wouldn't find out for a very long time.

Roquen and Retap walked up behind him.

"Manvapa neyar Marcus?" Retap asked Marcus.

"Potek," Marcus replied.

Roquen raised his eyebrows impressed, but Retap shook his head in dismay.

"Manen kuchuy waxa?" Marcus asked the two, still amazed that the bonds had been cut so cleanly.

Roquen shrugged with a smile. Retap turned away as adults often do when they know younger adults are discussing mischief they want no part in. As soon as Retap left, Roquen slipped Marcus's metal knife back into his hand with a wink and ever-present grin.

They found food at the Urinhyame camp which the Piucca split and hungrily devoured. That night the men took turns standing watch until the morning though Retap doubted the Urinhyame would return. Bullies and cowards rarely enjoy a fair fight, and the Piucca now had equal numbers and weapons.

None of the Narwa ever saw those particular Urinhyame again; the voice of the sun accepted neither apologies nor failures. When the two groups said their farewells and set off on their respective journeys, it was with heavy hearts. All felt the gravity of both the violence they had seen and the violence they knew to come.

The following four days of travel were grueling, especially for Marcus. Retap had the strength and wisdom of age, and Roquen had the energy of youth along with his considerable knowledge of forest travel. Marcus had grown far stronger and faster than before he met the Narwa but was no match for the two who were probably the fastest and strongest of what was once the Piucca tribe.

On the second night Marcus felt so exhausted he didn't even remember lying down, but he knew that the fruits and berries, along with occasional insects, were not enough to sustain his strength for too much longer. Roquen and even Retap looked tired, but not as ragged as Marcus felt.

That night Retap told Roquen and Marcus that he intended to stop by a village on the way. The stop would cost them half a day plus whatever time they stayed there, but they could rest and eat. Retap felt it would be good to warn nearby Narwa that there were Urinhyame in the area, even if the raiding party had fled. Retap also wanted everyone from that village to understand how important it was that they send fighting men to Ingole to resist the growing threat.

Roquen agreed, and so did Marcus, though in fairness they mostly wanted a chance to stop for a bit and maybe have meat instead of solely berries and insects gleaned during the trek. Marcus thought it odd that Retap would agree to stop but decided to enjoy the break.

When the trio arrived at the other camp, that of the Ohte, Retap's ulterior motive for the detour became clearer. After greeting the elder men of the tribe and detailing all that happened to the Piucca and how the Urinhyame had specifically wanted to kill Marcus, the Ohte tribe held council on what they would do. After Retap excused himself from the Ohte council meeting, Marcus and Roquen saw Retap engrossed in a private conversation with a woman Marcus and Roquen recognized from Ingole and the solstice festival where she and Retap had spent much time together.

Marcus asked about the woman later that night, and though Roquen had the manners not to ask, he listened with curiosity as well. Retap only replied that her name was Ell, and that she was important to him. He added that if the world were different perhaps she would be even more important to him. Marcus thought Retap would be a world class poker player if given the chance. Though Retap said nothing of it, Marcus sensed that Retap had sacrificed much in his life to do what he believed to be right, and a relationship with Ell was among those things. Now Marcus believed that Retap saw any window of opportunity he may have had for that normal life with Ell was closing.

The tribe of Ohte proved as hospitable as the trio could ask. The food, while in Marcus's opinion not as good as Piucca cooking, tasted delicious to the hungry travelers. After a surprisingly short debate, the Ohte decided they would send four men to Ingole to defend it. The rest would stay at the tribal camp. Marcus knew that this was far less help than what Retap had advised, but he made no argument and respected the decision of the tribe without complaint. The seven would leave in the morning, and Marcus rejoiced at a night's sleep. The Ohte men took turns standing guard that night, something that they commented would have been unheard of a few years ago.

That night was one of the first Marcus slept soundly in the last few days, and he paid for it with the same dream of the earth collapsing into the sun. Sometimes he was able to will Earth away, but that ended the dream with it drifting into space as a frozen ball and just as lifeless. No matter the outcome of Earth's fate Marcus continued to be amazed by how many stars existed in the vastness of space. Marcus grew up a fan of stories about time travel and space adventures. Though the former were rapidly losing appeal, staring at the endless stars made him long for the latter. In his dreams he heard the voice again "You must save humanity." Sometimes he tried to ask the voice how, but he never received any reply, and Earth would again go to its doom taking all humanity with it.

TAKEN BY TIME

CHAPTER TEN - SPARKS WITHIN SPARKS WITHOUT

If you can't resolve your problems in peace, you cannot solve them with war.
-Somali Proverb

When the trio arrived at Ingole, the scene was shocking. What had once been a bastion of serenity and order now bustled chaotically with refugees. Far more Narwa had come to Ingole than the area could support and wide spread squalor resulted. The Narwa also were unaccustomed to and resisted centralized leadership which led to the camp of people being run by multiple small councils, and one ineffective large council. Many Narwa hoped that the elders at Ingole would offer some leadership or guidance. Other Narwa openly opposed Ingole elder guidance on anything other than spiritual affairs. Regardless the elders remained notably silent. Marcus was not surprised by the silence; a shaman is a much different calling than a politician.

The gathering area had turned into a giant open-door council meeting. They discussed much but agreed on little. The only real significant decision they made was that the fashioning of spears would be allowed because they were tools and the time for using them had come. They would be discarded once hostilities ceased. The council also agreed that they should ask for more men from the tribes which had not sought refuge at Ingole. The agreement to ask for help was significant, the amount of help received, less so.

"Whime ala hus? Masse na Narwa?" Marcus asked Retap wondering why so few Narwa had come to defend Ingole despite more than a week having passed since the yearly gathering.

"Laia molomelta," replied Retap. He knew many of the Narwa, especially further from the Urinhyame and Ingole did not consider fighting, killing, or dying for Ingole to be their part in life.

"Laia molomelta?!" asked Marcus, "Au Ingole Narwa londa vanwa." Marcus said believing the destruction of Ingole would end the Narwa way of life for all. From a strategic view he also believed if the Narwa did not defeat the Urinhyame at Ingole the other Narwa tribes would be conquered as well.

Retap shook his head with a tiny smile. He knew there was so much Marcus still did not yet comprehend. To Retap Ingole was far from being the summation of the ways of the Narwa.

"Ingole erinqua la Narwa londa."

"Mana Narwa londa?" Marcus asked. Marcus wondered at the fact he had been with the Narwa for more than nine months, and never asked the question of what was the 'Narwa way' outright. He had always believed he knew the answer, but the more he learned the more he realized how much he didn't understand.

"Turuimmo... Panotar," Retap paused. "Prem."

Marcus had heard all but the last word before. Self-control he knew for certain was a pillar of Narwa life. Panotar didn't directly translate, but to Marcus meant the Narwa overall respect and acceptance of the plan and life in general. Prem was a word he had not heard the Narwa use before, and sounded foreign even as Retap said it.

Marcus hoped for an explanation but the return of scouts sent to survey the movement of the Urinhyame interrupted the conversation.

The report which the returning scouts gave only added to the gravity of what all the Narwa at Ingole already felt. The number of

Urinhyame approaching at least matched the number of Narwa presently at Ingole. Marcus couldn't help but think if all the tribes within a five-day walk banded together, they would outnumber the Urinhyame at least two to one. The scouts also confirmed that the advancing mass carried with them tomahawks and other weapons which used sharpened stone, like spears with stone tips and long knives. The Urinhyame were not moving particularly fast, and the scouts all agreed it would likely be another two full days before any fighting began. They also noted that the Urinhyame brought stores of food with them.

The report of the scouts led to another gathering to discuss what should be done for the defense of Ingole. Marcus had never seen such disorder. The Narwa continued to be respectful of other opinions to a fault. The discussion remained as egalitarian as any he had witnessed before. The system which worked so well at the level of a twenty or thirty-person tribe broke down under the strain of so many voices, no matter how well intentioned. At times when a few hundred gathered at Ingole for annual ceremonies such decorum worked when no real decisions were being made, but with a hostile force getting closer by the day, time was of the essence. Throughout the discussions men and women came and went as they either tired of the debate or wanted to think about it by themselves elsewhere.

Several hours of discussion flew by, and Marcus knew that those gathered were no closer to any decision than when they began. No plans for defenses or retreat had been agreed upon. None of them could agree on even the most important area to defend. If one wanted to defend the meeting area of the elders, another agreed but commented that to him the lives of those gathered for protection were more important. A third would then agree but note that the gathered could flee and seek shelter in the forest. They all agreed on the importance of protecting the cave, but also believed the magic of the cave protected itself.

No one gathered there had a clear idea of why the Urinhyame were attacking Ingole. The outcasts from the tribes had always formed their own communities since the first violations of the laws of the first red child. A lengthy discussion as to why they had only recently begun to cause trouble completely disengaged the gathering from the question of what should be done about it. Some said that the trouble had started because of the voice of the sun who was some sort of leader, perhaps a free Tavari. Others disagreed and said even outcast Narwa would never accept to be ruled. One of the older men stated that problems from the Et Narwa had been only a matter of time, once they took possessions and interfered with the natural growth of plants. Marcus knew enough of human history to understand that a society which believed farming to be deviant behavior would not stand much chance against the rising tide of human progress.

Marcus listened for several hours, gaining hope each time a good idea was brought up and then loosing that hope as the group's discussion would become side-tracked. The analysis of the issues astounded him, and Marcus had no doubt that the wisdom he witnessed would have taken each individual far. As for the group, things went nowhere. Marcus grew impatient and upset and looked for someone to blame for the circles the group talked in. After several hours Marcus realized the fault lay not with any one individual but with the whole assembly, maybe with the whole way of life. To make matters worse, no one had taken--nor would take--the authority to do anything about it. For a people who lived in a way where time floated easily by, Marcus felt with certainty they were now squandering a resource they could not replenish. The Narwa remained stuck in a way of life they could defend conceptually, but not pragmatically.

When he gave up all hope the group would resolve its endless debate, Marcus stood up meaning he wished to say something. Usually those who stood would be forced to wait for a while until attention shifted to them, but Marcus's unusual appearance, along with the rumors which followed the scar on his chest, gave him an advantage in being noticed. Word had also spread of his part in the rescue of tribe members. Marcus worried he would not be able to convey what he wanted but found the Narwa words came easily to him.

'I am Marcus. I came to the land of the red children not from another place, but from another time; a time very far from now. I have done my best to learn your ways, and it was only with great trouble that I realized these ways make a person's life better, their soul better, their interactions with others better. But these ways will not survive. Growing plants will allow the Urinhyame or another group to have more sons and daughters. Keeping possessions will allow them to have better tools to fight with; some you cannot imagine. Choosing leaders and accepting their decisions will make everything progress faster and further, even if not always for the better. One day someone will come with more men, better tools for killing, and more knowledge of it, and they will kill the Narwa and take their land. Your way of life may be better; I believe it is, but if you don't change, you, along with your way of life will surely die.'

For a moment the gathering stayed quiet. Marcus held a faint glimmer of hope that perhaps his words and knowledge of things to come convinced them. Perhaps the battle could be won, Ingole preserved, and Earth saved.

"Mana indome indome," he finally heard someone say. The sentiment was echoed again by several others.

When the murmuring stopped, an older man stood up.

"Malda wanyuy tena, la kawsay raica" he spoke plainly but with determination, and it was clear the words were not being said for the first time. Marcus understood; it is better to die right, than to live wrong.

At that point Marcus knew nothing else he could say would change what would occur between the Narwa and the Urinhyame, so he left the gathering.

Marcus departed the gathering area unsure of any destination. He started to walk in no particular direction at all, but unlike his previous scared and angry walk in the market so many months ago, he felt focused. His walking may have lacked a defined destination, but he was confident it would take him where he needed to be. Before long Marcus found himself walking among the Narwa refugees who had fled for fear of Urinhyame raids. While he expected to see fear, anger, or desperation on the faces of those forced from their homes, he saw dignity instead. The future of the Narwa may have been uncertain, but he knew they would face it with the same self-respect they had carried their whole lives. Marcus wondered if their respect for the Plan and embrace of fate and acceptance of even death would be their downfall.

After walking through the refugee areas Marcus walked back to the Ingole Rondo. He stared into the darkness of the cave that had tested his will as well as his values and reason. Marcus wondered if that power inside was that which the Urinhyame wanted and were willing to go to war over.

The woman Marcus had asked his question to on his first visit walked up next to him.

::Much power in the cave,:: she said speaking into Marcus's thoughts

::What is in there? Is that what the Urinhyame want?::

::Urinhyame don't want power. They want acceptance. They want revenge. They want many things, but they are not on a quest for power, not yet.::

::What is the power of Ingole?::

::The power of Ingole is the realization of the power within each of us. The crystal is a tool that facilitates that. The caretakers who built Ingole gave the crystal to the red children. It was a tool given to the caretakers by the first Tavari. It has the power to store, and to focus that power of the Fea.::

::The crystal changes our thoughts into energy and form?:: Marcus asked, continuing the unspoken conversation. ::But that's impossible... Energy, form, power-- these things aren't just created from nothing.::

The woman smiled, but Marcus heard her laugh. ::Oh, they were absolutely created from nothing, but for now we will agree things are not created from nothing anymore. Regardless, the original power that created everything is in you, in us, and its potential is limitless.::

::The Fea? The Soul?:: Marcus tried to reconcile his belief in a soul with his still confused beliefs regarding anything supernatural.

::Call it what you want. It was first and has many names. All energy and all form are created from it, and it is inside you. It is the part of you that came from the infinite. You lack the ability to control it, but that is changing. Those of us at Ingole have learned to control it and use the power in the cave. The Tavari are ancient and control that power better, but they have been limited here.::

Marcus continued staring at the cave. All energy, all matter being made up of one fundamental thing sounded a lot like advanced particle physics, but it also sounded a lot like prehistoric superstition.

::Remember the feeling from the cave, and the way you felt drinking the water there.:: The woman spoke into Marcus, and it felt like her words brought him back to that moment.

Marcus could see the shining water in the pool, and then in the cup as he brought it to his mouth. He could feel the water going down his throat and then through his body, touching each cell, and filling him with focus and energy.

::Good. Now focus on this pebble in my hand. Reach out and take it, but with your mind, not your body.::

Marcus focused on the stone. The smooth worn surface of such a mundane object hardly seemed worthy of the practice of magic.

Focusing on the pebble Marcus willed it to his own hand, but the small rock didn't move. Marcus did not expect it to.

::Don't think about what is in my hand. Think about the power that is in you,:: the voice of the woman told him softly.

Again, Marcus reached out, but this time brought his mind back into itself. He felt the energy from the cave coursing through him. The power felt like a fire that burned through his spine up into his skull and started to spill out through the crown of his head.

::Now move the pebble.::

Marcus reached out with his thoughts and touched the pebble, feeling its smoothness as he picked it up with a hand comprised only of his will. It rose the height of a fingertip and Marcus started to bring it to himself. With a shock Marcus watched the inanimate object being moved by power outside his understanding. His amazement caused the boy to lose focus. The pebble dropped to the dirt, just in front of the woman.

She smiled.

Suddenly he felt a slight chill and emptiness deep inside. To Marcus it felt like a combination of the feeling bad news can put in one's stomach, along with being hungry.

::I did that?:: Marcus asked incredulously.

::Of course. What you are feeling now is the loss of the energy, but don't worry it will return. It is all around you, waiting to refill the power of your Fea.::

Marcus wanted to try again, but he also felt exhausted by his effort.

Smiling, the woman reassured him, ::It gets much easier.::

Amazed by the small demonstration, Marcus's thought returned to the crystal, ::This power in all of us... with this power, and with human sacrifice... could someone use the crystal in the cave to destroy Earth by pulling it into the sun?::

::The sacrificed souls and the power of Ingole magnify and focus the intentions of the mind. In time there is no limit to what can be done,:: the woman answered Marcus

::So they could destroy the planet.::

The woman nodded, ::Yes. But in truth one could do far worse things.::

::I have to make sure the Urinhyame don't get it.::

The woman regarded Marcus thoughtfully, ::You must do what you think is right, of course.::

Marcus spent a little time trying to imagine what would be worse than Earth being destroyed by the sun, and a lot of time thinking about how to prevent it.

The rest of the day remained quiet, and Marcus tried to find things to do to keep himself busy. Whatever idle time he found was shared between replaying his fears of the doom of Earth, the destruction of the Narwa, or his own possible death trying to prevent either of those. Sharpening his spear for one more countless time with Roquen didn't fill much of the day.

Roquen touched the pointy tip and smiled at the sharpness.

"Soon Urinhyame find what Piucca do when no sleeping. After battle no more pray to sun."

"How are you so sure... the scouts said they may have as many men and better weapons," Marcus questioned.

"Narwa know good life. Not coward. Not lie. Live right way. Can never lose."

"I don't know if that's true or not, but I hope so. I know it sounds stupid, but between trying to save the Earth, myself, and the Narwa right now the Narwa seem most important."

Roquen smiled. "Marcus think with heart. Save Earth feel too big. Save Marcus feel too small. Marcus no worry. Save Narwa, then mereth, then save Earth."

"I hope you are right. Even with their numbers if we position ourselves on the hill and in the trees, we should be able to surprise them, and then attack with spears from above. Maybe with reinforcements we could surround them."

Roquen shook his head a bit confused. "No. Fight at enter. Flat ground. Make fight fair."

Marcus couldn't help but respect his friend's commitment to fair play.

"I'm sure you are right, and we'll pay these cowards back for what they did to Evad, Paa and the rest of our tribe..." Marcus grew serious knowing his friend wouldn't like the second part of what he had to say. "But if things go bad... I'm going to the cave and taking the power of Ingole far from here... where the Urinhyame can't get it."

Marcus based his plan on two big assumptions: One, he would not be a casualty of the war, and two, he would know what was going on around him. Those may have been optimistic assumptions, but when tasked with saving humanity one must stay optimistic. In fairness no one at Ingole understood how chaotic war would be. It is impossible for the uninitiated to understand the way conflict, rage, and fear confuse the passage of time, or how the fog of war clouds any perception of the surrounding world.

Roquen continued his thoughts on the upcoming battle. "Many Urinhyame know Roquen spear soon. Never come to Narwa again."

"Did the council ever decide anything?" Marcus asked.

"No. Nothing to decide. Battle decide all soon. Some thinking Urinhyame come slow to make bargain with Narwa."

"I think they are coming slowly because they know we will run out of food."

At this Roquen looked up considering the thought. The idea of keeping people locked up and short of food was even more dishonorable to him that the previous Urinhyame actions.

"We should use this time to make a lot more spears... and tomahawks, maybe shields too... or bow and arrows. Instead we are wasting time talking," Marcus said.

"Marcus worry too much." Roquen looked at his friend with a warm smile that contrasted with Marcus's mood.

After a short while Retap joined them from the council meeting. Retap informed them that the council agreed on nothing except that the Narwa men would gather on the west side of Ingole the next morning at the largest entrance to the grove. They would all have spears ready though none made with rocks, nor would they make tomahawks. No leader had been suggested, neither in election nor in spirit, but they agreed that one should go forward as a representative in an attempt to talk to the Urinhyame and bring them to reason. Retap did not sound pleased with the progress which had been made at the gathering but mentioned that there were still some discussing additional options and potential outcomes.

Marcus's sleep on the second night was interrupted by Retap in the middle of the night.

"Retoh!" Retap shouted and awoke with alarm.

Marcus and Roquen awoke as well.

"Mana?!" Roquen asked alarmed.

"La... la. Lare, " was Retap's only answer, and he went back to sleep.

The third day was the same but marked by the arrival of a few more Narwa who had heard news of the upcoming battle and sought to join it. Marcus didn't think the number of those who arrived, which was less than a hundred, would make much difference, but hoped every addition would help.

Less important to the outcome of the battle but more important to Retap, Roquen, and Marcus was the arrival of their friends. Layen, her father and her mother, along with Sivat and some from the Hyalma tribe enjoyed a fond reunion. Marcus was astounded that some of the Narwa who witnessed the atrocities of the Urinhyame first hand still declined to get involved. By this time the entire camp was restless and wanted for either the battle to start or to go back to normal life.

The third day also marked the beginning of food problems. There was enough food in the forest to support a large gathering once a year, and enough to support even the very large numbers there as refugees for a day or two. But now, after several days of eating, the bushes were picked clean of berries, and the trees which bore fruit were also bare. No one wanted to search for food in the direction of the Urinhyame, and in the other areas the animals which were worth eating had become scarce. Marcus's grumbling stomach wondered how much magic it would take to create enough weechs to feed all those gathered. Probably a lot he reasoned. Marcus knew that if the Urinhyame wanted to wait them out they probably could, however that would not be the case.

The same interruption from Retap and the same dream plagued Marcus's sleep on the third night. Marcus was already awake, but Retap again awoke from a deep slumber in the night shouting.

"Retoh!" he shouted

Roquen and the others awoke again. Retap would not speak about whatever he was dreaming of and told them to go back to sleep.

On the morning of the fourth day commotion filled the Ingole refugee camp. At first light the Urinhyame had sent a spokesperson to the area where the Narwa expected the fight to start. He gave the Urinhyame demands to the entire group gathered there. They were as follows: the Ingole elders would apologize to those who had been cast out of Narwa society and admit guilt for having done so. Second, the crystal in the Ingole cave would be retrieved and given to the Urinhyame, who referred to themselves as the rightful owners of the crystal and the land of the red children. The final demand was that the laws of the sun were to be the law of all Narwa and the prohibitions as well as the trials were to be eliminated. If the demands were not agreed upon by noon the next day, the Urinhyame would come and take all that they demanded by force.

Needless to say, great debate followed the declaration of demands. Unfortunately, none of the discussion made any real progress. Some Narwa wanted to agree to the first demand. A few wanted to agree to the second demand. Only one or two wanted to agree to the third demand and noted that they could still follow the Narwa ways, whether they were the law or not. Almost none wanted to agree to all the demands. The deliberations continued well into the night and began again the next day.

Marcus spent as much of the day as he could with the remnant of the Piucca tribe. He believed that one way or another, this would be the end of his time with them. Whatever fate had in store for him it did not involve returning to the life he had taken for granted with them. Layen and Roquen came to talk with Marcus after finishing a long talk with their parents.

"Roquen tell Tatya, Retap shout at the night," Roquen told Marcus, looking around to make sure Retap was not in earshot.

"I don't know what Retoh is. Is he having a nightmare?" Marcus asked, surprised that anything could affect Retap so much. The fact that Roquen would ask his father about the disturbance surprised Marcus even more.

"Retoh was Retap's brother but Tatya said he went searching for Amlug as soon as Retap became a man. He never returned." Layen gladly inserted herself into the conversation, and Roquen looked happy to be less the center.

"That would explain a lot about Retap," Marcus concluded. "Do you think it has anything to do with his father leaving the tribe? He sounded upset about that also when Naa mentioned it."

"Retap think leave tribe not good. Not good Narwa, not good Tatya." Roquen's insight into Retap's values of service to the tribe and especially family were clear to Marcus and Layen as well.

"But why is he having dreams about his brother here?" Marcus wondered, knowing neither of them would have any answer.

"Well I don't think there is any point in asking him. He won't want to talk about it," Layen reasoned, and so they let the matter drop.

The twins spent the rest of the day with their parents, and all the families used the day to appreciate one another's company. Rather than feel a stranger Marcus felt welcomed everywhere among the Piucca as well as the rest of the Narwa. However, his own desire for solitude and thoughts of his family far away kept him from most of the gatherings.

Marcus found Retap, who evidently also preferred to be alone and had grown tired of the endless council meeting. Marcus, though still young, deduced correctly he possessed more knowledge of military history than the rest of the camp combined. He urged Retap to tell the council that if they were not going to accept the demands, they should attack before dawn. The Narwa would be able to catch the Urinhyame by surprise and may gain a psychological advantage over sun worshipers by battling without the light of the sun. Retap smiled at him, and told him it was a good plan, but not the way of the Narwa. He asked if Marcus was going to fight against them when the Urinhyame attacked.

"Nahto," Marcus answered with an emphatic yes.

"Anni?" asked Retap.

"Nahto," Marcus answered again. He would be honored to fight beside Retap, as members of the same tribe and, he expected, as close to Retap would come to having a son. Marcus knew that Roquen and his father would be side by side, and all Narwa would likely fight as close to family (members) as they could. Marcus truly didn't want to die, but if he had to, he was glad it would be with people who cared for him and who he cared for as well.

After the demands of the Urinhyame had been presented, the minutes seemed to drag on, but dawn came before Marcus felt emotionally ready for it. Marcus told Layen of his plan to prevent the power of Ingole from falling into the hands of the Urinhyame.

"No need save Ingole. Narwa defeat Urinhyame, then feast," Roquen said. Marcus could tell his friend was annoyed at even a suggestion of defeat.

"I am not sure we should go about interfering with a power that has been safe for thousands of years," Layen said.

"I don't want to, but the elders agree that the power there, in the wrong hands, could do awful things. Do you want that power to go to people who make human sacrifice?" Marcus asked.

"No of course not... But what are we going to do with it, just take off running? To where?"

"I don't know, but if we leave it here the Urinhyame are going to get it. It's a big world... maybe we drop it into the ocean... or try to destroy it. Anything to keep them from using it to pull Earth into the sun."

"Did you tell the Ingole elders of this plan? Do they think it's a good idea?"

"They know," Marcus said, and the conversation was left at that.

Marcus embraced each member of his extended family and said what he hoped would be temporary goodbye.

"I don't know how, but know I'll see you again soon," Marcus said to Layen.

Roquen and his father said a loving goodbye to both mother and daughter as the same scenario repeated itself in many of the families gathered at Ingole. Weeping and long speeches were not the Narwa way, and Marcus saw the emotion expressed more in simple warm eye contact and embraces.

Eventually the men, as well as the women who were determined to fight, gathered spears and went out to prepare for battle still a few hours before noon. Marcus didn't know if they went so early because they thought there would be much to prepare for, or if they could no longer endure the protracted farewell with loved ones. There was in fact very little for them to do. They had tried to eat what was available, and drink before what they expected would be a long day. Most of them were not hungry. Whether fear or excitement, things other than food and drink filled the stomachs of the Narwa.

Marcus had intended to line up on the northernmost end of the line and was pleasantly surprised when he arrived to see that Roquen and his father were already in the area he would have chosen. Marcus worried how much he stood out from the rest of the Narwa with his lighter skin, and if that would attract negative attention, especially since he knew they had tried to kill him once already. In the end it didn't matter; older men shuffled him to the back. Marcus found himself standing in a bit of a hole next to Retap which prevented him from seeing much as well as from being seen. He eventually realized his hidden position had not been made by coincidence.

When the spokesman for the Urinhyame, who made it clear he was not the voice of the sun, arrived the Narwa had no answer. There were in fact some still debating, and those waiting to fight sent a runner to ask them for an answer.

"I can't believe we don't have an answer," Marcus said.

"Have answer. No. No and never," Roquen said echoing the thoughts of many gathered there.

"Yeah... Even if you tried to compromise they would keep demanding more. That's how this type of thing always goes... or least how it always will go."

Nevertheless, a representative from those who were still meeting came out. He started his reply by emphasizing he could not speak for all Narwa but gave a reply nonetheless.

The Narwa would offer an apology in exchange for peace but would not admit to wrongdoing. The Urinhyame would be welcome at Ingole, but they would have to respect the customs there. Also, the Narwa would keep their rules, but the outcasts were free to do as they felt best. The representative from the Narwa council expected that the spokesman for the Urinhyame would take the offer back to the camp for discussion. He did not. He told all those gathered that they should prepare for battle and destruction that they brought upon themselves. Any who wished to flee should do so immediately.

The field itself was amazingly green. Its serenity contrasted with the specter of violence growing around it. The scattered grey stones stood testament to the fact that, although lifeless, they would bear witness to the battle and endure longer than all the petty conflicts of men. The grass, which had been watered by the rain the night before, waited silently in the still air for that darker liquid, even more valuable to men than life-sustaining water, which would soon wet the ground.

CHAPTER ELEVEN – BATTLES LARGE AND SMALL

"War is an ugly thing, but not the ugliest of things: the decayed and degraded state of moral and patriotic feeling which thinks that nothing is worth a war, is much worse."

-John Stuart Mill

T

he Narwa did not have to wait much longer for the Urinhyame to arrive. Marcus thought to call them soldiers since unlike the Narwa they prepared for war but looking at them advancing he could see they were not. The only notable difference between them and the Narwa was that their spears had sharpened rocks attached and most also had at least one tomahawk. All of the Urinhyame also wore a yellow sun painted on their foreheads. Many also bore yellow suns painted elsewhere on their bodies. Outside of the weapons and the yellow markings, they were identical to the Narwa who were facing them.

The Urinhyame tried to advance with confidence, though it was visibly a false confidence to anyone who looked closely. After all, no one on either side had ever been to war before. Even those who had attacked the tribes never encountered much resistance. Many of the Urinhyame looked at one another for confirmation or perhaps some sign. They received the call to stop about fifty meters from where the Narwa formed a line, with the oldest and strongest near the front, the young or weak near the rear.

The two sides stood looking at each other for a few minutes, and Marcus found it hard to believe they were prepared to kill and die for whatever differences they had. The air was still, and for a few moments an eerie silence covered the area. Marcus could hear and smell several people relieving themselves prior to the violence, though he did not realize then that it was involuntary. Marcus himself shivered a little and felt sick to his stomach. It wasn't simply that he didn't want to die. He didn't want Roquen, Retap, or any of the Narwa to die. In truth, he didn't even want any of the Urinhyame to die. He estimated a thousand on each side, and he couldn't imagine so many dead people. He knew he didn't want to.

Finally, a shout came from a voice well behind the Urinhyame company of men. A shout went up from the rest in reply, and any chance for peace vanished as they charged forward. The distance covered by those charging forwards was short, but the time seemed to be stretched as Marcus watched them rush into the fray. Moments of the battle would be forever frozen in Marcus's mind. Strangely, however, whenever he would reflect on what actually happened that day it would remain a confusing haze.

Many of the over-exuberant Urinhyame were quickly impaled on Narwa spears. Narwa were familiar with death, but not with the killing of humans. Such a senseless loss of life immediately weighed on those responsible. The battle at Ingole would be the first and only significant one of a civil war that would never really be won or lost. There were brothers on each side, as well as fathers and sons, and countless pairs who had known each other before some event tore them apart. Those children of the outcast not born into Narwa culture had a particular zeal for the violence. Thiers was a hatred which comes from a lifetime growing up in the presence of anger and resentment. Often those who knew each other avoided clashing directly. Just as often they sought it out. Marcus didn't recognize the Urinhyame who came rushing toward Retap, but Marcus believed Retap did. Marcus saw his mentor locked in battle, but then lost track as his own concerns became more pressing.

For his part Marcus held onto his spear tightly and pointed it towards the onrush of bodies. He hoped no one would impale themselves on it, though he knew in his head this was the preferred outcome from a tactical view point. A youth a few years older than Marcus ran toward him. The young man was clearly older and stronger than Marcus, but not hopelessly so. Marcus would always remember that face, which struck him as stupid and brutish, in contrast to the quiet nobility of most Narwa faces. In his adversary's hastily made belt Marcus could see two tomahawks, one of which danced around as if it would soon free itself and end up in the dirt. The bottoms of both tomahawk handles were sharpened to a point which struck Marcus as odd since he had never seen that done to a tomahawk either in museums or on television.

Blood pounded in Marcus's ears as he felt all the muscles in his body tense up. As the two squared off and circled around each other, Marcus would jab his spear forward while the Urinhyame youth would jump to avoid it and attempt a jab of his own.

"Ahurin!" the Urinhyame would shout at Marcus with some of his spear thrusts. Marcus wasn't sure if the shout was meant to weaken the resolve of the listener or strengthen the courage of the shouter. It took him several minutes to realize it was a battle cry to the sun.

He heard the shouts but little else. To Marcus's panicked mind every detail of his opponent was magnified, and everything outside of the two of them was a million miles away. Intellectually Marcus knew this same scenario was being replicated around him with hundreds locked in combat and hundreds dying. Marcus could see none of that as well as he could see the yellow sun on the young man's fore-head painted almost comically large. The wood on all his weapons had been sanded by course rocks and oiled so the grain stood out. Marcus thought he saw the tiny individual grains of wood each time the spear came near him. The stone tip was made from a rock which had been split after being repeatedly hit by another larger rock, and its edges sharply honed over many hours of tedious grinding. The workmanship was in vast contrast to Marcus's spear which wasn't much more than a very sharp tree branch.

"Ahurin!" his foe howled the first time the rock tip of his spear drew a tiny amount of blood from Marcus.

Marcus knew the older youth was stronger than himself and wasn't sure how he would be able to come out of the contest victoriously. He also didn't know how long they would continue exchanging impotent jabs. Marcus failed to make contact with his opposition, but a few times the edge of the rock tip glanced against him. He was bleeding though he did not feel much, nor could he inspect the wounds. They circled each other as the Urinhyame youth sought a quick victory over Marcus, who was content to play towards a draw in hopes someone else would be able to assist him.

They continued their dance around each other with no real progress until amid one of Marcus's slowing spear thrusts the Urinhyame grabbed his spear. When he did, he gave Marcus the nasty grin which bullies have been giving those smaller than themselves since time began.

"Ahurin!" the young man shouted with glee looking up to the sun.

Marcus did not hesitate when both of the youth's hands were occupied at his sides with the spears and his mind distracted by his victory cry. Marcus released his hold on his own spear and leapt forward hitting the sun worshiper in the face with his fist as hard as he could. Marcus had never hit someone square in the face with such force before. He marveled at how solid the head felt and how much his hand seemed to melt into flesh. Even behind the intoxication of the adrenaline he could feel how much the contact hurt his hand and hoped it hurt his adversary more.

The Urinhyame's nose erupted in blood, and he stepped back while dropping the spears and pushing Marcus away. As his opponent wiped at the blood, Marcus could see the first hints of fear in the older boy's eyes, but they were quickly displaced by rage. The boy reached down and pulled the lone tomahawk from his belt. Marcus could see that this stranger intended to take his life.

The larger boy swung the tomahawk threateningly towards Marcus staring him down through the tears from a broken nose which mired his vision. The Urinhyame tossed his weapon from hand to hand toying with the younger weaker fighter. He took another swing with his tomahawk and let loose a little laugh.

Gloating over his larger size and weapon, the bloodied attacker moved forward.

"Ah-u-rin!" came once again from the youth's mouth, and by now Marcus couldn't help but think the shout had become more annoying than intimidating. Marcus caught a glimpse of the other tomahawk which had shaken free and was now at its owner's feet. The larger boy continued to dance around, which seemed silly to Marcus since the Urinhyame possessed a size advantage and a weapon, but bullies always want to savor the smell of fear on those they have made afraid.

Marcus was afraid. Afraid he would die. Afraid he had let down the Narwa. Afraid he had let down his family, who would never know what happened to him. He was also afraid that he had let down himself. Marcus was afraid, but he also remained focused. As his will to live fed that focus, it pushed those fears further back in his consciousness until only the intensity of his desire to persevere remained fixed on the threat before him.

If he couldn't defeat the larger combatant, Marcus at least wanted to slow him down. He made a kicking motion at his attacker's shins, though he knew contact would hurt his unprotected toes more than the leg of the sun worshiper. His opponent jumped back in surprise, but the kick didn't succeed in anything other than angering him further. Marcus bent down and picked up a handful of dirt, wishing it were the tomahawk a few feet away, and flung it at the tomahawk wielder. Marcus would have been surprised to know he wasn't the first or last to throw dirt clods in life or death battles. At having this final insult hurled at him, the Urinhyame's temper boiled over. He rushed forward blinded by blood, tears, and dirt, as much as his own rage.

The shout of "Ahurin!" sounded even more filled with rage, and any composure the young Urinhyame had before was lost.

The tomahawk which had landed in the dust early in the conflict finally made a contribution to the violence. Patience was rewarded as rage was punished. Time seemed to slow as Marcus watched one foot of the Urinhyame land on the rock head causing the handle to tilt up. The handle lifted into the air catching his other foot. In a tumble the assailant lurched forward and tried to catch himself evidently forgetting he held a weapon with two dangerous ends in his hand. He landed with a sickening thud as the tomahawk in his grip betrayed him. Marcus heard his adversary make two coughs and saw the blood from underneath the body start to spread out on the thirsty dry ground.

Marcus dashed forward and grabbed the tomahawk which had sent the larger boy sprawling. He stood physically ready to strike, though unsure if he was mentally ready. The Urinhyame before him made one attempt to get up and collapsed again. Marcus felt a combination of feelings; joy mixed with pity as well as relief. He was so engrossed in staring at the casualty before him he almost didn't see the figure of a second attacker running up to him. Marcus ducked low as he lunged forward only missing the swinging of the opponent's tomahawk already stained with blood by a fraction of a second.

The Urinhyame, this one a full adult, appeared bewildered at missing what he had been sure was an easy target. He carried that look to the grave as a Narwa who Marcus hadn't seen ended the Urinhyame's life with a spear thrown from just a few feet away. Marcus saw it was his own weapon which had been thrown on the ground earlier, but he decided to leave it. Marcus looked at the Narwa who saved him without speaking. The Narwa man grabbed the fallen Urinhyame's tomahawk and another spear from the dirt and went to involve himself in another engagement with the expressionless face his people prized.

As Marcus observed the carnage, he could see there would soon be enough weapons for any who would want them. Scanning the chaos Marcus found Retap wrestling with an Urinhyame. Neither of them had weapons. Marcus could not locate anyone else he knew and started toward Retap in hopes he would be able to help. By the time Marcus got there the larger man had Retap on his back and was choking him. Marcus grabbed a tomahawk and tried to envision himself driving it into the back of the enemy skull. The frozen moments weakened his resolve and when he reached the man's back, he hit him as hard as he could with the blunt side of the head of the weapon. The man rolled over, not dead but certainly not conscious anymore. Retap gave Marcus a thankful nod and staggered to his feet.

The two surveyed the battlefield. Two things were clear; there would be a lot of dead, and the Narwa would not be victorious. This was not to say the Urinhyame would be clear victors. At least four out of every five Urinhyame who joined the battle would die there or in the coming days of wounds and infection. Even fewer of the Narwa would survive.

Marcus's concern turned to Ingole Rondo and the power there. Once the remaining Narwa were subdued, Marcus knew the Urinhyame would go to the cave if they were not there already. Looking out on the carnage of the battle Marcus wondered why the power to destroy the earth couldn't have been used to prevent the bloodshed instead.

"Marcus Ingole Rondo," Marcus said with a heavy heart.

Retap nodded.

Marcus took off at a run in the direction of the cave. Retap followed, though Marcus could tell he did not want to leave the field of battle before all was finished.

"Marcus!" As soon as he heard the voice, he knew it belonged to Roquen. His friend came trotting up to him. "Ingole Rondo. No Urinhyame take Ingole."

Roquen's ever present smile had been replaced by fatigue. On the whole battle field Marcus could see no one more covered in blood than his friend.

Retap asked him where his father was, and Roquen's only reply was to look at the sky and then the ground with a heavy shine in his eyes.

Retap nodded. The three continued as quickly as they could in the direction of Ingole Rondo as the battle entered its third hour, not over, but decided.

Marcus and the others approached the cave with caution. All three expected that the Urinhyame would send a party in an attempt to take the power from there before the battle ended. As Marcus got closer he could see no one outside or around the cave, not even the Ingole elder usually present. Unsure as to whether the elder had left of her own will or been taken somewhere, all three approached cautiously. Retap motioned for them to split up and approach the cave from different directions in case a trap had been set.

Marcus arrived first and tried his best to stay hidden. Soon he was able to make eye contact with Roquen and Retap who arrived not long after.

They agreed that Marcus should enter the cave and retrieve the crystal, while the others guarded the cave entrance. If any of the Urinhyame should arrive, they would try to alert Marcus. Though it was unlikely they could fight them off, it would allow Marcus time to destroy the crystal if that were possible.

As Marcus entered the cave, he couldn't help but note the difference between the present and his first exploration of the cave. When he first entered during the trial, the cave had been an unknown which filled him with fear. Now the cave acted as a refuge from the violence outside.

After a few steps the physical and mental fog he remembered from this first time in the cave confronted him. Marcus almost fell as he tripped over something he didn't remember from his previous visit. When he kneeled down into the heavy mist to see what his foot had struck, he saw the face of a man with a yellow sun on his forehead. Now down on his knees, Marcus could see many of them dead in the cave. Marcus wondered if they were his test this time; if maybe dead Urinhyame was what the cave was tempting him with. He picked up a tomahawk, just in case they were real and perhaps more were ahead. Marcus thought at times he heard someone in the cave with him, but the heavy fog's effect on his mind made it impossible to know for sure. As Marcus progressed a bit further, he was glad to see the illusion of his family; not because he thought they were real, but because he didn't want to believe that anyone's death, even Urinhyame, was what he desired.

Walking past the mockery of his family didn't take much time, and again his head cleared. He tossed the very real tomahawk aside and stared at the crystal's glowing brilliance. Using the cup, he drank again of the water which revived his spirit and helped to wash away some of the horror of the day. As Marcus lifted the crystal out, it lost its glow. The water surrounding it still radiated from the power the crystal had imbued it with, but no longer seemed as alive., Marcus speculated that perhaps the two interacted to create the power in the cave. In any case he knew time was not his friend while in the cave, and so he made as quick of an exit as he could.

Marcus expected his previous temptations to be gone with the removal of the crystal from its place of power. Curiously they remained though the allure had been overcome. On his fourth trip through the mist Marcus came to the conclusion that the deaths there were from asphyxiation. Some fumes from the rock or perhaps the plants poisoned the air and the mind. The now dead Urinhyame had tarried too long with their temptation and lost consciousness. They died still believing they had found happiness. Marcus walked out of the cave and took in the fresh air. He felt strong from drinking the water, and Retap and Roquen were where he had left them. They both took an awed look at the crystal.

Marcus was about to tell them they needed to take off running immediately when he was interrupted by a familiar voice in his head.

::Thank you, Marcus. I knew you could do it.::

Marcus knew the voice of Ahsigna even before he saw the Tavari's face.

::I really need you to give me that, and in exchange I'll send you home, just like we talked about.:: The Tavari spoke into Marcus's head again. As Ahsigna came out of the grove, Marcus could see Layen with him clutched by her forearm.

"You want to use it to destroy Earth, to kill everyone!" Marcus shouted aloud though Ahsigna was speaking into his mind, as well as everyone else's.

Ahsigna feigned surprise at the accusation. ::Actually, I was just going to give it to these savages and let them make human sacrifices until they pulled Earth into the sun,:: he said nonchalantly. ::I thought it would be a fitting end for mankind; destroyed by their own desire and ignorance.:: Ahsigna looked at Retap and Roquen with disdain. ::But first I am going to use it to spread truth and repair some injustices. I think you should be able to appreciate that.::

Marcus wasn't entirely sure what Ahsigna was raving about, but it didn't sound good. "I'm not going to let you have it. I'll destroy it. Or we will destroy you."

::You can break the crystal, but you can't destroy it. On the other hand, it is entirely possible that you could destroy me with the crystal. But then who would get you home?.:: Ahsigna smiled dryly. ::Besides why do you want to get involved in this? I saw you down there fighting. You almost got yourself killed. For what? One group of ignorant humans fighting another about whether or not they can keep trinkets or grow berries?::

"It isn't like that. They are my people now, " Marcus said looking at Retap, Layen and Roquen. He thought of Ingole and the traditions and practices which he knew had made him a better person since his arrival.

::Look around, these people's way of life is pretty much over, Marcus. As you knew it would be.:: Ahsigna gestured toward Ingole with a shrug. ::The world is moving on. They didn't get out of the way, so that's what happens.:: Marcus could tell Ahsigna couldn't care less about the loss of life.

The smell of the smoke coming from Ingole caught his attention before he saw it. He knew he had to resist thinking about what was happening and would happen there and concentrate on the task at hand.

::Give me the crystal, Marcus, and go home. Don't get dragged into some mess you don't understand by powers beyond your comprehension.:: When Ahsigna smiled and spoke to him that way Marcus couldn't help but be amazed at his beauty and charm. ::I am trying to help you, Marcus. This business of saving the Earth is beyond you. You're going to get killed and bring grief and death to the people you care about.:: Ahsigna explained it all so sweetly Marcus wanted it to be true.

Despite his distrust of Ahsigna he could feel his resolve weakening. He asked himself how much he really believed in all these ideas of magic anyways. He was just a kid from California, and despite magic caves and ant stings he still wasn't even old enough to drive.

::I'll even promise not to let the sun worshipers use the crystal. They can sacrifice each other on pyramids or in fires, and they will be just as happy. And see? Now you've 'saved' Earth. Congratulations!:: Ahsigna said mocking him and his quest.

"What are you going to use the crystal for?" Marcus asked again hoping for a clearer answer.

At this Ahsigna's face grew darker, and he lost much of the convincing charm he had displayed since his arrival.

::I'll use it to open the eyes of everyone here to the true nature of their creator, of their abandoner, and this facade of a plan. I'll use it to undo every single piece of that Plan I can. I'll do to this creation what was done to me and show them the failure of this and everything else that is part of this damned failed scheme. Every man and all my brothers and sisters here in exile will see the lies and feel my suffering.:: By this point Ahsigna looked as somber and bitter as anyone Marcus had ever seen.

Marcus could see the pain on his face, and though his words alarmed Marcus, he wondered what had happened to cause such deep scars on this Tavari soul. After seeing the strength of Potek Marcus knew he would not be able to fight against a Tavari even half as strong. He wondered if it wouldn't be better to give it up than to die and have it taken in the end regardless. Ahsigna could sense the boy's resolve weakening.

::Now give it to me. Such a power in the hands of these animals is a waste. They use it for tricks, when it has so much more potential.:: He started walking toward Marcus.

"La. Lalume." Retap stated firmly stepping out to block the Tavari's path toward the boy holding the crystal.

::I'm done reasoning with savages,:: Ahsigna declared shaking his head. In an instant he pulled out a dagger and in one smooth motion hurled it forward into Retap's chest. The dagger impacted Retap's chest with a sound that would stick with Marcus for a long time. Retap looked down and observed the instrument of death with the same stoicism he had observed in life. Despite his great efforts he slowly collapsed to the ground.

::You don't have any say in what this magic is used for now,:: Ahsigna gloated looking at his victim with disdain.

"Retap!" Marcus shouted. He wanted to run forward to see if he could help but was afraid of letting the crystal get any closer the Ahsigna.

::Alright, Marcus, who's next? Ladies first?:: Ahsigna sneered as he grabbed Layen and pulled out another knife.

As Ahsigna spoke, the sky started to grow cloudy. Ahsigna turned his gaze skyward as he felt the first drop of rain hit his face, and Marcus could tell the Tavari knew he had made a miscalculation. He shoved Layen from his side, and she rushed to the hemorrhaging Retap.

Potek dropped from the sky with a crack of lightning and landed a few feet from Ahsigna, whose arrogance had vanished. The sun shone off Potek's massive frame, and his body coursed with lightning.

::What are you doing here? This doesn't involve you!:: Ahsigna shouted at Potek.

::I didn't get involved until you put your knife in that man. You know our rules; you can look, and you can talk, but once you touch I have the right and the duty to oppose you.::

::You are a fool and a slave. If you care about some pathetic human so much you can share his fate.:: With this Ahsigna drew another dagger from inside his robe and launched it at Potek. The larger Tavari raised his club with blazing reflexes and the blade lodged there for a brief moment before falling to the ground.

::If I am the slave, then why are you the one who is so miserable, brother?:: Potek countered squaring off and holding his weapon at the ready.

::Like I said, because you are a fool. You can't see the truth. Can you?:: With that Ahsigna's form glimmered before splitting in two. Each form drew a dagger, and they smiled in unison.

Marcus had been certain it would be a quick fight, but now he wasn't sure how Potek would fare with two enemies to contend with.

::Tricks from the servant of tricks and lies. Did your new master teach you this?::

::He isn't my master! I am free, and you are just a foolish slave.:: The Ahsigna to Potek's left continued to shift to the left and the one to his right farther to the right. They spread apart trying to catch Potek between the two of them.

Potek tried to keep an eye on both of them when they simultaneously lunged at him. The thunder god leapt forward avoiding the one on the right but the one on the left caught him with a slice to the shoulder. It appeared Tavari blood was not unlike human blood as red drops swelled from the slice Ahsigna's knife had made. For his part Potek didn't take any note of his wounds.

::The only disappointment in killing you will be knowing that you really aren't afraid to die. Can't wait to go back to your prison, can you?:: Ahsigna sounded as though he gained some confidence from drawing first blood.

::It was your home once also. You were complete there, or have you forgotten? I'll help you remember!:: With a crack of thunder, he raised his club high before bringing it crashing down on the Tavari who had spilt his blood. Ahsigna collapsed under the immeasurable force of the club, and as he did his twin disappeared. Potek readied his weapon high again to bring it down on his foe, but before he could deliver a killing blow, Ahsigna rolled away and out of reach.

::I was as much a fool then as you are now. But now my eyes are open. I can choose now. What will you choose?:: Again, Ahsigna glimmered and he separated into three identical forms; all grinning, all wielding knives with a stain of blood.

Just as the two had been able to form a pincer on Potek, the three now encircled him. Despite his best efforts, eventually they surrounded him, the grin on all three growing as Potek realized the depth of his disadvantage. Unable to avoid the synchronized lunges from all three sides Potek took a significant slash below his ribs.

The two other facsimiles of Ahsigna disappeared and the one in front dashed out of reach and began to taunt Potek. ::So strong, but such a fool. Unable to see the truth, or maybe unwilling. It's a shame your dead body will be stuck here in time. I'd love to use it as an example for the next slave who gets in my way.::

With that he divided into three parts again and started to surround Potek. This time Potek didn't wait to be surrounded but lunged at the form in the middle swinging his club wildly. He went flying through the illusion, and as he did, the true Ahsigna, now behind him on his left, jumped on him, thrusting the dagger into his back. The clouds overhead grew darker as more blood spilled from the larger Tavari.

The wound clearly effected Potek, but he managed to shake off the smaller fighter. Ahsigna now felt in control. He backed up and divided himself again, and the three illusions laughed in unison. Potek swung wildly, but the nimble Ahsigna was able to evade again to keep his distance.

::I am going to kill you and use the crystal to wreak havoc on these foolish humans, and the rest of creation for the next five thousand years.:: He laughed again though Marcus thought there was still a deep sadness and pain beneath the laugh.

As he, or they, were laughing, a rock passed through the center Ahsigna form. When Marcus turned to look where it had come from, he saw Layen knelt down next to Retap with a handful of rocks. Marcus, Roquen and Layen had been watching the fight, the former both aware that they were well out of their league and respecting one on one combat. Layen harbored no such concerns for conventions and tossed another rock. This one bounced off the chest of Ahsigna, who looked shocked that anyone would throw rocks at him especially in a way which would clearly not hurt him. Ahsigna, Marcus, and Roquen all looked at Layen in confusion.

Potek did not look at Layen at all. As soon as the rock revealed the true Ahsigna, the god of thunder focused on the form before him. As Ahsigna was distracted a truly massive bolt of lightning came down and struck him, charring his skin and clothes. The attack dazed Ahsigna, and Potek did not relent. Leaping through the air he brought the full force of his now electrified club down on his enemy.

His club came down squarely on Ahsigna's chest and Marcus thought the smaller Tavari would be obliterated. Now unconscious, Ahsigna did not move. Potek stared at his unconscious brother at his feet. ::You were given a chance to repent, but you cannot be allowed to interfere with The Plan. I sentence you to die.:: He said the words sadly, and Marcus could tell Potek took no joy in them, nor did they hold a sense of revenge, only duty.

As Potek pointed his club skyward and the heavens filled it with lightning, Marcus could see the power intensify. Staring at the bolt of lightning he was aware that everything around him seemed to be slowing down. At first Marcus thought something Potek or Ahsigna were doing slowed the flow of time, but they appeared as effected by it as everyone else. As Marcus wondered why he remained unaffected, he saw a form in a blur of grey running towards Potek.

The stranger looked even more out of place than either of the combatants. He wore what resembled a dark grey gi that Marcus had seen martial artists train in but with a hood covering his head. The stranger also had his face wrapped up so only his eyes were visible, though Marcus couldn't get a good look at them. The stranger quickly drew a sword which looked insanely sharp but of surprising simplicity. From what Marcus could tell, it was not much more than a piece of metal with twine wrapped around the base to create a handle. The sword was thicker than a katana, but smaller than European broadswords. The stranger moved blazingly fast to Marcus's eye but was made all the faster by the fact everything and everyone but Marcus and the stranger still moved in slow motion.

Before Marcus could scream, the man in grey drove the sword into Potek's chest while his club was raised overhead. At the impact of the blade, time resumed its normal flow. Marcus stared at the frozen giant certain the sword had pierced his heart. He saw the stranger remove his sword and pull Potek down looking in his eyes as the giant Tavari collapsed onto his back. The sword had gone completely through him, and Potek knew he was dying. The swordsman looked into Potek's eyes and said some words softly which Marcus did not hear clearly but sounded very strange to him. Marcus couldn't hear what the man in grey said, but Potek's face changed, and held a tinge of joy edging out his anguish. The dying Tavari turned towards Marcus and whispered his last thoughts, audible only to his killer.

Potek's body shimmered and started to fade. The grey clad stranger kneeling down next to Potek placed his left hand on the wound on Potek's chest. He was wearing a left-handed glove of unstitched leather that lacked a mate on the opposite hand. The glove was made of a type of leather that looked ancient but not old or damaged. Marcus noted the man was missing his small and ring finger on the gloved hand.

With his killer's hand still over Potek's wound, the Tavari's form flickered again and then disappeared. The man in grey stood up as he placed his sword back in its simple sheath on his back. The swordsman nodded at Ahsigna while a light rain began to fall.

"Leave this one alive; you will need him later," he said as he turned and approached Marcus. Marcus looked towards his friends for help but Roquen and Layen were huddled over Retap who was talking to them with the little life that remained in him.

"I know the power of the crystal; come closer and I'll destroy you." Marcus tried to sound as confident as he could, but knew it sounded hollow. Roquen stood to help his outmatched friend, but with a look and a gesture the man in grey froze him in place. Marcus could see the fear in his friend's eyes as some supernatural power locked Roquen in place.

"You neither know the power of the crystal, nor how to use it. But I do," the man in grey said approaching Marcus.

Marcus wanted to move away from the approaching stranger to prevent him from taking the crystal, but he remained fixed in place. No magic spell held him captive, other than his own fear. As the stranger reached out his left-hand Marcus could see that he in fact only had an index finger and a thumb. These two remaining gloved fingers reached out and took hold of the crystal. Marcus was frozen but held on tight, determined not to let the stranger take the crystal from him. To Marcus's surprise when the man in grey grabbed hold of the crystal, he did not pull it away but only tightened his grip.

The glove, on what was left of the two fingered hand, glowed as did the crystal. Marcus could see the gloved hand tightening and squeezing on the crystal as the glow from the two in unison intensified. Frightened, Marcus looked up into the man's eyes, but they were as emotionless as eyes could be.

Suddenly the crystal shattered. The broken pieces crumbled out of Marcus's hands onto the moist dirt still being sprinkled with the gentle rain. The crystal had split into seven pieces which were identical except for their colors. The crystal which had been white was reduced to pieces each with a tint of color instead of the dazzling pure white beauty now destroyed. The stranger carefully picked out three of the shards and put them into some hidden pocket in his clothing. He then walked over to where Retap lay dying and gave the man a long look. After a quick glance at Layen and Roquen he turned to the east and walked away into the forest.

The mixture of anger and sadness in Marcus finally boiled over. He didn't think about how easily the man in grey might slice him in half, or even if he could beat him in a fair fight. Marcus charged after the killer hoping to strike him with enough force that he would share some of Marcus's pain.

Without looking the man's fist swung around and backhanded Marcus sending him sprawling onto the ground.

"You have other things to worry about," the empty voice ordered without turning his head.

"Marcus! Hurry!" shouted Layen who had been attending to Retap as best she could during all the fighting.

Marcus stood up and wiped the blood from where he had been hit. Glancing back with anger at Potek's killer, Marcus ran over to where Roquen and Layen anxiously huddled over Retap. Marcus could see life draining out of Retap with each passing breath.

Retap smiled up at him. "Pano."

Too much blood had been lost, and Marcus and Retap both knew his time had come to an end. Marcus began to cry, but Retap stopped him.

"La... La," he whispered softly. "Enyal mana Retap cennada Marcus. Turuimmo... Panotar... Prem... "

Marcus nodded. "Hanta," he said as he clasped his mentor's hand. He had no doubt he would fulfil Retap's demand to remember his teachings.

Retap's eyes closed as he departed the world of the living with a last rare smile.

Layen laid his head down flat on the ground, and Marcus knew that Retap had spoken his last words.

"We need to leave here, Marcus," Layen said standing up. Roquen stared at the growing flames of what had been Ingole.

"Mamya," Layen said looking first at Roquen and then looking at the ground.

"Tatya." Roquen looked at the ground as well.

Though he couldn't communicate between them as well as the twins could, he knew both their mom and dad were dead.

"I don't think the crystal can be repaired, but if the swordsman took shards, we should too." Marcus picked up the remaining pieces and wrapped them in leaves.

"Urinhyame come here. Ahsigna wake up soon," Roquen said as he removed Ahsigna's dagger from Retap. Marcus picked up the one Ahsigna had thrown at Potek earlier and handed it to Layen.

"I don't know where we can go where they won't find us," Marcus replied despondently.

"We do," Layen replied looking at Roquen. "We have to keep those away from Ahsigna." She motioned to the shards. "Only one we know stronger than a Tavari is Amlug."

"How are we going to find a flying dinosaur? I don't think it's like tracking weech," Marcus said.

"Retap knowed where Amlug is. That what his father went look for when he left the tribe. That where his brother, Retoh, went." Roquen said.

"If we hurry the mountain is three days from here going to the rising sun. Then we climb this mountain from the path to the great water." Layen said.

Marcus looked over at Ahsigna laying soundly unconscious, then at Roquen and Layen. They could hear the sound of a group of men approaching from Ingole's grove now in flames. Without any further hesitation the trio took off running in the direction the man in grey had gone to the east, though they could see no trace of him.

CHAPTER TWELVE - FRIENDS OR FOES

Behold now behemoth, which I made with thee; he eateth grass as an ox. Lo now, his strength is in his loins, and his force is in the navel of his belly. He moveth his tail like a cedar: the sinews of his stones are wrapped together. His bones are as strong pieces of brass; his bones are like bars of iron.

-Job 40:15-18

Marcus and the twins spent their first day after the fall of Ingole at a near frantic pace trying to put distance between themselves and their presumed pursuer. All through the night the three continued on silently wondering if each strange sound from the forest would be followed by a dagger identical to the ones Layen and Roquen now carried at their hips. Marcus kept feeling for his own pocket knife to ease his fears.

The second day they continued their frantic pace not stopping for food despite their bodies and minds growing equally exhausted from travel and thoughts of being chased. They did not stop until late that night. Layen and Roquen collapsed too tired to dream, but immediately upon falling asleep Marcus found himself staring at Earth orbiting the sun.

Familiar with the dream from so many frustrating iterations Marcus watched Earth circle the sun for its allotted time. As Marcus came to the part of the dream where he knew his home would start the decent to its doom, the boy's mind felt too exhausted to interfere. To his relief Earth came no closer to the sun. He watched the beautiful blue and green orb circle a few times more. Then all of the joy Marcus felt at his accomplishment drained from his tired mind as the home of mankind drifted from orbit into the vastness of space. Marcus's tortured unconsciousness replayed the dream for the rest of his night.

At the end of the third day they could see the mountain matching the description from Retap's final instructions. Far larger than any that Roquen or Layen had seen before, the mountain dwarfed the surrounding landscape.

"Do you think he is near?" Layen asked on the third night as they exhaustedly ended their day.

"I've been thinking about that, and I don't think he is even following us," Marcus replied.

"Marcus take crystal. Layen help Potek beat Ahsigna. Roquen think Ahsigna coming," Roquen answered very confidently.

"I would think so too, but Ahsigna can travel far faster than us. So, I think that either he can't find me or doesn't want to find me. I agree he would want revenge, so maybe he can't find us."

"He found you at Ingole and when you first arrived in the cave, why wouldn't he be able to find you now?" Layen asked.

She asked the very same question Marcus had been asking himself. He didn't like the answer but knew he owed it to his friends to be open and honest.

"I think I may have called him or someone who sent him." Marcus's disappointment in himself was clear.

"What!? Why? How?" Layen asked shocked at the admission. Roquen looked at his friend with confusion and some suspicion.

Marcus immediately went on the defensive. "Not on purpose of course. But listen, the first two times he showed up were the two times I felt most sad, alone, and lost. I was falling apart. I asked for any help from anyone, but I didn't really think that would mean him. I was praying to heaven, not a depressed, angry, fallen angel... or whatever he is. It's crazy that I could somehow just say something, and he could hear from anywhere."

"You traveled time, moved a rock with your mind, and saw the Tavari of Thunder die, but you think someone hearing your prayers is crazy?" Layen wondered what it would take for Marcus to really open his mind.

"I know, I know... it's just that all of this still seems a bit unbelievable," Marcus admitted.

"We should be careful what we say, just in case you are right. And even if Ahsigna isn't following us, the Urinhyame might be," Layen added trying to let her frustration with Marcus go.

Marcus nodded his head in agreement.

"Did you see how Potek just disappeared... no body or anything?"

"Naa told us that Tavari don't leave bodies. When a Tavari dies its body stays frozen at that moment in time. It's because they don't really belong here and only their Fea kept them."

"Well, it would be nice if Potek was still around," Marcus said. "We could use some help."

"Better no Potek, no Ahsigna, no grey man. All trouble start from stranger." Roquen said.

"Sorry," Marcus looked at his friend. He knew Roquen had not meant him in the accusation, but he felt guilty none the less.

Roquen laughed and gave his friend a forgiving hug.

The group traveled all the next day, but at a slower pace and reached the base of the mountain not too long before nightfall. The three were glad to have reached the mountain without incident, but at that time nothing could have made them happier than the small weech Roquen managed to kill for the group to eat. The hunt put Roquen in a much better mood, and the food made all three of them feel as though they could face the challenges of climbing the mountain the next morning. As far as facing what they found on the mountain, that was a different matter entirely.

"Well, this is the mountain three days in the direction of the rising sun," Layen started as they hungrily devoured their dinner.

"Great water that way," Roquen gestured towards the south.

Layen nodded her head. "We can head that direction and start up the mountain tomorrow."

Marcus paused in thought. "South isn't the direction of the great water though. I know the sea is south from the Piucca camp, and from Ingole. But the great water is really east of here, on the other side of the mountain."

"Narwa only know one great water," Roquen answered.

"It is the same ocean... just that the largest part is east of here. We can try climbing the mountain from the south though."

"No. If the great water is to the East, we should start from there. Maybe starting from the South is why Retap's brother never came back."

"Or maybe he started from the South, found a dinosaur, and it ate him. I feel like encounters with dinosaurs or Amlug or anything with huge teeth probably don't usually end well."

"'Maybe' doesn't matter. You know where the true great sea is, and that's where we should start climbing the mountain from."

"For mountain only direction matter is up," Roquen added equally annoyed at superstition and technicalities.

"If the direction wasn't important, then why did Ingole tell Retap's brother about it?" Marcus asked to no one in particular.

The company of the crystal shards fell asleep with bellies full from having devoured the pork and with confidence full from finding the mountain. Each fell into a deep sleep too tired to worry about any possible pursuit. Marcus replayed his dreams of Earth spinning out into the emptiness of space. Sometimes he would be able, by sheer force of will, to prevent it from losing orbit and spinning into icy darkness. However, Earth would then invariably crash into the sun just as it had in his dreams since the first trip to Ingole.

"So, do you want the good news or the bad news?" Marcus started their conversation after a few hours of walking the next day.

"Good news is food?" Roquen asked with fake excitement.

"Is this about Earth still being doomed, even though we saved it?" Layen asked.

"How did you know!? Are you having the dreams also now?" Marcus asked, excited that they shared his burden of knowledge.

"No, but you still talk in your sleep. And it's really annoying to hear 'Nooo, not Earth!' every night." Layen's impersonation of Marcus's voice made all three of them laugh, despite the heaviness of the subject.

"Better 'Earth... nooo...!' instead 'Mary... yeeeesss...!' Marcus before Ingole," Roquen added, his version of Marcus's voice more absurd than his sister's.

Marcus turned deep red at the thought of his high school crush. He also couldn't believe that the three of them could make jokes and laugh in such a dire situation with so much at stake.

"Well anyways..." Marcus continued embarrassed, "I think I saved Earth from being pulled into the sun, but now it freezes in space... and everyone still dies."

"Marcus saved? Retap make Potek come... Layen help Potek beat Ahsigna... Roquen find mountain... Marcus saved Earth?" Roquen continued to tease his friend.

"Okay, well I got the crystal from the cave," Marcus defended himself.

"The cave where it had been safe for hundreds and thousands of years?" Layen took her turn teasing Marcus.

"... whatever..." Marcus laughed at himself as well.

It took most of the day to circle to the east side of the mountain, and the trio started their accent the following day. Marcus wasn't sure if he should be more concerned about not finding Amlug or Amlug finding them. Finding a living creature, the size of a commercial airplane seemed at first to be a pretty easy task. However, the mountain was fairly large and full of hiding places and to search the whole of it might take a very long time. It would be very easy for Amlug to be hidden amongst the rocks, crags and crevices. Additionally, they were dressed for the warmth of the South American forest, not ideally prepared for a challenging climb involving significant elevation changes. Fortunately, the mountain itself turned out to be not as cold as it had looked from below, and Marcus was glad they were there nearer the summer solstice than the winter. Green and lush vegetation covered most of the mountain, though the shear faces of stone prevented life from taking hold in several areas. Without the birds and the trees, the most notable sound of the mountain was its silence.

"Where Amlug?" Roquen asked with a little impatience after only an hour of walking up the mountain.

"That's a good question. Retap only gave the directions that his brother was told by Ingole to look for Amlug," Layen answered.

"Maybe Amlug gone." It sounded to Marcus as though Roquen was preparing himself for disappointment more than thinking the creature had left. Marcus knew Roquen wanted to see Amlug up close.

"Are there more than one, or is this the same one we saw that day by the stream?" Marcus asked, sure that Layen knew as much as there was to know about Narwa dinosaur lore.

"No one really knows. There are certainly more than just one, but I think only a very few in the land of the Narwa." Layen said.

"One of my last talks with Retap I asked him what he thought was the Narwa way... He said Turuimmo and Panotar... which I think I understand."

"Understand Turuimmo and Panotar not easy..." Roquen added thoughtfully.

"I know... but at least I know what they mean. What did he mean by 'Prem'"?

"That's an old word. It's kind of means like a big love... or first love. Like a love for everything... but not like desire how you sometimes say love." Layen answered.

"Are you guys going to be okay? I mean about your parents and everyone... "

Roquen nodded softly.

"We will be... eventually. And Prem is part of that." Layen said and it was clear she didn't wish to discuss it further.

The three of them walked on for several more hours. The ascent proved moderately difficult, but as they climbed in altitude they were treated to a breathtaking view. Marcus had enjoyed the view from the top of the mount at Ingole, but that took less than an hour of climbing to achieve.

With every hour which passed without a sign of Amlug Marcus expected someone to question the decision to approach from the East. The trail that originated from the South had looked far easier than the one they chose, as the mountain had a much more gradual slope from the southern direction. Marcus and his friends walked along a cliff side of a ridge which would from time to time give them glimpses of the easier path below.

The sudden howl of monkeys prevented Marcus from apologizing for the more difficult path. The three paused and listened. The sounds came from an area below the trail they had been following.

"Monkeys up here in the mountains?" Marcus asked, looking at the two.

"Sound angry monkey," Roquen replied.

"It's coming from up ahead. Let's see if we can take a look without being seen." She looked at her brother and added, "Be careful."

Roquen smiled with a shrug at her in return.

As the trio continued, the howls of the monkeys grew louder and sounded menacing. Roquen approached a cliffside above the sounds and motioned Marcus and his sister towards him. The three lay on their bellies peering over the cliff.

Down below they saw five Urinhyame. Several loud and angry monkeys encircled their foes. The men were much larger and brandished weapons, but the monkeys moved quickly and easily avoided the men's attempts to harm them. After each howl the number of monkeys grew as they emerged from the caves and crevices which surrounded the area along the path the Urinhyame had chosen.

Huge ferocious teeth snapped at the men and their weapons. Every few seconds a member of the troop darted in at the surrounded Urinhyame who had thus far been successful keeping them at bay with their weapons. As the number of monkeys grew, it became clear the tactic would not be successful for much longer. Already there were two dozen hungry and angry simians.

"Urinhyame follow," Roquen whispered.

"I bet Ahsigna sent them. I guess that's why you don't take the southern path." Marcus couldn't help but smile at seventh grade geography saving their lives.

"Let's go. I don't want to watch this," Layen whispered. She would forever remember the Urinhyame as the ones who killed her family and destroyed the Narwa way of life, but she would not relish watching them die what all three knew would be a gruesome death.

Carefully the three crawled away from the ledge. The violence may have been below, but they knew more carnivorous monkeys could easily inhabit other areas. Marcus, Layen, and Roquen continued on in cautious silence.

Late in the afternoon Marcus grew hungry for some of the meat they had brought with them. He could tell Layen was exhausted by her silence and was about to suggest they stop for a while when Roquen paused abruptly.

"There." Roquen pointed to an elevated plateau which looked less than an hour of more climbing away. Marcus could see a flat spot near the peak of the mountain looking out on the vast land below.

"How do you know? Did you see something up there?" Marcus asked, sure his friend had a good reason for believing they were near, even if he couldn't tell what it was.

Roquen didn't say anything but increased his pace.

"I don't see anything up there," Marcus whispered after his friend trying to catch up.

"No see. Smell," Roquen replied, now in a much quieter voice.

"I can't believe we are going to see Amlug. I don't think anyone has able to find one in hundreds of years. At least they haven't survived if they did." Layen's excitement at seeing the creature up close gave her a clear boost of energy.

After less than thirty more minutes of travel, Roquen stopped and pointed to a spear which laid old and rotted on the ground.

The growing strength of the smell of something strange did put a healthy bit of caution into Marcus but did not match the excitement at the prospect of seeing a genuine dinosaur up close. As a small child he dreamt of seeing one in real life, and all the movies, books, and stories only fed his desire. Now that he might actually be coming close to one, he felt giddy with anticipation. Marcus wondered if they would come upon the creature sleeping, or if perhaps it was already aware of their presence and preparing to attack. He imagined multiple scenarios in his head, but none of them began with the creature speaking to him. Which is what it did.

"Who. are. you?"

Marcus looked around at his friends whose shocked faces showed that they clearly heard the voice as well. Marcus said nothing but tried to continue forward as quietly as he could. Marcus knew the voice had been audible, and not just spoken into his head. Roquen clutched a Tavari dagger, which Marcus was sure made him feel better, though he doubted it would be effective against a creature a thousand times their size.

Marcus, Layen, and Roquen rounded another stone face of the mountain and found themselves looking directly into the eyes of the largest creature any of them had ever seen. The body of the giant beast blended into the green grass beneath it. The thick skin pulled taunt across the huge muscular frame of the shoulders and hind legs and looked impenetrable. The wings folded neatly over the back. Marcus thought the head resembled a Tyrannosaurus, and he could see the huge teeth which jutted from its closed mouth. Running down from the neck and covering the underside of the body were scales which looked like rows of small thick shields. Claws with digits each the size of a small man rested on the ground and looked as though they hadn't moved in months. The entire body, which did not resemble a Tyrannosaurus but one of the huge grass eating giants, laid almost lifelessly still. The color matched so closely the vegetation, it almost appeared as though the beast were part of the landscape despite the vitality that the muscular frame implied. A thick tail curled up behind the beast in perfect concentric loops.

Eyelids open halfway revealed black slits on saucers of gold from which Amlug observed the world. The eyes which resembled those of a cat or snake held the most telling sign of life. They seemed much more alive than the eyes of the snake which terrorized Marcus months ago, but more sinister and unfeeling than those of a cat. As he looked into those eyes, he could start to feel himself fall into a trance.

"Who are you?!"

The voice asked again, more demanding this time. Marcus could feel the deep voice booming in his bones. No part of the beast that Marcus could see moved when he heard the voice, which sounded like it came from all around him.

"I-I-I am Marcus, and these are my friends. We just-"

"I know your name, foolish boy. And I know why you are here. I asked, 'Who Are You?' "

Marcus looked sideways at Layen and Roquen who looked as confused as Marcus felt. Layen shrugged her shoulders, and Roquen just nodded to Marcus that he should answer.

"I am a time traveler with a broken crystal?" Marcus answered without the slightest hint of certainty.

"No. You don't know how to travel through time, and you don't have all of the crystal. Doing it once on accident doesn't make you a time traveler."

Marcus was perplexed. He couldn't think of any better answers.

"Who are you?" Marcus asked, hoping to stall for time and inspiration for a more acceptable answer.

The beast's eyes narrowed on Marcus.

"Who do you think I am?"

"A giant talking dinosaur?"

With this the beast's head rose up several feet above them and shook the mountain with a roar from jaws which opened exposing rows of teeth each as long as a man's forearm and glistening white. The skin which had been the green of the grass quickly faded to the greyish red color of the rock. The wings which had been folded neatly spread out revealing a massive span. The gaping maw sucked in a deep breath of air and expelled fire in a blast which impacted directly behind Marcus and his friends. As the blast of fire scorched the earth, the ground shook, and Marcus feared the mountainside might collapse on them.

"A dinosaur? I am further removed from those mindless beasts than you are from the rodents that inhabit the cracks of this mountain."

The voice boomed through Marcus's body and shook him to his core. As quickly as the fire and shaking started, everything became still again. The giant torso of the creature lowered itself down in eerie silence, assuming both its prior position and color.

"But you fancy yourself a time traveler, so perhaps your answer isn't completely wrong."

"Please, tell us who you are." Marcus tried to sound as flattering as possible.

"I suppose telling you my tale now has saved me time before."

The voice spoke the statement so convincingly Marcus didn't have time to note that he had no idea what it meant. The head once again rested on the ground and the body looked as still as when they arrived.

"I was once a creature like you describe. We were giants, and we ruled this land for longer than your kind will. The conclusion of our reign came in the form of a rock from the heavens. It brought the end of my kind, but the first arrival of the Duta, or Tavari as you call them. It also brought delicious amtra fruit."

The story paused as Marcus could tell that the giant's mouth was reminiscing on a tasty treat.

"My kind had always fed on one another. That is the way of life, but those of us who ate the amtra fruit were changed; those we consumed became part of us. We changed. We grew. The few of us who remained evolved into something more."

"That's why you look like a bunch of different dinosaurs. You're some kind of super hybrid dinosaur." Marcus was unaware how much of his childish enthusiasm for dinosaurs was shining through.

"You have a better word for me."

"Dragon. Amlug means dragon..." With that Amlug smiled a toothy smile exposing more of the fearsome teeth again. Marcus had been certain dragons were not real a year ago, but he had been even more sure about time travel and magic. Now he wondered if this dragon was good or evil, and learned reading thoughts was second nature to the beast.

"We are not good or evil. We see the future and the past, we have no fear, and we commit no transgressions. That is solely the burden of man."

Marcus tried to fathom an existence without fear; it seemed impossible.

"I am a watcher and a thinker. I am what remains in the present of a distant past. I am incredible power, and I am just as meaningless as a blade of grass."

Marcus wished he had more time to contemplate that answer, but Amlug was waiting for Marcus's reply.

"Now tell me who you are or prepare for the inferno."

Marcus thought how best to mirror the answer he had been given.

"I am a lost traveler. I am on a quest to save Earth and all who live there."

The giant head moved closer to Marcus, and he could feel the moist breath from the nose of the dragon. The eyes narrowed and focused on him.

"No, you aren't. But it was an honest answer, so I will accept it."

Marcus didn't know why the dragon would not agree with either part of his answer but decided to move on to more immediate concerns. Everything about the encounter was confusing and he only wanted to protect the crystal and leave with his life. "Will you protect the crystal from Ahsigna or whoever wants to use it to destroy Earth?"

"No."

Marcus paused a moment after the reply thinking Amlug would explain, but silence stretched emptily.

"Why not?" Marcus asked, confused and upset.

"Simply put I don't care if Earth is destroyed, and I don't want to deal with unwanted visitors."

"Earth destroyed Amlug destroyed too!" Roquen added to the conversation for the first time.

The giant piercing eyes focused on Roquen, and Marcus thought he saw a hint of a toothy smile on the inhuman face.

"Even if I were not to be killed before this Earth is destroyed, I would not agree. Everything has to end sometime. Stop fighting the inevitable."

"Ahsigna wants to use it to do disrupt the Plan... to cause suffering all over, for everyone." Marcus wasn't sure how to appeal to dragons but thought something as ancient as Amlug would have some attachment to the Plan, whatever it may be.

"Does he? Well good for him. It is irrelevant. The Plan is what it is. Suffering will be; it will come and it will go. That is the nature of life."

"All life destroyed; innocent people, animals, dragons, everything. Destruction and misery for all living things. Are you saying that doesn't matter?" Marcus argued.

"Of course, it matters. It matters to everyone it happens to. It mattered to millions of unborn spiders this morning that you inadvertently stepped on and killed their mother. It matters that the swine you ate yesterday will not reproduce and feed villagers who will go hungry. Every single little thing matters. But none of it is important. Nothing lasts."

"Doing the right thing is important!" Marcus protested

"Only to the one who does it. Which hardly counts in the balance of trillions of lives."

"But Ahsigna is evil; you don't understand," Marcus pleaded.

"No. You don't understand. Good, Evil; they are inconsequential to me. The one you speak of; his view of life makes him miserable. So be it. Find a way of life that works for you. Or don't. Either way it is not important to me or the rest of reality."

"We will do what we have to without your help then," Layen protested.

"Roquen no need Amlug help," Roquen shouted defiantly. The dragon looked at him again, and Marcus again saw a faint grin that he was sure meant Roquen would either be engulfed in flames or eaten alive.

"I didn't say I wouldn't help you."

The creature eyed them intently.

"I will help you open a door to a different time. For a price."

Marcus looked at the giant beast with some suspicion, wondering what they could offer it that it would be unable to take by force. All they had were the shards of the crystal, and he was certain if Amlug wanted, he would just kill them and be done with it. He looked at his companions who appeared just as confused as Marcus.

"What price?" Marcus asked hesitantly.

"Next time you come you must bring amtra fruit."

The beast paused and Marcus couldn't help but wonder how delicious such a fruit must taste to continuously sidetrack the dragon.

"Uh sure... next time I come I'll bring amtra fruit," Marcus promised, despite having no intention of returning to pre-historic South America. He also did not have any idea what amtra fruit looked like or where to find it.

"Excellent. Though shattered as it is now Shila has great potential. Use a piece that remains and focus on what you want. Where you want to go. I will supply the strength you lack."

Marcus opened the leaf with the remnants of the crystal. The blue tinted shard held the most color so he selected it. Holding it in his hand he tried to picture the shimmer he experienced in the cave before being transported from the time he knew.

"Decide what is on the other side of the door, boy."

Marcus's heart leapt. He thought of the world he left behind, his parents, his friends, all the convenience the modern world offered. Then he remembered the words which had dogged him in every dream since he first saw the crystal: 'You must save humanity.' Marcus knew saving humanity meant not going home. His heart sunk at the thought. He knew Layen and Roquen could never go home as well. The thought of a dead Retap, Roqued, Enn, and all the slaughtered Piucca as well as the rest of the deaths of the Narwa at Ingole came crashing in on him. The crystal glowed a bright blue and, in a flash, Marcus was no longer next to a dragon and his friends.

When Marcus reopened his eyes from the brilliance of the flash, he stood alone on a perfectly flat dusty expanse surrounded by a heavy blueish fog. As Marcus looked up he saw above him was not a sky but what appeared to be an enormous crystal ceiling. On the other side of the blue tinted glass Marcus thought he could see Layen, Roquen and himself frozen and looking in through the crystal sky. Marcus looked around with wonder at the strange but empty world he found himself in.

"Hello?" Marcus called into the heavy mist.

No answer came in return. Marcus willed himself to stay brave. He thought of Retap and tried to remember all he had learned. As he did, the fog swirled into the form of his lost mentor. The ghostly Retap faced Marcus with the slight smile Marcus remembered from the best times with Retap. Out of the fog a swirl of a dagger came, headed towards Marcus. The cloudy figure of Retap stepped in front to protect Marcus. Then the figure clutched his chest where the blade struck, and Marcus watched the scene of Retap's death unfold again in the blueish fog.

"NO!" Marcus screamed at the death he was unable to prevent a second time. He ran towards the falling body, but his hands brushed through it like so much vapor. Marcus knelt down next to the body as it dissolved back into the mist. Heavy tears fell down Marcus's face. He gazed into the mist which had been a facsimile of Retap. Now it surrounded him with the battle at Ingole as hundreds of Narwa and Urinhyame around him died.

"Nooooooo..." Marcus wept. The deaths of so many soon faded away and the mist became the Piucca camp, and he could see all those who had taken Marcus in and given him shelter and friendship in a strange place. The whole camp was fast asleep, and Marcus noticed Retap and Naa missing. Layen and Roquen were not in their normal sleeping spots as well. The heavy mist then whirled into the shape of a tomahawk and then the rest of the body of the one wielding it emerged.

"Noooo... No! Not again. Please!" Marcus watched the as Urinhyame of fog murdered the sleeping Tahmi and Kahmi. Marcus cried into his hands and hung his head to avert his eyes from the massacre he knew would be played out. He heard Huo's voice looking for him and remembered all these deaths occurred because the Urinhyame had been searching for him. The tears raced down Marcus's face, mixing with the dusty ground creating sludge. The more Marcus cried, the thicker it became. Marcus raised his face up again just in time to see Semaj reaching for his children before being cut down by the Urinhyame with the screeching voice.

"Nooo..." Marcus sobbed. The ground where Marcus knelt was now thoroughly soaked and Marcus's legs started to sink into the thick goo. He paid it no attention and made no attempt to fight the tears which added to it.

"Marcus?" he heard the beautiful voice he had ached for in the past months. "Marcus?" his mother called again.

"Mom?" Marcus looked up. He saw his mother searching frantically; calling his name out, running through the city and forest.

"Mom! Mom, I'm here. It's me," Marcus desperately called into the fog.

The cloudy apparition of his mother did not respond. She continued running and searching for her lost son; calling his name, but unable to hear his reply.

"Nooooo..." Marcus cried again. Marcus looked down at the muck that his body had been sinking into which now reached to his chest. He struggled to stand up but his movements only succeeded in making him sink deeper. Each time he made an attempt to lift himself out of the brown slime, he found nothing solid and only continued his descent into the muck.

All around him scenes played out from his memories or imagination. Each one stacking on to his sadness as he slipped deeper into the ground which lacked any solidity. Marcus watched his mother frantically continue her search as Ingole burned; the Piucca and the rest of the Narwa being killed and their way of life lost. Marcus tried to fight against the mud, but he was already up to his chin and couldn't take his eyes of the scenes reenacting in the dullness of the blue mist. The deaths of the Piucca and Retap played out again in the fog. He glanced over at his mother one last time as the taste of the mud entered his mouth.

Marcus saw Retap's dead body look over at him. When the body spoke, he didn't hear the voice of the one who had taught Marcus, but rather Marcus's own voice.

"You must not fear."

The words were nearly lost as the mud slipped into Marcus's ears as he tried to breathe above the rising sludge. He remembered the respect for the Plan Retap carried to his death, and Marcus's love for his mentor inspired him to do the same. He knew if not for Retap's death, Potek would not have saved them from Ahsigna. If not for Retap's life, Marcus knew he would still be the same sad, angry, selfish, fearful boy he had been when he arrived. Marcus's sadness at Retap's death was transformed into respect for his life and the part that even his death played in the great Plan Retap dedicated his life to. As the change in his heart took place, Marcus felt his foot push against something solid enough to lift his head above the mud enabling him to take a deep breath.

"You must not fear."

Marcus looked at the Piucca and Urinhyame bodies; of all those who had died at Ingole. Even the Urinhyame had his respect for having died for something they believed in. The loss was no less horrible, but Marcus knew it held meaning and that limited the sadness he felt at such loss of life. Marcus was able to push against a soft but solid mass of mud with his other foot, raising him a bit higher in the mud.

"You must not fear."

Lastly, he looked at his mother sobbing at the loss of her son. The grip of sadness and dread of defeat tried to take hold of Marcus again, but he fought back with the love and resolution his mother had always shown him. If he truly was tasked with saving humanity, Marcus knew his departure from his parents was unavoidable. While they may now be physically separated from him, he knew that the examples he had taken from them could never really be lost.

"You must not fear."

With a final resolute step Marcus lifted himself out of the mud, which had almost engulfed him with the weight of his sadness. The forms which had brought him so much grief when he viewed them before dispersed as did the fog. Before him was only a glowing blue light. This light glowed with a brilliance that contrasted the dullness of the blue which previously lit the interior of the crystal. Marcus walked towards the glow passing through it and back into the world of pre-historic South America.

Marcus was back exactly where he had been holding a blue crystal trying to make a door in time open. A slightest glimmer of a door started to appear. It resembled the heat mirage he remembered from the cave but was miniscule.

"Now tell me boy, where will this door take you.?"

"To whenever we can stop the Earth from being lost," Marcus answered trying not to break his concentration.

"Retoh!"

At Amlug's command a Narwa man emerged from around the corner. He resembled Retap but his appearance was more unkept and wild. Most of the right side of his body still showed the mark of an ancient burn.

Marcus's focus stayed on the door which grew gradually more visible though still tiny.

"**Amlug qapta tar, Retoh?**"

The dragon rose up to its full height.

"*Nahto. Retoh qapta tar sin yando.*" Retoh replied with the same resolute face his brother had always kept in the face of danger and death.

Marcus didn't have time to ask what agreement was being fulfilled between Retap's kin and the beast. The bargain was concluded with death as an eruption of fire spewed from Amlug's mouth. Though they stood a fair distance from the flames, the heat singed the three travelers. Retoh was instantly incinerated.

Marcus lost concentration on the door and turned to look at the maelstrom of fire that obliterated any trace of the man who had stood before it. The dragon remained perfectly still in concentration for a moment then shifted its huge head looking where the tiny mirage created by Marcus flickered in and out of existence.

"**And now I have kept my bargain with you as well, Marcus. You will bring me amtra when you return and as a token of your pledge I demand a kiss.**"

The last demand surprised Marcus as much as anything else he had encountered. Marcus turned towards Layen. For her part Layen looked as if kissing a dragon to save the Earth wasn't a deal she could accept.

"No..."

Layen appeared relieved, and she and Roquen looked at Marcus.

"**And you still reek of fear. But this one...**"

The giant fearsome toothy smile flashed across the dreadful countenance which looked designed only for dealing death. The dragon lowered his head directly in front of Roquen.

Marcus was as surprised by the demand as he was by his friend's stepping forward and placing the most normal kiss on the cheek of the dragon.

The head of the dragon shot up and the entire length of the beast rose to its hind legs. The wings which were previously folded opened wide and for the first time since their arrival the three could see just what immense power they were dealing with.

"A door out of this time is there. Now go! "

The mirage of a door which Marcus created had grown large enough to accommodate the travelers. They each took a look at one another both in fear of what the door might hold, and in joy that they could escape Ahsigna and continue the quest to save the Earth.

"Go!"

Immediately a huge jet of fire came bursting from its mouth scorching the earth and grass behind them. With two huge beats of its wings the fearsome dragon lifted itself off the ground just overhead of the three shocked onlookers. They tried to run to their right in the direction of the door, but a swipe from the enormous power of Amlug's tail sent giant boulders--each many times larger than a man--flying in front of them.

"What the hell?!" Marcus protested.

The only response he received was another blast of fire impacting the ground a few feet in front of them and tracing its way toward the three who split ranks to avoid being incinerated. Marcus and Layen dodged to the right and had a clear path to the door. Roquen went left and faced the dragon alone.

They hesitated to leave Roquen behind, but he motioned for them to make a run for an escape. As he did Roquen picked up a stone and hurled it at the dragon. The head was too high in the air but the stone was able to ineffectively strike the dragon in the breast. Now the terrifying beast truly smiled. As the smile faded, its huge right claw came crashing down, and Roquen barely jumped out of the way in time. The force of the impact drove the claws deep into the ground, and the beast remained momentarily stuck.

Roquen used the opportunity to catch up with his friends, and the three quickly ran past the dragon's perch. Without a glance back Roquen, Layen and Marcus stepped into a door to another time.

EPILOGUE - BETWEEN FRIENDS

A man in a grey gi walked onto the plateau from where a dragon surveyed with eyes half shut the vast lands below. The man sat down on a rock next to the colossal beast and also took in the view as the sun went down.

"They just left as you said they would. I let them have a little fun before they did though. "

"I know," the man said.

"Of course you do."

The man in grey merely nodded his head.

"All goes well on your quest. "

"I knew it would before I started," the man replied vacantly.

"Makes things a bit empty..."

The man again nodded his head in agreement. "I am a bit empty."

"They believe in so much. So much fire in them; they want desperately to believe they can make a difference, to do something important."

"Like you said, nothing is important," the man in grey replied looking at the giant next to him.

Opening a canteen, the man pulled out some large berries that were floating on the liquid inside. "Well, almost nothing."

The dragon's eyelids shot up in recognition. The fearsome maw with huge razor-sharp teeth opened, and the man threw the berries onto the waiting tongue. They looked comically small and insignificant compared to the hugeness of the beast. The mouth snapped shut and the smile that formed on the terrifying mouth proved the berries' significance.

"Mmmmmmmmmm. Always a pleasure to work with you."

The man took a long draught off the canteen and repeated the process of feeding the remaining berries to the eager dragon.

"Our next meeting will be our last, you understand," he said although he knew the dragon already remembered it as well as the first.

The dragon lazily rose on its hind legs and stretched itself up to full height.

"A savage send off with lots of amtra. "

"For me it already was."

With this Amlug took a deep breath and spewed forth an inferno that made his attacks on Marcus's group seem trivial. The man in grey braced himself against the force which directly impacted him.

When the flames receded the man was unhurt, though most of his clothing had been reduced to ashes, leaving only the two fingered leather glove and a grey hooded tunic. The exposed skin revealed a patchwork of tattoos of primitive designs and runes as well as scars both small and large. For his part the man in grey didn't seem annoyed at the loss.

"Congratulations."

NARWA LANGUAGE

aguyje (grateful)
ala (not)
alli (strong, resilient, healthy)
Amar (Earth/World)
an (more)
anni (next to)
ara (day)
au (without)
aykiy (escape)
bapo (tasked)
cennada (taught)
chika (true/correct)
drimea (onion-like blulb plant)
enyal (remember)
endome (cave
er (one/unity)
erinqua (alone)
et (out/banished)
gaity (follow)
guapy (sit)
guar (jaguar)
guat (move)
hakay (anything)
hammat (destroy)
hanta (Thank you)
Hosta (ceremonial gathering)
hucha (transgression/crime)
hus (more)
hyalma (shell)
hyam (pray)
hyame (worship)

iasy (moon)
imi (in)
kapakocha (sacrifice)
kawsay (live)
kinsa (three)
koara (today)
koero (tomorrow)
kuarasy (summer)
kuchuy (cut)
Kurusa (Southern Cross)
la (no/don't)
laia (Is not)
laique (thyme-like herb)
lakiska (sad)
lalume (never)
laurenque (yellow flowered tree)
lek (to lose)
lennaye (will go)
limbe (hurry)
londa (ways)
lore (sleep)
lula (lie or deception)
lum (time)
malda (better)
mamya (mom)
mana (what)
mandu (strange)
manen (how)
manvapa (who)
masse (where)
mereth (feast)
merne (wanted)
mita (boy)
molomelta (another's burden)

muboia (snake)
na (other)
na (yes)
nar (fire)
nahto (yes, emphatic)
naicele (pain)
nakuy (fight)
neyar (talked)
nyaro (rodent)
Ohtat (man {ceremoniously})
ohte (egg)
pakay (hide)
Pano (Plan, order to universe)
panotar (respect for the Plan)
panta (guilty)
phakia (angry)
pytuna (night)
qapta (agreement)
qurriy (run)
raica (wrong)
raxi ({more} dangerous)
rehtie (save)
reqsisqa ({close} friend)
rondo (cave)
rucs (break)
sin (now)
suyay (stop/wait)
tar (fulfilled)
Tatya (dad/father)
tena (right)
turuimmo (self-control)
Urin (sun)
uywa (creature)
vanwa (lost)

wanyuy (die)
waxa (bonds/ropes)
whime (why)
yachay (know)
yando (also)